A GOOD CONFESSION

A GOOD CONFESSION

Bridget Whelan

This first world edition published 2008
in Great Britain and in 2009 in the USA by
SEVERN HOUSE PUBLISHERS LTD of
9–15 High Street, Sutton, Surrey, England, SM1 1DF.
Trade paperback edition published
in Great Britain and the USA 2009 by
SEVERN HOUSE PUBLISHERS LTD

British Library Cataloguing in Publication Data

Whelan, Bridget
  A good confession
  1. Catholic Church - Clergy - Fiction 2. Irish - England -
  London - Fiction 3. Widows - Fiction 4. Love stories
  I. Title
  823.9'2[F]

  ISBN-13: 978-0-7278-6720-9   (cased)
  ISBN-13: 978-1-84751-095-2   (trade paper)

All Severn House titles are printed on acid-free paper.

Typeset by Palimpsest Book Production Ltd.,
Grangemouth, Stirlingshire, Scotland.
Printed and bound in Great Britain by
MPG Books Ltd., Bodmin, Cornwall.

This novel was completed with the financial assistance of the Arts Council, England South East. Their bursary bought me the time to write, revise and revise again. I am also deeply grateful to my agent Jonathan Conway whose unwavering support gave me the confidence to do just that.

Dedicated to my mother Anna (Nancy) Lyons and in memory of my father James Lyons (1921–1999).

London

July 1961

'How long have you known?' Cathleen's voice was playful. Standing at the kitchen window, she heard the door swing open but didn't turn around. The old children's game rang in her head as the floorboards creaked under his weight: one step, two step. He was behind her. Three steps and she could feel his breath on the back of her neck.

'Known what?' asked Jerry. Across the tar-black roofs they watched the early morning sun silver the dome of St Paul's.

'Us.' She smiled up at him. 'That there would be an us.'

'Since the first time I saw you.'

'Don't say that!' She jerked away as if she'd been slapped. 'Jerry, you mustn't ever say that.'

Cathleen's mind snapped back to that first time. Giddy with nerves, her feet fighting with yards of nylon net underneath her long, white dress as she walked up the aisle. And Jerry? He had been standing at the altar all in white himself, wearing vestments embroidered in gold thread, waiting to marry the man he loved as a brother.

'I'm an eejit. Forgive me?'

She nodded.

Back then Jerry had been a mellow voice turning the Latin phrases into poetry as I fumbled through my vows. Back then I was Mick Brogan's girl and Mick Brogan's wife. It was only after I was Mick Brogan's widow that there could be a first time for us.

'When did *you* know?' He moved nearer.

'For absolute sure?' Cathleen smiled. 'At the First Holy Communion. Not in the church, when you were making the sermon, but later in the hall when everyone was having tea. I reached for something . . .'

'A butter knife.'

'Only I wasn't looking and I touched your hand. I didn't move. And you didn't move. It was then I knew we were going mad together.'

One

'Tell her to come.'

This simple message had been telephoned through to the corner shop; but it was not something that could be delivered by the boys in short trousers loitering outside, nor was it a crumb of gossip to be chewed over with anyone who came in for their daily paper. Reg, shop proprietor and owner of one of the few telephones in this battered corner of London, knew that he had to do this himself.

He reported the staff nurse's words faithfully to Cathleen Brogan while feeling for the sweets he always carried in his pocket. Other people swore by a cup of tea in a crisis or a nip of brandy, but Reg preferred the slow comfort of toffee. On the steps of the Brogan's house, however, he discovered he had nothing to offer. He had run across the street in shirtsleeves and braces, without jacket or trilby, without anything except the message that tore the colour from the young woman's face. She held on to the front door as if she had been hit. Behind her two little girls crouched on the brown linoleum stairs that led up to their rooms at the top of the house.

Reg shifted his weight from one foot to the other; finally he said, 'I'm sorry for your trouble.' It wasn't a phrase he'd normally use but his Irish customers said it often enough.

Sorry for your trouble. Sorry for your trouble.

Cathleen flinched at the words. Afterwards Reg remembered that he had only heard it said after someone had died.

Cathleen left her two frightened daughters with her sister Mary and hailed a taxi to Bart's Hospital. When she got there someone else was in her husband's bed, someone whose face was the colour of wax. The hair, that should have been brilliant with

Brylcreem, was a mousy shade of brown. She stretched out a hand and hesitated. It looked touchable, but it belonged to a stranger.

'I'm so sorry.' A nun with a girl's waist and an old woman's face stood quietly to one side. 'The priest's been.'

And then Cathleen knew that the man lying there, with soft hair and fish blood lips, was the Mick she had first seen foxtrotting across a crowded dance floor in Holloway. Mick, who liked a few pints on a Saturday night, and every other night if she'd let him; Mick, who could carry a hod of bricks for twelve hours without complaint, but had to be nagged out of bed in the morning. Her Mick. Her husband. Her life.

Cathleen nodded to show that she understood Extreme Unction had been given. Now all she could do was wait. 'Do you think he knows I'm here?'

'Perhaps,' the nun sighed. 'But, even if he doesn't, I think he must sense that he's not alone.' She touched Cathleen's hand lightly. 'I think he knows he's safe.'

Cathleen turned her face away. What a word to use, she thought, when none of us are safe. The nun produced a spare set of rosary beads from somewhere within the folds of her habit, and together they began to pray.

Hail Mary.

Mary was home with the girls, Cathleen thought.

Blessed art thou amongst women.

That's what Mick said about himself, especially when he had a pint in his hand.

Our Father.

How could she bring the girls up without a father? How could Mick leave her behind when they had so much to do?

Thy will be done.

I'm not giving permission. Cathleen's lip trembled as she reined in her thoughts, afraid that she might run crying from the ward.

'Did he ask for me?'

'I think I caught one word before you came.' The nun touched her hand. 'It's hard to be certain but I think he said Bell. Or perhaps Bella.'

Cathleen sank back in the chair: it meant nothing. She gave up all pretence of praying, leaving it to the nun. A few minutes after three o' clock Cathleen jerked as if she had been startled out of a deep sleep.

'What is it, child?' The nun was still by her side; the rosary beads put away. 'Shall I call someone?'

'No, but I think he had a dog, Belle, when he was a boy. I'm sure he told me about a dog called Belle.'

The nun nodded. 'Yes, that'll be it. Yes. Take comfort in it.'

'Comfort?' They had been whispering, but now Cathleen's voice grew louder. 'He has two little girls at home. He has a mother who hasn't been off her knees since she knew he was ill.' She trembled. 'He has me.'

'I know, child, I know. And how could the poor man leave you at all? Not with a good heart, surely?' Cathleen started to cry softly. 'No, he's gone back to innocent times. A country boy, was he?' Cathleen nodded. 'Gone back to playing in the fields, God love him.'

Cathleen wiped her face on the handkerchief that she'd tucked into her sleeve before leaving home. Mick's tied up to ugly machines that aren't doing one bit of good, she thought. In his head he's a kid again, and me? I'm nowhere, lost entirely. But even as the thought came to her, it was swept away by an image that was suddenly as vivid as a photograph. She saw again their reflection in a gilt mirror on the wall of a Camden Town dance hall and leaned forward.

'Remember your blue suit, Mick? You saved for a year to get it. Remember my slingbacks? The ones I kicked off walking home because they made my heels bleed? Weren't we the gorgeous ones?' she whispered, and kissed his forehead.

Tipping her chair forward, Cathleen's whole being became tuned to the pitch and fall of Mick's breathing. It was as if they were walking a hilly road together. Occasionally the rhythm broke and floundered, only to rally again. Three times it stopped. Three times a shudder from somewhere deep within started the tempo again.

Let go, Cathleen thought. There's no coming back from this. Go and play in the fields, Mick.

And finally he did.

Smithfield meat market was bloody and buoyant in the grey hours before dawn. White-aproned men dragged marbled carcasses from lorries. They were quick to make lewd suggestions at the sight of a young woman, but the words shrivelled on their lips when they saw Cathleen's face. She was cut off from the life and death around her. Even the cold couldn't penetrate the coat that should have been too thin for the early hours of a raw winter morning. She wasn't sure how she was walking, or where she was going, because no part of her mind made her feet turn into the broad thoroughfare of St John's Street, but like long-serving horses her shoes seemed to know their own way home.

'What will I do? What will I do?' Cathleen murmured as she passed the bakery and Reg's shop.

They had seven pounds ten shillings saved in the Post Office and a fridge on hire purchase. They can take that back, she thought. She knew it would never be warm again.

The insurance would cover the funeral, at least there was that. She had kept up the payments regularly even though Mick had resented the milky-faced collector who called on Friday mornings. 'Aren't we young?' he would argue. 'Aren't we strong?' Mick would have preferred the couple of bob in his own pocket; or, better still, in the pocket of the bookies' runner who dodged up and down Chapel Market in well-worn gaberdine.

Cathleen stopped, key in hand, outside a Georgian house whose elegant proportions were divided and subdivided, hacked and slashed into a motley of rented rooms. She stroked the grimacing lion's head on the front door. Years of touches had worn away the grime to reveal a brass snout. Mick had called it Ned, why she didn't know, and now she wished she'd asked. He and the girls waved it goodbye when they went out. There's nothing inside me to keep the story going, Cathleen thought. Ned and Mick would die together.

She was careful not to wake the sleeping house, climbing four flights of stairs in her stockinged feet. Her younger sister was asleep in an armchair but she woke with a cry when Cathleen touched her shoulder, as if she had dreamt the news and didn't need telling.

'What are you going to do?' Mary wailed.

'I'll manage,' said Cathleen. 'I'll manage.'

Two

The house was quiet. Mary had sobbed herself back to sleep and the children were an innocent huddle of limbs. Cathleen, standing in the kitchen, felt herself drifting back out into the street that was slowly stretching itself awake: back to the hospital. And for a moment she was overwhelmed by guilt. She wanted to run, just as she was, run and hold Mick again because, after this, there would be no more holding. She tried to steady herself with a cigarette. The occasional drag, taken from one held between Mick's fingers, used to remind her of warm tweed and she wanted that comfort now, but when she inhaled it was like dragging a sharp, metallic thing deep into her lungs.

How? The question felt like the beat of a throbbing headache. How could a man like Mick die? He was young, not yet thirty. He was strong, his body honed from years of hard work on the building site. The most he'd ever suffered was bronchitis his first winter in London, and a couple of cracked ribs celebrating the night Anna was born.

She'd questioned him, Cathleen reminded herself that she had done that much at least. But no, he denied any injury, or anything to explain a travelling pain that moved from one side of his back to the other. Some days he had a stomach ache, some days he didn't. It grumbled on and despite it Mick worked every day on the new block of flats the other side of Rosebery Avenue that were the talk of the place. People he hardly knew would stop him in the street to ask if they really were putting in metal sinks with a gadget to eat up tin cans. Like something out of *I Love Lucy*, he would assure them.

For Mick the main bonus of working so near home had been the few extra minutes it gave him in bed. They were sweeter than all the other hours of the night, he would declare, especially on dark mornings when there was frost on the inside of the bedroom window and he would wake to see his breath cloud the air. Silencing the alarm, he'd duck back under the eiderdown and blankets to entwine himself in the long folds of Cathleen's nightdress. But in those last weeks she was left on the edge of the bed, stroking a back arched against pain.

I would rage at him for chewing aspirins as if they were sweets, she reminded herself And every night I would tell him to go to the doctor. And every night he'd complain that the radio was too loud, and the meat was too tough, and the children too noisy.

Tacit Donovan, the ganger on the Clerkenwell site, had lost patience. Mick had been pulled aside one morning and asked why he was late two days running. Only Tacit hadn't said it like that. He'd wanted to know if the streets needed to be well-aired before Mick Brogan could venture out.

'He's a fellow Kerry man, which is a kind of insurance,' Mick reported. 'But all the same I'd be a fool not to heed the warning.'

Cathleen went over to the window and looked down at the street below. It was still dark and the shutters on Reg's shop were closed but she could make out the corner where Mick would turn into their road at the end of a shift, head back and whistling. And there I'd be with a kitchen full of steam, she thought, condensation running down the walls, trying to sterilize the baby's bottle, hush a crying toddler, dry wet nappies, soak the dirty ones and darn a ladder in my best pair of stockings. I'd be ready to flare at him if I smelt drink on his breath, or found a bookie's slip in his pocket. Or if he said just one word out of place.

And what would he say? Always the same thing, with his hands on my hips. 'What more could a man want.'

Always the same smile too.

She glanced up at the shelf by the sink. Half hidden by a box of soda crystals was a wedding photograph in a cheap tin frame. It hadn't been such a big group in the Dublin church: Brogans on one side, Cooneys on the other. Mick's mother, slab-faced in funeral dark clothes, Cathleen's two younger brothers gawky next to Mary who was striving for a bit of schoolgirl glamour. Bridesmaid Angie beamed from ear to ear, in the long green dress that she had made herself to hide her calipers. Her arms were goose-bumped – she hadn't been able to master sleeves – and the uneven darts in the bodice gave her a lopsided look. Poor Angie, thought Cathleen of the girl who had been her best friend from childhood: polio at three, dead at twenty-two, a year after her satin glory.

Everyone agreed that the photograph wasn't good enough to stick in the family album but Cathleen had always liked it. She didn't care that her mother was a blur – captured telling someone off – or that she herself was frowning against the glare of the sun. It was Mick's expression that she wanted to keep and she took the picture down now and looked again at the generous mouth. If I concentrate I can almost hear him laugh, she thought. Did he know that these were the good times? And that they wouldn't last?

There was an echo of Mick's laughter on another face. Directly behind her young husband, but slightly to the left, was the priest who had married them. Father Jerry: the sainted cousin and repository of all Brogan virtues. Her tears came steadily now, in a constant flow that washed her face, and she wished she could remember what had made them laugh.

Three

Cathleen had found Mick sitting at the kitchen table six days earlier.

Neither of them had been in the right place. Mick should have been digging the foundations of a lift shaft and she should have been shopping for the evening meal. But it had been a muddle of a morning and outside the butcher's Cathleen suddenly remembered that she had left her purse on top of the dresser. Bribing her youngest daughter with the promise of a visit to the park later, she hurried home to discover Mick sitting in their kitchen.

'Not feeling so good.'

The words were chopped off at the ends and his fingers gripped the underside of the kitchen chair.

He's crucified with the pain, Cathleen thought running to him. She put her hand on his forehead.

'Crucified with the pain and burning up.'

Those were the only words she seemed to use that day. It was what she told Reg at the corner shop when she asked to use his phone, and she repeated it to their family doctor who promised to come as soon as he could. She said it again when she spoke to her younger sister.

Mary had pulled a face when she spotted Cathleen and Geraldine through the window of Crawford's Antique Emporium, a small shop in Camden Passage smelling of dust and mouse droppings. She hurried out to meet them brandishing a pair of Victorian sugar tongs.

'Go on,' she hissed. 'Look like you've a mind to buy them.' She glanced inside the shop. 'Old Man Crawford's on the prowl.'

Cathleen opened her mouth to say something but, as her sister turned to show off the kick pleat on her pencil skirt, she felt tears come into her eyes.

'What's wrong?' Mary twisted around. 'It's not Mum, is it? I thought she was going to explode this morning but why should I eat the fried egg she planted in front of me? I saw her wipe the fag ash off the side of the plate.' Mary looked more closely at her sister's face. 'Oh God, is it Mum?'

Cathleen shook her head as Geraldine spoke for her.

'Daddy,' the little girl whispered, drawing on the pavement with the toe of her shoe. 'Daddy funny.' And then she hid her face in Cathleen's skirt.

'Mick's been taken to hospital.' Cathleen found her voice at last.

'Motherajaysus!' Mary gulped and suddenly looked much younger than her nineteen years. 'An accident? Oh God, is he hurt?'

'No.' Cathleen bit her lip. 'He's ill.'

The two sisters stared at each other. They had been brought up to regard hospitals with a deep-seated suspicion that they hadn't quite managed to shrug off. It's where the poor go to die, their mother had told them when they were growing up in Dublin. And even after their move to London, she would shake her head knowingly when her children protested that things were different now and the National Health Service was the best in the world.

'I'm going to him,' Cathleen continued. 'Only there's the girls.'

'Don't be worrying.' Mary swept her niece up into her arms and turned to face the shop's dark interior. Although Cathleen couldn't see anyone among the glass domes of stuffed birds and mounted stag heads, she presumed that somewhere in the shadows Mr Crawford was listening.

'Bit of a crisis,' Mary called out. 'I'm after having to help with the children.' She turned back to her sister. 'Off with you now. I'll take Geraldine around to Mum and one of us will get Anna from school.'

'Your boss won't mind?'

'There's a fear of him,' Mary assured her. 'Off now.'

'Jaysus! His liver?'

Cathleen nodded. Her mother's voice was rising in pitch and volume.

'Good God, has that man of yours been keeping secrets?'

'What?' Cathleen's head jerked up. She had crawled into an armchair after returning from the hospital: it was the first night she and Mick had spent apart since they married.

'Isn't it amazing what a smile can hide. Did you never suspect? Or have you been hiding it from us too?' Kitty demanded.

'I'm hiding nothing.' Cathleen spoke without emotion. 'Mick's never had the money to ruin his liver.'

'They're all liars, men. Do you know how much he earns? You don't! And if he said, you couldn't believe him. Ach, they're all cheats.'

'It's an infection,' said Cathleen as if her mother hadn't spoken. 'An abscess caused by infection. The doctor explained.'

Kitty, moving to and fro in the Brogan's sitting room, bumped into the heavy mahogany dining table that stood in the centre, nearly knocking over a standard lamp. 'Infection? Is that what they're calling it?' She spun on her heel. 'Men covering up for one another, that's what that is.'

'Mother,' Mary warned, standing in her path.

'Ach, it's an instinct they're all born with.'

'You're not helping.' She gestured in Cathleen's direction. 'Just for once could you shut up? Could you?'

'What a thing to say to your own mother.' Kitty glared, but stopped moving. 'You've an awful mouth on you.'

Mary turned to Cathleen. 'What are they going to do? Are they operating?'

Cathleen shook her head. 'They don't think so. Penicillin, that's the thing. Before penicillin there was no hope.' Silently Cathleen started to cry. 'And I know it wasn't the drink because I asked.'

She looked up at her mother and sister. 'It came into my head too, although I don't know why. I must be my mother's daughter.'

Kitty opened her mouth and then thought better of it.

'Sometimes there's no one to blame,' Cathleen continued. 'Sometimes people just get ill.'

'We'll go down to church tonight.' Kitty's lips were set in a grim, determined line. 'There's benediction on. Not you, girl. You're wrecked. You don't want to be going anywhere. Me and Mary, we'll take the girls. The boys too if we can gather them up.' She spoke of her adult sons as if they were puppies. 'A few prayers for Mick, God help him.'

'Don't bother,' said Cathleen. 'If you want someone to blame, that's the place to look.'

Four

'WHy does Daddy have to go to Leytonstone?'

Cathleen turned from the brick of butter she was attacking to look at her daughter's face. Anna was chewing a strand of hair as she drew shapes in the condensation on the window. She made the East London district sound strange and faraway.

'It's where Catholics are buried.'

'But why is it so far?'

'Because there aren't so many Catholics in London that there can be a cemetery around every corner.' Dear God, thought Cathleen, you could never guess what was going through a child's mind. We're burying her father tomorrow and all she's thinking about is the journey.

'Do you mean there's people in London who aren't Catholic?' Anna pulled more hair into her mouth

Grandma Brogan looked up in surprise. 'Doesn't the poor child know she's living in a heathen country?'

Cathleen paused, not sure how to answer. Her mother-in-law had arrived by taxi early that morning with tears in her eyes and a suitcase that the pair of them had struggled to get up the stairs.

Cathleen's own eyes felt as though they were filled with hot sand. Four days and nights she had worked, sleeping little, eating less, and now all she wanted was to knock the bright eager questions out of her daughter, that or hug her and never let go.

Cathleen had polished windows until they squeaked, cleaned inside and outside of cupboards, spent hours on her knees washing the kitchen floor with water so hot it hurt her hands.

At night ironing had become a substitute for sleep, and she discovered herself pressing things she had never even thought of ironing before: gym knickers for Anna that looked exactly the same afterwards as they had done before; an old brassiere, grey from washing, that she had no intention of wearing again; and Mick's work shirts that were not fit to be given away. And everything she did was accompanied by noise. After the BBC closed down she would twirl the radio dial through the poetry of foreign stations: Stuttgart, Leipzig, Oslo, Luxembourg, preferring speaking to singing, but even static was better than silence.

'Go downstairs to the sitting room and let the television warm up. *Watch with Mother* will be on soon.'

'What day is it?' Anna's eyes widened with pleasure. 'Oh, I hope it's *Picture Book* day.' Cathleen gently brushed the strands of hair away from her daughter's face and looked across at the woman who was taking up most of the room at the kitchen table. Cathleen read her disapproval.

'People can be scandalized if they like,' Cathleen said as her chin jutted out, 'but it's better to have the child entertained than me snapping at her.'

'It's *The Flower Pot Men*,' Anna called up. 'But that's my next favourite.'

'Ah, you have to do what's best.' The old woman glanced across the room at the drawing Anna had made in the steam. Although the lines were already bleeding into one another, the stick man's happy smile could still be seen. 'The poor dote doesn't have an idea what's going on.'

'I've told her.' Cathleen was defensive. 'It was hard, but I did. I didn't want the girls hearing it from someone else.'

Grandma Brogan nodded. 'You did everything right, I'm sure. She has the words off pat, but they haven't got inside yet. There's knowing,' the woman sighed. 'And then there's knowing.'

Cathleen nodded. They were silent for a moment, looking at each other, and she sensed that Grandma Brogan wanted to say something else. The details of Mick's illness had been fine-tooth combed into some kind of order before Anna and Geraldine had woken up to discover that the grandmother they had never met was sitting in the kitchen.

'I suppose you're wondering why I'm on my own,' Grandma Brogan began hesitantly, staring at the floor. The pink of her scalp showed through the thinning ash-grey hair. 'I suppose you think it's very odd.'

Cathleen shrugged. She had given up supposing anything. People came and went. Neighbours she had never spoken to called to shake her hand; some didn't even knock but left a gift outside. Yesterday she found an apple pie that was still warm on the stairs.

'Maeve was desperate to come, you must know that.'

Cathleen nodded. Of course, Mick's sister would have made the journey if she could. They had only met once but every fortnight she wrote, and every six months a brown paper parcel would arrive, crammed with hand-knitted cardigans for the children that were always the wrong size.

'Only didn't a wall-eyed heifer give her an awful kick a week last Thursday.'

Cathleen tried to pay attention to the story of a leg that ballooned to twice its size, that needed a trip to Tralee for an X-ray and was broken in two places, but the thought of a week last Thursday crowded everything else out. He was talking then, Cathleen thought, telling me off, saying I was making a fuss. A week last Thursday we both still thought he was coming home.

She became aware that Grandma Brogan had said something else and was expecting a response. The old woman's eyes flitted around the room as her hands fumbled with a set of rosary beads.

'I'd bought the two tickets. I don't know if I'll get a refund now, but I bought two without asking. After all . . .' She paused, her fingers agitating the beads. 'After all, with his father dead and Mick his only brother you wouldn't think it was a question that had to be asked.'

Her voice dropped to a whisper and Cathleen had to strain to hear. 'And I'd only been as far as Dublin twice in my life and then always with a crowd.' She shook her head. 'I never thought Thady would let me come on my own. I never thought he'd let Mick be buried without saying goodbye.'

'But you came,' said Cathleen gently. 'And I'm very glad you did. Can I take your coat now? You'd be more comfortable.'

'In a bit, when I'm warmer.' The old woman pulled the vast purple coat around her like a blanket. 'The boat was awful cold. And people were saying it was a good crossing and a mild night, but if that was good, I'd never want to know a rough one.' The old woman nodded gratefully as Cathleen poured another cup of tea. 'I've been cold since I left Farran. I think I've been cold since I got the news.' The old woman paused. 'Father Jerry! Have you heard from Father Jerry?'

Cathleen shook her head.

'He might come. It's an awful long way but he might come. There's hope yet.' She poured some of the tea into the saucer and blew on it. 'He said the Mass when himself died,' she added, referring to Mick's father. 'It was a terrible great comfort.'

'I don't suppose he even knows that Mick . . .' Cathleen's voice faltered as she looked across at the weathered face, cross-hatched with lines. There were still some words she found too hard to say.

'Oh, but he does! I went into town specially to send the telegram – I knew you'd have no time for it. But Father Jerry had to know. Didn't he and Mick get on famously? Like real brothers.'

An imperious knock on the kitchen door startled both women.

'Mrs Brogan! Mrs Brogan! Are you in there?'

Both women answered yes, as the door swung open to reveal the parish priest, a scrawny little man with a scratching of grey stubble on his cheeks.

'The funeral,' he gasped out of breath. 'The funeral will have to be postponed.'

'Why?' Cathleen faced the priest with a bread knife in her hand.

'Why indeed.' He rubbed his hands. 'Not of my doing, I can assure you. But when all's said and done it will work out very nicely.' He turned on his heel. 'Aha, a face I don't know. And you would be?'

'I'm Mick's mother.'

'Another Mrs Brogan! Ach, this is a terrible business, but you'll understand the need to hold back the proceedings once I tell you about the telephone call I'm after taking. An international call, mind. And couldn't I hear him as clear as a bell. This very afternoon the call came just as I was sitting down to my dinner. But did I mind a bit?'

'What call, Father?'

'Now if I said Verona, I'm thinking that you wouldn't be too far behind me. Am I right?'

'Father Jerry!' The old woman's face lit up.

'Aha, you have it, m'am. Father Jerry Brogan. A charming man.'

'Oh he is, he is.' Grandma Brogan nodded furiously. 'A lovely man.'

'And what a close family you all are! He explained it all to me – it was a long call, do you see. Much more than a cousin, he was saying. Anyway . . .' The priest looked around and allowed his gaze to fall on the kettle. 'Wasn't he packing his suitcase as we were talking? And with God's grace and the wonders of air travel he will be with us all tomorrow. But not in the morning. Oh no, that can't be done.' He shook his head as if they were about to argue. 'Marvellous things they are, but they won't get him here for the morning Mass.' He coughed again. 'So I put it back.'

'And how are we to let people know?' Cathleen's voice rose as she thought of the consequences. 'There's flowers arriving. There's cars booked. There'll be men coming off the building site who'll lose a whole day's pay when they only bargained on a morning . . .'

'Yes,' the priest agreed. 'There are things to do, no doubt about that. I myself have had to rearrange my schedule. I've offered every amenity to Father Brogan, of course. Even volunteered to stand down in my own church. And I can tell you not every parish priest would do that, but he wouldn't hear of it. So, Mick will have a concelebrated Mass. The curate will help out as well as myself. Think of that, three priests on the altar!'

'Father Jerry here!' Grandma Brogan clutched the priest's arm in excitement. 'It's what I've been praying for.'

'And I've already sent word to Tacit Donovan.' The priest swung around to Cathleen. 'So, you see these things can be done.'

'But perhaps I don't want them done.' Cathleen held his gaze for a moment. 'Perhaps I just want to bury my husband.'

With difficulty Grandma Brogan hoisted herself up from her seat at the table and walked stiffly towards Cathleen, holding out her arms. For a moment Cathleen didn't understand what she wanted: the two women had never touched. The closest they had got was a shy butterfly kiss on the cheek the day she married Mick.

'Father Jerry's coming,' Grandma Brogan repeated and engulfed Cathleen in the coat that smelt faintly of mothballs. 'We won't feel so lonely with Father Jerry here.'

Five

R eg was the first to spot the arrival of the undertaker's limousine. Cathleen's mother, Kitty, got in first, still smoking and, judging from the way her head was bobbing up and down, still telling someone off. Two men with black armbands followed, and it took a while for Reg to work out who they could be. It nagged away at him until he saw Cathleen's sister urge them to get a move on; it could only mean that they were the brothers. He couldn't put a name to either one but they had been in the shop a couple of times and he remembered shy, smiling men who mumbled over their change.

Cathleen herself looked very fine, Reg thought, with the kind of black hair that stood out in a room of black-haired people, just as it stood out now against the glossy paintwork of the hearse.

He put on his trilby and jacket and flipped the shop sign: he could afford to close for a few minutes. At a slow, steady walking pace, the procession of cars manoeuvred out of the side street and edged into the traffic. As the hearse turned into Rosebery Avenue, Reg stood to attention and took off his hat to salute Mick Brogan.

The coffin dominated the church. It didn't matter where Cathleen looked, she could see it. Placed on a pedestal in front of the altar rails, three Madonna lilies were arranged on the lid, their waxy trumpets gleaming white against the ochre veneer.

Cathleen glanced down at the watch Mick had given her when they got engaged. A few bits of marquisate were missing from the rim of the dial. She should have looked after it better: she should have been more careful.

Ten to two: the church was filling up.

She and the girls sat on their own in the front pew. Her sister Mary was directly behind with their mother and Grandma Brogan. There were a few people she didn't recognize but mostly it was parishioners, faces she was used to seeing on Sunday mornings. Cathleen wished that good manners hadn't kept Pat and Christy Brady right at the back. They ran a pub in Amwell Street and were the first friends Mick had made when he arrived in London with nothing but a few pounds in his back pocket. They had given him a bed when he hadn't been able to find lodgings, bailed him out when his wages didn't stretch an entire week and loaned him the money for Cathleen's watch. 'It was a good investment,' they told her later. 'We knew you'd keep our Mick on the straight and narrow.' She looked at them now, stiff in their best clothes, Christy with a bit of paper on his chin where he'd cut himself shaving. Cathleen had never seen them apart and longed for the warmth of their company. Me and Mick always thought we were going to be like them; growing old together. She bit her lip hard and turned away. Perhaps it was best that the Bradys had decided to sit at the back.

Five to two and Tacit Donovan entered, followed by a long line of men. They looked as though they were in uniform, each man in his Sunday best of a dark suit and tie. Tacit directed his men into the pews on the left-hand side of the altar, but before he took his own seat, he walked over to where Cathleen was sitting. She tried to prepare herself. He would say something, she thought, and then I've got to say something back and this is what it will be like all day. And I need to have that something ready in my head, although thank you would surely be enough. Thank you for coming, she whispered to herself.

Tacit stood in front of her. She hadn't seen him out of his workman's clothes before. He's only a few years older than Mick, she thought, and wondered why she had never realized that before. Tacit took one of her hands and held it for a moment as a look crossed his face. You know, Cathleen thought, you know how wrong all this is. I shouldn't be sitting in church on a weekday afternoon. None of us should.

Then he was gone, touching the coffin's polished surface with the tips of his fingers before melting into the rows of men on the other side of the aisle.

Two o'clock and people began to shift in their seats and fidget.

There were coughs, throat clearings and nose blowings. Anna
tugged at Cathleen's coat and spoke in a fierce whisper.

'Is Daddy in there?' She pointed at the coffin. Cathleen nodded
and attempted to put her arm around her daughter but it was
shrugged off. 'It's the wrong colour.'

'It's wood colour, child,' hissed Kitty from behind. 'Don't be
showing your mother up. If you can't be good you'll have to sit
with me.'

'It's horrible yellow,' Anna persisted. 'And I am good. Aren't I,
Mummy? Aren't I always good?'

'Always,' murmured Cathleen, feeling Anna's forehead. It was
cool but her cheeks were flushed and her eyes shiny. She had
been chewing her hair again and sucked the tight brown curls
on either side of her face into a slick, ragged mess. Cathleen
glanced down at Geraldine burrowing into her right side. She
seemed fragile, all elbows and knees. Cathleen drew both children closer to her.

At ten past a couple of men standing at the back stamped their
feet. There was a chill in the air and a smell of damp.

'Where's this priest then?' Kitty demanded. 'Where's this Brogan
fellow?'

The main door opened and everyone turned. A young man
scuttled up a side aisle, a stray from Tacit Donovan's brigade.
Cathleen noted the eyebrows grey with cement dust, and she
ached for him and the shirt that looked clean enough but had
obviously, even from a distance, not been near an iron in a
long time. She opened her missal and tried to read a prayer
to the girls but stopped after a few words. She couldn't trust
her voice.

And then everyone was on their feet and she was left sitting
there, clinging on to her daughters, as if they were in danger of
being swept away by the organ's bellow. The Mass had begun.

'Isn't he the spit of Gregory Peck,' Kitty whispered.

Cathleen didn't want to look up. It wasn't a day for heroes or
good looks. It was a day for holding in and holding on. Cathleen's
grip on Anna and Geraldine tightened as together they rose to
their feet.

'*Requiem æternam dona eis.*'

The voice from her wedding day. She forced her head up. Yes,
it was Father Jerry.

Grandma Brogan squeezed her shoulder. Cathleen was glad that the old woman was so easily comforted but she knew what was to come. After the gospel, after the church rang out with the response to the *Kyrie Eleison*, after the smoky sweet flumes of incense, there would be the sermon. It didn't matter who said it. It didn't matter if it was the parish priest with his bobbing Adam's apple or the shy curate. Or even Father Jerry Brogan with a Kerry swing to his voice that made each word sound as though it were lifted from a ballad. It would be about Mick and it would be wrong.

Don't tell me Mick was devoted to the Mass, Cathleen thought as Father Jerry climbed the steps to the pulpit. That's what they said about my friend Angie when everyone knew the only thing she was devoted to was sticking pictures of Grace Kelly on her bedroom wall. Don't say he loved the Eucharist. Mick Brogan loved a bet and a pint and me.

She bowed her head as the sermon began.

'Mick and I played together as children and his house was like another home to me.' Cathleen heard her mother-in-law's sudden intake of breath. 'And when I see all your faces, I know that this matters.' The priest spoke quietly, holding out his hands in a gesture that took in the whole congregation. Cathleen looked up.

'Being here matters.' Father Jerry's voice was stronger, his words carrying clearly to the upper balconies and the back of the church. 'Because Mick Brogan mattered.'

He held the pause for a couple of heartbeats.

'The world goes on outside,' Father Jerry continued. 'There's trains still running, men working, women cooking. Ordinary life goes on but in here, in this church, right now, it stops. Not for long, but long enough to say goodbye.'

Cathleen felt the priest's clear grey eyes on her and couldn't look away.

'I know that no words can comfort his young wife or his mother who has travelled all the way from south-west Ireland to be here. But Mick is home now, not home to Farran – the village where he grew up – or to the home he made for himself in London. But to the home we're all going to where we'll find one another again.' The priest looked around the church and then back at Cathleen. 'We're on the same journey and Mick has gone on ahead.'

'Didn't I tell you he has a terrible way with words?' Grandma Brogan whispered. The old woman was crying. Cathleen put a hand to her own face and was surprised to find that it was wet.

Six

'Summer in Farran,' promised Cathleen. She stood next to her mother-in-law beside the open grave while the wind whipped at their coats. On three sides they were hemmed in by red-brick terraces, on the fourth by the growl of slow-moving traffic. 'We'll come next summer,' Cathleen repeated and she was rewarded when a hand reached out for hers.

'Ah God, if you only could.'

The note of desperation in Grandma Brogan's voice made Cathleen wince. She and Mick were always going to visit but somehow never did. It should have been one of their stops during their honeymoon but Mick had fallen in love with Dublin and, after the wedding, they had a few precious days of hotel life with the pair of them acting like tourists in the city where she had grown up. Farran would wait. But the next year she was pregnant and the year after that there was no money to spare for holidays. And then pregnant again.

Clouds filled the sky above the cemetery and the first drops of rain released a fresh, earthy smell from the newly dug grave. Father Jerry, without the purple vestments he had worn in church, stood at the edge, his tanned face contrasting with his simple black cassock. He spoke softly and the unfamiliar Latin words merged with the sound of rain. When Father Jerry raised his hand, Cathleen turned away instinctively. It sounds like a baby's rattle, she thought, as the first spade of earth was thrown on top of the coffin.

'Daddy won't like it here.' Anna broke free and edged forward. 'Make them stop.' She turned an angry face to her mother. 'You know Daddy doesn't like the dark.'

The little girl flung herself into the folds of her mother's coat, lashing out with a foot.

'Don't leave him here,' she ordered, her eyes and nose streaming and her small fists hammering at Cathleen's chest. The two grandmothers pulled her away; Grandma Brogan with tender clucking noises as if she was a sick calf and Kitty with a swift tug on the arm.

It was raining in earnest now and, as Cathleen knelt down on the wet grass to be at the same height as Anna, she wished that her eldest daughter hadn't grown so big. She wanted to pick her up and whisper lies about everything being all right. Instead, she pulled the wet strands of hair away from the child's face and kissed her forehead. Anna was still gulping mouthfuls of air but she had stopped struggling and Cathleen straightened up to find Geraldine by her side, eyes wide in fear. She turned away from the grave and dragged her children out of the cemetery.

At the gate Cathleen looked back. A dozen umbrellas were up. Only Tacit Donovan was still bareheaded as he led a line of men to the edge of Mick's grave.

The damp wintry afternoon had turned into a wet wintry evening by the time Reg realized that Cathleen was back. The sweet jars in the shop window cast pools of colour on to the counter and through the lemon sherbets he was able to make out her slim shape as she emerged from the limousine. Reg hesitated. He'd intended to pay his respects and had already rehearsed what he was going to say several times in front of the mirror, but in the glow from the street lights Cathleen looked a smaller, frailer version of herself.

And he hadn't expected so many people.

Cathleen stood by her bedroom door and pressed her cheek against the cool wood. On the other side was a houseful of guests, and she could hear the clink of glasses and an undercurrent of talk from downstairs. The Bradys, thank God, had taken over. They would see to everything while regulars at The Sleeping Dog would go thirsty. Christy Brady had called on Cathleen two nights earlier with a barrel of beer in the back of his van.

It might not settle in time, he had warned, as he upended it on to a table in the corner of the sitting room, but I think we have a chance. And it will surely make for a grand send-off. He had to blow his nose loudly to hide the catch in his voice. After he left Cathleen realized that the barrel was in the same position as the Christmas tree Mick had put up last year.

There were only two rooms on the top floor of the house:

the big double bedroom that she and Mick had shared and next
to it a kitchen. Cathleen opened the door to let in a sliver of
sound. A muffled cheer came from the floor below and she shut
it again, guessing that the first pint had been drawn.

*Wouldn't Mick have loved that? Wouldn't he have loved draught beer
at home!*

I can't do it; I can't face them.

'He was a mad thing carrying on.'

A man's voice sliced into her thoughts. It was very near, just
the other side of the door.

'And after we won I got him up on my shoulders. He held
the hurling stick high above his head and we ran around the field
chanting and cheering. Mad things both of us.'

It was the priest. Cathleen pushed open the door. Father
Jerry was facing her and talking to a knot of people on the
landing.

'That's a good memory,' said Grandma Brogan softly. She had
her back to Cathleen and hadn't heard the door open. 'Mick
always loved going to your matches.'

'Cathleen!' Father Jerry moved forward, making the glass of
foamy beer in his hand froth over. 'We disturbed you?'

She shook her head. 'Go on,' she said quietly. 'Please, it's all
right.'

Grandma Brogan looked at her face and then guided her gently
by the elbow into the kitchen. With a frown, pursed lips and a
shake of the head, the old woman was like some guard dog that
still had some bite left in its bark.

'Look after her,' she beckoned to Father Jerry. 'You're the only
one who's any good for her now.'

Cathleen tried to say something.

'Sit easy,' Grandma Brogan instructed. 'The children are minded
and you have to mind yourself.' The kitchen door creaked shut.

'Do you want to talk?'

Cathleen shook her head and studied the wood grain on the
kitchen table. The edges of Father Jerry's accent had been rounded
off by his years abroad. There were shades of Mick in it, but not
enough to hurt.

'We could pray together if you prefer.'

'No, I don't!' She blushed at the passion in her voice. She
would never have dared talk to a priest like that before. 'All I
want to talk about is Mick . . . And I can't talk about him at

all.' She looked away. 'I want to hear about when he was a boy but I'm jealous of your memories. He didn't tell me everything. He didn't know he was going to run out of time.' She swallowed hard. 'But most of all I want to shout like Anna. I want to hit someone. I'd like to hit Mick right now. He shouldn't have left us.'

'It's all right to be angry. I understand.'

'Do you?' She sat up straight, looking at him. 'Do you really think you understand?'

'A bit. Not all of it, not nearly all, but yes, enough to understand the terrible pain.' The same grey eyes that looked at her from the pulpit held her now.

'Then tell me why.' A stab of energy gouged through Cathleen. Her chin jutted forward.

The priest's voice dropped. 'That's something we weren't meant to understand. I do know that if you start blaming God, or the hospital, or the stars in the sky, the pain will get bigger. And it won't even be about Mick any more.' They sat in silence, a ticking clock marking every second. 'I miss Mick,' Father Jerry continued. 'You can take that as a bit of blarney and I wouldn't blame you. After all, the last time I saw him was the day you two got married. If I said I always thought of him as a brother you wouldn't think me much of a family man.'

Cathleen looked away. What could she say? The last time Mick saw his mother was at the wedding.

'But I had the idea of him with me always. My kid brother,' he sighed. 'I thought we would have a chance at being grown up together.' He held out a hand to her. 'I'm saying this because I hope that we'll be family. Me. You and the girls. The Brogans of Farran.'

'A long-distance family. Us in London. You in Italy and the Brogans in Kerry.'

'Part of being Irish, I suppose.' He shrugged ruefully. 'And I don't plan on being in Verona forever.'

Mary was at the door, peering in. 'Are you all right?' She looked from her sister to the priest.

'I'm . . .' Cathleen struggled for a word. 'I'm managing. Come on in and get to know Father Jerry better. He's family.'

When Reg crossed the street he saw that the front door to the Brogan house had been wedged open. The Italian family that lived in the basement had lined the entrance hall with chairs and were now handing out cups of tea and slabs of rich, dark fruit cake. From somewhere upstairs a lone tenor voice was singing. The words dissolved into each other and Reg couldn't be sure if it was English he was hearing. He climbed the stairs, following the song, brushing past men sitting on the steps, their suits still damp from the afternoon's rain. One got up to look in the box Reg was carrying.

'Tizer! To a wake!'

Reg pulled his trilby down on his forehead and hugged the box close to his chest. The sitting room was crowded. Reg sniffed the air cautiously. Yes, it even smelt like a pub. The dining-room table, pushed to one side to give more room, was loaded with food. He wondered if that was where he should leave his own small offering. He was still trying to decide when he noticed one of Cathleen's brothers standing in front of the window, his prominent ears glowing a rosy red. At first Reg thought the young man must be watching out for someone, but then he realized that this was the singer he had heard from downstairs.

'God didn't give you much, but at least he gave you a mouth to make music.'

The young man's ears got redder. Kitty was in an armchair by the fire with a cigarette in one hand and a glass of liquid in the other. It was the colour of cough candy, thought Reg, but he guessed not the taste. Little Geraldine was asleep on her lap. There was no sign of Cathleen.

A woman charged over to him. Her grey hair had been restrained into a tight perm and her red glasses had been knocked askew.

'I don't know who you are −' she thrust out a hand − 'but I do know you're welcome.' She peered into Reg's box and turned to her husband. 'Christy, come here and see this!'

Reg stood very still and straight. He would go now, without another word. He would leave quietly and he wouldn't hold it against Cathleen Brogan or the little girls. But he would go if there was another comment about the contents of the cardboard box.

'What's this?' A softly spoken man joined them. He seemed to be made of soft edges, from the rounded ball of his nose to the slack muscles of his belly. The box was presented to him and he emitted a long, low whistle.

'If there was one thing needed. And sweets!'

'Exactly! Aren't we saved!' Pat put her arm through Reg's while Christy took the box away. 'That's generous. The girls will love this and they're not the only ones. I'm a publican's wife –' she nodded in Christy's direction – 'but I could go one year to the next without having a drink and it wouldn't bother me in a pig's eye! You're a friend of Mick's that I know just from the look of you. But who are you?'

'He's from across the road.' Kitty's words were beginning to slur and she spilt some of her drink as she gestured in the direction of Rosebery Avenue.

'The shop?' Pat Brady glanced at the clock. 'Closed early, didn't you?' Reg was forced to acknowledge that he had.

'Good man yourself. And people talk about the English!' Pat looked around as if she had been in the middle of an argument before he came in and now she had the very piece of evidence to clinch it.

'Will you have a little something to keep the damp out?' Christy was at his elbow and Reg, after some pressing, agreed to a whiskey.

He looked up to see Cathleen framed in the door: her green dress the colour of grass at night; jet black hair falling in waves from hair grips that had forgotten how to do their job and the light from the hall glowing amber behind her.

So many colours and none in her face. She's going to fall, Reg thought. And who's going to catch her?

Seven

'If the father won't provide . . .' The young man behind the desk didn't bother to glance up. He was about Cathleen's age and she could see the tide mark around his neck that marked where his flannel had reached. He was holding out a form.

'Fill this out. Instructions printed at the top. Next.' A middle-aged woman jumped to her feet; Cathleen hesitated.

'I don't think this is right . . . it's not that he won't.'

The other woman was glaring at Cathleen and muttering under her breath. For the first time the man looked up. 'Is he living with you?'

'No!' Cathleen suddenly felt panicky. Geraldine was beside her, sucking her thumb and listening. 'But he didn't leave us. He died.'

A look of irritation crossed the man's face. 'Should have said.' He fumbled through the papers on his desk and, reaching out for his pen tray, became aware that Geraldine had moved nearer, watching everything he did.

'Get her away, can't you? There's important documentation here. Right, death certificate.'

'I don't have it. The landlord wanted it; so he could change the rent book. I'll have it by the end of the week.'

'I can't do anything without a certificate. Next.'

'About time.' The woman elbowed Cathleen out of the way, but before putting her own papers in front of the clerk she turned around. 'Think you're better than us, don't you? Because your bloke's in the graveyard and not living in the Caledonian Road with a fancy woman.' She nodded towards Geraldine. 'I've got three like her at home. And they eat just as much as poor darling orphans. Only difference is mine have to see their dad lord it around town while I'm scrabbling around after a new pair of shoes.'

Cathleen stepped back, tugging at Geraldine who seemed unwilling to move. She pulled again, more roughly, forcing the child to turn and follow.

Outside sleet was beginning to fall. This is life now, Cathleen thought, pulling Geraldine's bonnet tightly around her head, and tying her mittens in place. And I'm no good at it. Why did I let the rent collector take the certificate? Because he asked, that's why. I'm a fool. Should I get a copy? She paused, making a calculation in her head. Buying another copy plus the bus fares to get it would be at least as much as a dinner for the three of them; and then there was the milkman on Saturday morning, he'd want paying. Still, she had that safe in the jam jar at the back of the dresser. No, she didn't! A tight, sick feeling twisted in her stomach as she remembered that she had used the jam jar money to pay the rental on the television. And already she owed two weeks on the hire-purchase for the fridge.

'Mummy! You're hurting.'

Cathleen let her daughter's hand drop. The gas meter. She'd forgotten the gas meter. Mick had always brought shillings home for that; a shiny pile of them on a Thursday night, more than enough to last the week. And when the meter man came and left a rebate it would be Mick's treat.

'Mummy, I'm tired.'

'Pick your feet up,' Cathleen snapped. 'You're scuffing your shoes.'

'They hurt.'

Cathleen remembered the sour face of the woman in the National Assistance office spitting out insults. New shoes were something she didn't want to think about either.

When they got home there was a letter on the doormat and it brought a tired, half-smile to Cathleen's face. She was glad to see the familiar copperplate handwriting and smudgy postmark of the Irish postal service; at least Maeve wouldn't be demanding money, or asking where Mr Brogan was, and why wasn't he supporting his family any more.

She opened it as she warmed her hands on a mug of tea. Geraldine was playing underneath the table with pictures of people that Mick had carefully cut out of a clothes' catalogue. These were her family: a backcombed blonde in tight black sweater was the mummy and, as the pages of blue notepaper slipped from the envelope, it sounded to Cathleen that in Geraldine's game Mummy told everyone off.

The cows are still milking, Cathleen read and her smile widened. She knew what to expect, a selection of tiny details from her sister-in-law's life sprinkled with 'Please God's' and 'Thank God's'. The last line was always about her son: Seamus had a cough on Tuesday night but after a bit of linctus he seems better. P.G. Or: Seamus went into town for a haircut and we had a very fine day T.G.

Cathleen scanned to the end. Yes, here was this month's announcement: Seamus is looking forward to it too. That seemed very little for Maeve to say about her only child. Cathleen leafed quickly back through the pages to find out why, and her own name leapt out at her.

There is no talk now but that Cathleen and the girls are coming. It is all we can think of and the winter won't seem so harsh knowing what the summer will bring. God bless you for this and I know you will get your reward in heaven because it is the greatest thing you could do for our mother and for all of us and I thank God that Mick married such a lovely girl.

'Mummy?' Geraldine was tugging at her dress. 'Are you crying again, Mummy?'

The shop was busy but Reg, glancing over his shoulder at the window lined with sweet jars, noticed Anna kicking the railings outside her house. Squinting through the distorting glaze of barley twists and pear drops, he could make out the child's scowling face. He glanced up at the clock. She was cutting it fine if she was going to get to school on time.

A woman was talking about a knitting pattern. Yes, yes, he nodded, making a note of the order with the stub of a pencil he kept behind his ear, but he was only giving it half his attention. Out of the corner of his eye he spotted Cathleen, dashing out of her front door. Her coat was unbuttoned and Reg tutted to himself as he served the next customer. He had felt a chill wind that morning when he collected the pile of newspapers from the shop doorstep and his print-stained hands were still cold. He looked again and this time saw the youngest girl trailing behind, a dark veil of hair falling in front of her face – no time for ribbons this morning.

Grabbing a copy of *Bunty* from behind the counter, Reg suddenly opened the shop door.

'Here's a treat for you.' He shoved the comic into Anna's hand but was looking at Cathleen, shocked at the smudges beneath her eyes and the greyness of her skin. Reg realized that he hadn't seen her close up since she had stopped buying a daily paper. 'Let her stay in the shop.' He nodded towards Geraldine. 'I'll mind her while you get to school.' A small pinched face looked up at him in horror. 'It's nice and warm in here,' he added, as an icy blast stung his ears and the tip of his nose.

'Will you . . .?' Cathleen coaxed. 'I won't be long.'

'I don't want to be left,' wailed the little girl. She was inside her mother's coat now, pulling it around her.

'Read it already.' The comic was back in Reg's hands.

'Anna!' Cathleen's cheeks flamed with sudden colour. 'There's no helping us,' she mumbled in embarrassment. 'But thank you. Thank you.'

As Reg turned back into the shop, he saw Anna race ahead on strong, athletic legs, not looking back to see if her mother and sister were following. He glanced again at the shop clock. The girl might just do it, he thought.

Cathleen called out in alarm as Anna crossed Rosebery Avenue by herself. The six-year-old stepped out into the traffic and brakes screeched as an angry taxi driver made an emergency stop. The desperation in Cathleen's voice forced the child to wait but she did so with bad grace, jigging up and down in impatience.

Children were already lining up in the playground when they reached the school gates, ready to march into the hall. The headmistress blew the referee's whistle that was swinging around her neck. She insisted on silence at the start of the school day and the look she directed at talkative mothers at the school gate was every bit as fierce as the one she wore when inspecting her pupils.

Geraldine tugged at Cathleen's coat and pointed at her sister who had caught up with the rest of her class. The girl was frowning in almost brutal concentration, her lips clamped together in a tight grimace, while her right hand was raised high in the air. Pain, was Cathleen's first thought, and she stepped forward to claim her back and take her home.

'Please, Miss.' Anna's voice carried clearly in the playground and the headmistress turned slowly, looked her up and down, frowned, and turned slowly away again.

'Please, Miss!' There was agony in the voice now and the child's hand stretched to the rooftops. It was too late. A steady stream of urine splashed down on to Anna's shoes, puddling the tarmac. The children in front turned around and those in other lines inched forward, pointing.

This time the headmistress spun on her heel, freezing the playground with a short blast on her whistle. Something inside Cathleen lurched as she watched her daughter being marched to the toilets. Anna's face was now so pale every freckle stood out as if she had been splattered with coffee. Cathleen stepped forward, desperate to do something, but not sure what. Without turning around she could feel the nudges of the other mothers and hear the giggles and grunts of mock disgust from the children.

Get them into the hall, she prayed, but without a command from the whistle the school was paralysed.

Anna emerged from the squat red-brick outhouse, the wooden

door clanging behind her. She held her head high and didn't look to the right or the left as she rejoined her class. The headmistress followed with a small damp bundle wrapped in newspaper. She handed it to Cathleen without a word.

'Let me take her home . . .' It was a feeble appeal and one look from the headmistress withered Cathleen into silence. She turned away as a skinny boy in short trousers, his bony knees red with the cold, started to sing: 'Dirty Anna's in a fix because she's wet her knix.'

'I can't do a thing right.' Cathleen gulped down the hot sweet tea Pat Brady put in front of her.

Cathleen had never been to the Brady's pub out of hours before but, standing outside the school gate, she knew she couldn't go home. Without a word, she turned sharp left and walked against a cheek-stinging wind towards Pentonville, first depositing the damp parcel in the nearest rubbish bin. Geraldine struggled to keep up and was gulping for air when they reached The Sleeping Dog. The child's nose was running and her eyes were wet with tears as Cathleen's chilled knuckles knocked nervously on frosted glass. The door was flung open and Christy Brady, in an old baggy cardigan and with white stubble on his chin, urged them to come in. Inside the curtains were closed and the soft, sallow darkness smelt of beer; Cathleen's face crumpled when Pat appeared, pink curlers in her hair and slippers on her feet.

'And then there's Christmas,' whispered Cathleen. Pat's strong arms were around her; rocking her gently. 'And I haven't the money for it. Or the heart.'

Eight

Father Jerry leant out of his office window and looked down at the grey-pink rooftops stretched out on both banks of the river Adige. It was a cool, dry day with a sky that still had a trace of the summer in it. The air smelt of frying garlic. He glanced back at his desk, frowning at the ream of watermarked notepaper neatly placed on one side. There were letters to be written: decisions to be made.

And this surely was the easiest of all. In his hand were two dog-eared English pound notes and he half smiled as he felt the crumpled texture between his fingers. He had intended to send the money to Cathleen from London airport when he had discovered the notes in a pocket, and had cadged an envelope and stamp from the airline staff – using the combination of clerical collar and a wide smile – but then the address had eluded him. He could have described it well enough: soot-blackened bricks, dogs' mess on the pavement, dirty milk bottles on the doorstep, two minutes from a theatre, three from the station with a religious name. He clicked his fingers in annoyance. What was it called? The Saint? No, The Angel.

Flung into a crisis as soon as he had arrived back at the seminary, he had forgotten all about the money until now. The evening before his return a favourite student, just months away from ordination, had announced that he was getting married. As Spiritual Director, Father Jerry's task was to minimize the shame as he eased Salvatore back into the world. Meetings with the family were fraught. If the circumstances had been different, he might have been amused at the suggestion that as a non-Italian he didn't fully understand the disgrace. In Ireland the young man would have been called a spoiled priest, and carried the label to his grave. It was hard to shake the image of the young man's grandmother, yellow and shrunken inside her black widow's shawl, sitting in a corner with her face turned to the wall.

He shook his head. He had done what he could for them; what about Cathleen? Hers was another face that had stayed with him and he found himself thinking of her often. She and Mick must have made a good-looking couple. Had they been good to each other? As a priest he was often privy to the running grievances that seemed to make up so much of married life: each couple with their own hymn of complaints, composed and added to over the years, but always sung to the same tune: O Father, he's not a hero; O Father, she's not a princess.

Father Jerry glanced back at his desk. The bishop required an answer. At their last meeting it had been made clear that as a Kerry priest he had spent enough time in Italy. He had expected to be ordered home but instead he had been given a choice: a vacancy had arisen in a parish on the west coast near Dingle. 'The church needs a new roof,' the bishop had written in a terse, economical scrawl, 'and the land is too poor to support the families that live off it. Every year the biggest crop is the young who leave for America and Britain.' There's more to it than that, Father Jerry mused. He had climbed the mountains and walked the boreens of Dingle as a young man just before his own ordination. He remembered the thunder of the surf and how close he had felt to God.

The alternative was very different. It was a new venture and he would be his own boss. The budget would be tiny and the whole enterprise was untried, untested and would probably fail within the year. And it was in London.

Father Jerry inhaled. He could smell tomatoes now, as well as garlic: it was nearly lunchtime. He would miss Italy but he had been here long enough. Mick's death had made the decision for him. A Kerry priest should serve the people of Kerry, be where they needed him most, sharing the day, sharing the struggle. And there was only one place he could do all that.

London.

He looked down again at the pound notes in his hands. Sending them as soon as he had located his address book would have been a nice gesture, simple and uncomplicated. But now, weeks later? Would Cathleen think he was being condescending? The big priest doling out charity. He put the notes back in his wallet. No, he wouldn't take the risk. He'd write at Christmas, send the money then, maybe adding a bit.

And at Christmas he might even have some news.

Nine

'The world hasn't gone and cancelled Christmas so neither can you.' Kitty focused all her attention on her eldest daughter. They were sitting at Cathleen's kitchen table while Mary slouched against the door frame, pulling faces behind her mother's back. 'I've already decided about the dinner,' Kitty continued, scowling. 'It had better be at my place, although you can still do the cooking, Cathleen. Sure, the boys wouldn't stand for a slice of turkey otherwise.'

Cathleen nodded. It would be cramped and uncomfortable and she didn't know how she'd manage on the three small gas rings of her mother's ancient cooker. But yes, better at her mother's place because it wouldn't be like last year and all the other years of her married life. She wouldn't take the heavy damask table-cloth out of its cedar wood box after Mass on Christmas morning: she wouldn't lay the table with her once-a-year wedding-present plates. And she wouldn't nag Mick to hurry up and carve the turkey.

'And then there's Christmas Eve,' Kitty continued.

The words knotted in Cathleen's stomach. She turned away so her mother wouldn't see her face.

'Don't be going on at her,' Mary interrupted. 'She's done wonders. Only last Sunday I saw a jacket that once belonged to Mick on the back of that chap with a limp from Rosoman Street.'

'Oh, but she hasn't given it all away. There's a pile of old clothes on the dressing table.' Kitty turned on her youngest daughter. 'Torturing herself, that's what your sister's doing.'

'They're just the ones not good enough to give away, that's all,' Cathleen mumbled. 'I'll get rid of them. Soon. I will.'

'Those little girls only have you now,' Kitty continued. 'If you break, they break.' She picked up a brown envelope lying on the kitchen dresser. 'What's this?' Without waiting for an answer, she pulled out the typed letter. 'Mother of God, they can't do that! All that money put in, week after week.' Kitty scrutinized Cathleen's face. 'You weren't going to tell us, were you? They'd have it took away and we'd be none the wiser.'

Mary read the letter over her mother's shoulder and glanced towards the fridge that dominated one corner of the kitchen. She opened the door to look at the turquoise interior. 'It's so lovely. How could they take it away from you after all this time?'

'Because it's not ours – not mine – until the last payment. Now you know what buying on the never never means.'

'We'll not stand by and let the bastards take it off you.' Her mother was brisk. 'I can let you have a few bob now, and the boys will chip in. I'll make sure of that and—'

'You'd only be throwing good money after bad. I can do without.'

'Girl, you can't give up.'

Giving up seemed just about the best plan Cathleen had heard in a long time. All that mattered, she decided, was to have the fridge taken away on a day Anna and Geraldine weren't at home. She didn't care about the neighbours, but she didn't want the girls to see the repossession men cart it downstairs.

'Anyway, we'll be in desperate need of it over Christmas,' Kitty insisted. 'Is your sister-in-law sending the turkey?'

'I don't know.'

'Oh Lord save us, you'd better find out before every butcher's window is bare.'

'It's ages away yet!' Mary protested.

'It's clear that you've never had the planning of a Christmas. Always put in front of you as if by magic! Ages indeed!' Kitty was ready to leave. 'And I'll say it again, you can't ignore Christmas Eve either.' She flung the remark over her shoulder. 'That's another day that hasn't been cancelled.'

On Monday morning Cathleen was summoned to the head-mistress's office and instructed to leave Geraldine outside. The heavy panelled door shut on her daughter's anxious face with a resonant click.

'I presume you'll want a place for her in the new year?' The headmistress, a thin, angular woman, was leaning against the door, as if Geraldine might force her way in.

'Yes, oh yes.' Cathleen looked up eagerly. 'We've had her name down since she was a baby, and there's nowhere else.'

Through the walls came the muffled sound of young voices singing. The headmistress tilted her head to listen as *Adeste Fideles* penetrated the office. 'Class Five going through their paces,' she explained. '*Gloria, Gloria,*' she sang suddenly, her nostrils flaring. '*In excelsis Deo.*'

'Is that all? Cathleen got up to go.

'No, it most certainly is not.' The headmistress motioned her to sit down again and took up her own position behind the desk. 'You must be aware that our classrooms are not infinitely extend-able. Sometimes hard decisions have to be made, even about sisters. No, it's your other daughter I wish to discuss.' She looked intently at Cathleen. 'She has a musical capacity and was selected to sing at the carol concert. It is a great honour for so young a child. But little Miss Brogan has told her teacher that she's decided that she doesn't want to sing. Those were her very words.'

'Oh, right.'

'We need to nip this kind of wilfulness in the bud. I see that Anna has always been a top-table child. She came to us with many of her letters learnt and a facility for reading. That was your doing, I presume?'

'Well, she loves it so. It wasn't teaching her at home so much as not stopping her.'

'It's much better if parents don't interfere.' The headmistress leant forward to emphasize her point. 'I'm not saying any harm was done but teaching really should be left to the school, as a matter of principle. Otherwise confusion.' She let the word linger in the air between them, making it sound like a sin.

'And look what's happening now. No longer a top-table child. The class teacher says she stares into space. Little Miss Brogan, the brightest girl in the class, is above all the work that the rest of us have to do.'

'I was going to ask you about that. I didn't realize that only the top table are allowed to go to the toilet.'

'What has that got to do with anything?'

'Last week she came home very upset. She says she had her hand up but wasn't allowed to go. What with the playground and everything . . .' Cathleen studied the floor. 'I didn't want any more embarrassment for her.'

'I am sure that Anna didn't complain when she *was* sitting on the top table and her hand *was* noticed. Excellence is rewarded in this school and children are taught that life is serious. Less daydreaming and Anna will be back in her old seat again. Now really, I must press on.'

Cathleen scrambled to her feet. The headmistress frowned. 'We expect parents to do their duty. Can I rely on your support? Will you work with me in bringing little Miss Brogan back into line?'

Cathleen nodded and thought of Anna at the kitchen table that morning. She'd snatched a slice of toast from Geraldine and then pinched her viciously for telling. Without thought, Cathleen had lashed out, although she'd never smacked either of the girls before.

Geraldine was waiting obediently outside. Her apprehensive face fractured into a grin at the sight of her.

'Mummy, you were ever so long,' she whispered.

'I'm glad that we've had this little talk.' The headmistress rose to her feet. 'Of course, you're aware that Catholic schools in London are crammed to the rafters. We don't have nearly enough places for all the children.' The headmistress glanced at Geraldine and then back at Cathleen. 'We do understand each other, don't we? And let me assure you that this one doesn't need to know her alphabet as long as she knows how to keep her knickers dry.'

Cathleen nodded and held Geraldine's hand tightly as they walked down the corridor towards the exit.

'Look,' whispered Geraldine as they passed a classroom. The door was ajar. 'They have paints. I expect I'll paint a lot of pictures when I'm here. I'll paint with my new friends.' She looked up. 'I will have friends to play with, won't I?'

Cathleen nodded. They were now very near the entrance lobby and she was about to push the swing doors open when she hesitated, seeing again the red marks on Geraldine's arm that morning. Slowly, she turned around and faced the way they had come.

'Please, let's go.' Geraldine tugged on her hand

'Stand there,' Cathleen ordered. 'And don't even blink.' She hurried back down the corridor, almost breaking into a run. *I can't think about this. I've just got to do it.* She knocked on the headmistress's door and turned the handle before she heard an answer.

'I'm sorry . . .' Cathleen took a deep breath. 'I should have said that Anna doesn't feel like singing. I'm sure she will again, but it's not a singing time for any of us. And you don't have to give her lessons on how hard life can be. She discovered that for herself the day she buried her father.' Cathleen swallowed and made an effort to stand up taller. 'When Anna Brogan's hand goes up I hope someone sees it. I think it deserves to be seen.'

'I don't want it to be Christmas,' Anna whispered that evening, as she crept onto Cathleen's lap. A pile of cards had already arrived. Cathleen wasn't hiding them. She wasn't doing that. It was just that she hadn't got around to putting them on the mantelpiece.

'Perhaps we should have just a bit of a one for Geraldine's sake.' Cathleen glanced across at her younger daughter sprawled on the floor in front of the television. Anna nodded slowly.

'You'll have to help because I don't think I can do it without you.' Anna nodded again.

Although how a six-year-old was supposed to get them through Christmas Eve, Cathleen didn't know, especially as the memory of last year and all the other years was waiting like a trap on the edge of her vision, ready to drag her down.

On Christmas Eve Mick would be late home and the girls would be too excited to go to bed but somehow we'd get them there and all four of us would hang up their socks.

Last year, Cathleen's lip trembled as she remembered, was it really the best year, or am I kidding myself? Last year there was a crowd here and Mick lit the Christmas candle and made a big fuss about how it had to be seen from the road, because every Irish home was an immigrant home that had someone missing. And the candle was a sign to anyone away from their family that they could come inside and be made welcome. As he said it, just as the words were out of his mouth, there'd been a loud knock on the door that frightened the life out of us, until someone called out: 'That was quick.'

The roar of laughter put the candle out and it was only the Italian man from the basement flat. I was scared he'd come about the noise, but not a bit of it. He'd heard singing and wanted to join in and brought a bottle of sweet wine with him. And then he opened his mouth and out came a voice that rattled the windowpanes and, although his song was full of foreign words, somehow we understood and clapped, and Mick said he never realized we'd been living on top of Mario Lanza all this time.

About then I dished up the cubreens with thick slices of soda bread and I was clapped as loudly as if I was an Italian tenor myself.

That was last year.

Cathleen was staring sightlessly at the television and suddenly became aware that Anna was pulling at her.

'We better have Christmas,' Anna announced gravely, getting to her feet to join her sister. 'Because Santa Claus will come anyway.'

Ten

Maeve was plucking a turkey at the kitchen table in the Brogan farmhouse. All year she had tended her little flock, although she hated the sight of their raw, red wattle and the screech of the young birds as they strutted around the farmyard like bullying schoolboys. Now, though, her efforts were being repaid. She had a turkey to send to London, a turkey for the parish and a turkey for their own table. She was struggling to remove the last of the pin feathers when the back door slammed shut. Maeve flinched but didn't look up.

'And who am I feeding with that?' Standing in the doorway was her brother Thady.

'Oh now, don't go on.'

'Is it for the little widow, Cath-leeen?' Thady moved to the kitchen table and drummed his fingers on the surface. 'God in heaven, we grow widows in this family!' His loose, wet lips broke into a grin. 'Youse women don't know how to look after your men at all. And do I have to feed her as well?'

Maeve said nothing as she bent over the mauve-fleshed carcass.

'Go on, spit it out. In whose oven is that turkey cooking? Who's going to pull that wishbone?'

'Ah, Thady. You know these are my birds. You know I do this every year . . .'

'How much land do you have?'

'What?' Maeve looked up into her brother's face, startled at the sudden change in tone. From sarcasm he seemed to have leapt into a fury.

'How many acres is it? How many fields? How many blades of grass? Where do your precious birds feed unless it's on my land? You, living by the side of the road in a cottage not worth the name, no better than a tinker.'

'Leave her alone.'

Seamus had come into the room without either of them

noticing. He stood in front of his uncle, stronger and younger. His fists were clenching and unclenching as his mother started to whimper. The boy's eyes never left his uncle's face and the two men were breathing heavily.

'You lazy little git, what have you been doing all morning?'

'Your chores and mine.' Seamus' fists were still working like a pump.

'I was looking for you to mend the gap in the hedge.'

'I've done it.'

'I better see the mess you made.' Thady stomped out of the room.

'I want out of here.' Seamus turned away from his mother's timid, outstretched hand. 'And I want away from him.' He spat out the words. 'It's all right, Mammy.' He went over to Maeve's chair and knelt down beside her. 'I won't leave you to suffer Thady on your own.'

'You're a good boy,' Maeve whispered, stroking her son's chestnut hair. 'You're a gorgeous boy.'

Eleven

Cathleen watched as Tacit Donovan passed by Reg's shop and stood at the zebra crossing waiting for the traffic to slow down.

She was at the kitchen window at the same time every evening. Mick was never going to saunter down the road or wave from the corner, but it used to be his time for coming home and that made it her time now. She couldn't go to the cemetery every day, but for a few minutes every evening she could wait for Mick.

She thought of it as something secret, not realizing that both children knew when to avoid the kitchen. Although Anna was still struggling with the big hand and little hand on clocks, both children could tell the time by the expression on their mother's face, and the way sometimes her lips moved in silent conversation.

When Cathleen saw Tacit she knew he must have come straight from the building site. She glanced at her watch. Yes, he was bang on time. He was wearing a good overcoat but underneath she guessed was an old suit of the kind that all the men wore when working. Mick called it his third best and it was still hanging in the wardrobe. Tacit would probably have a thick jumper under his jacket; moth-holed, darned at the elbows and unravelling at the seams. She still had three of Mick's, hidden away in her dressing-table drawer.

Tacit was crossing the road. He must be walking up to the Angel to catch a train, she thought, and turned away.

The doorbell rang.

'I'll get it,' Anna yelled from the room below. Cathleen heard voices and feet on the stairs and then Tacit was in the kitchen, shaking hands and saying yes to a cup of tea.

She realized she was wrong as soon as he started to take off his coat. His suit was smart, the shirt starched and she was sure that the gold tie pin had never been near a cement mixer. Cathleen only realized that she was inspecting him when she looked up to see a slow smile spread across his face.

'I haven't been changing my job, if that's what you're thinking.'

'Or won the pools?'

'Business.' He shook his head dismissively. 'A lot of standing around, telling each other how grand we are. The flats are finished.'

Cathleen nodded. 'Are they nice? Mick thought they would be. And with all the gadgets . . .'

'Nice rent. More than fifty bob a week.' He frowned. The way he looked around the kitchen made Cathleen feel that he was the one doing the inspecting now, making an inventory of the painted walls and the warped window frame wedged shut with an empty Senior Service packet. 'I'm in need of advice, Cathleen,' he continued. 'Mick always said you had a head on your shoulders. The thing is the job was on time. A mite early in fact. It's the way I like it. I don't want those business fellows saying, Late again, Paddy.'

Cathleen nodded. She would be surprised if anyone had ever made a jibe like that in Tacit's hearing. It was well known that Donovan's jobs always came in on time.

'Thing is there's a bit of a bonus coming. I have Mick's here but I was wondering if I should give it to the men now? Or, seeing it's so close to Christmas, would it be better to wait?' He drew out of his pocket a fat brown envelope and placed it on the kitchen table. He pushed it towards her.

'First I heard of dead men getting a bonus,' she said softly. Tacit shifted slightly in his chair but his face remained expressionless. 'First I heard of the men getting a bonus at all,' Cathleen continued. 'Would you want me to tell the wives in Chapel Market and at Mass on Sunday? So they know what's coming. That'd stop the men from drinking it away.'

Tacit looked at her steadily as a muscle twitched in his jaw. 'Mick was right,' he said at last. 'It was a clumsy lie.' He paused and then gestured towards the table. 'There's two weeks' money there. And I'm not picking it up again.'

He was on his feet and at the kitchen door. As he reached for the handle, he turned to Cathleen who still hadn't moved. 'And if you want to know where it comes from, well the ganger does get a bonus. And that's another thing I'd rather you didn't spread around Chapel Market.'

He'd reached the ground floor while Cathleen sat at the table, mesmerized by the bundle of notes. Suddenly she was racing after him, clattering down the stairs. He was almost at the front door when she called to him over the banister. She said his name so urgently and with such passion that he was forced to turn around.

'Tacit,' Cathleen began. She was out of breath and her words jumped and collided into one another. 'Thank you, Tacit. Thank you.'

The fridge is safe, she thought as she walked back up the stairs. And Santa can come.

There were more Christmas cards on the doormat the next morning. She recognized the writing on most of them. One was from Maeve and Cathleen sighed when she picked it up. There was no pleasure in reading how wonderful she was, when sooner or later she'd have to say she wasn't wonderful at all, and break the promise made over Mick's grave. The other envelope had an Italian stamp and she opened it first. They were family, Father Jerry had said and, right now, she rather liked the idea of family that didn't tell her off or want anything. Inside was a handsome Christmas card of St Peter's Basilica and a letter: four pages of bold writing on thick paper. She took it out and five English pound notes floated to the floor. Cathleen looked at the money in amazement; it was a month's rent.

She scanned the letter. It wasn't like Maeve's ramble that seemed to come straight from her mind to the page, or Grandma Brogan's careful, stilted prose that had been drummed into her as a schoolgirl. It was more like a conversation and she noticed he'd made a mistake on the second page, crossed it out and rewritten the word. Family, she thought. He must have meant it and that crossing out seemed to prove it more than the letter itself, or the money. He wasn't looking to impress. He was just writing, that's all, and he was as relaxed about it as he had been when they talked together in the kitchen, or when he was in the pulpit preaching.

Forgive me because it isn't a proper present and only money.

Only money thought Cathleen. Only money indeed!

It's not for me to tell you what to do with it and there may be a hundred things you need, but I hope that at least part of it will be spent on something foolish, because things like that can make any struggle easier.

How like a man, thought Cathleen. Or, at least, how like the man I had. Wouldn't Mick have known how to spend this fiver? He'd have argued me out of all my sensible schemes and made us feel rich for a few hours. She smiled at the thought, but her smile faded at the realization that the letter would never have been written, or the money sent, if Mick had still been alive.

Still, it was a good thought from Father Jerry. Cathleen held the notes tight. There was no question of being foolish. She knew exactly what she would do with the money. It would pay their fares to Ireland and that meant she could open her other letter with a light heart because they would have their summer in Farran.

As she put the priest's Christmas card in pride of place on the mantelpiece she read his postscript for the first time: 'No date yet but I should be in London soon.'

A flying visit, she guessed. However short, it meant that she had something to look forward to. She felt the cream, watermarked paper between her fingers. It was a rich letter to give so much.

Twelve

All the women went shopping on Christmas Eve.

Kitty had an opinion on everything from the waxy tangerines piled high on stalls groaning under the weight of Brussels sprouts to the bride's doll that was on sale in Woolworths. Geraldine looked at it wistfully as she had done for the last three weeks. Mary and Cathleen exchanged glances. There was one just like it hidden at home, ready for Geraldine's stocking tomorrow. Anna would discover the handbag she had asked Santa about, and the books and colouring pencils she wanted, and there were new dresses for both of them.

While Kitty's back was turned a scarf was purchased and tucked into a shopping bag next to the box of Eat Me dates and a pound of Brazil nuts. The children had already wrapped an Adam Faith EP for Mary, and for Mummy there was a large bottle of perfume with a wonderful plastic eagle on top, its gold wings stretching upwards.

'Apple fritters,' declared Mary. 'We must have apple fritters going home.' The children giggled as they stood in front of the vat of bubbling oil that turned the cold air sweet. They squealed as they burnt their fingers on the crisp batter while biting into the soft, gooey flesh.

'It's going to be all right,' Mary whispered. Cathleen nodded, linking arms with her sister and smiling at the thought that back home another surprise was waiting for the girls. Her brothers had gone out earlier and bought a Christmas tree. It would be up, with lights twinkling by the time they got back and tonight they would decorate it with the tinsel they'd just bought. A beef casserole was simmering away in the oven and there would be a mound of colcannon to go with it. They would all have supper together and it wouldn't be like last year, but it would be all right.

After they crossed City Road the girls ran ahead. The optician knocked on the window and waved and Reg was at the door of his shop with bags of Maltesers for both of them. The man who ran the bicycle shop mumbled something and gave the girls sixpence each.

They crossed Robert's Row together and then the girls were in the house, racing upstairs. Geraldine charged ahead, eagerly hiding Nana's present by hugging it to her chest. The adults could hear the squeals from the sitting room.

'They've found the tree.' Kitty grinned. 'I always say there's nothing like a bit of spruce at Christmas.'

Geraldine came out on the landing, her face radiant.

'He's come! I knew he would. I knew!'

'Ah, the dote. She thinks Santa's been already.'

'Daddy's come home.'

Geraldine's words sliced through Cathleen like a razor blade. In the half light of the landing she saw her daughter's thin legs jig up and down in excitement. All this time, she thought, as she grabbed her and held her still, all this time she was waiting for him to come back.

Later Geraldine insisted that nothing was wrong. The tree was lovely and she knew Daddy was in heaven. She'd forgotten for a moment, that was all. With wet eyes and a mouth forced into a thin, twitchy smile, she begged everyone to stop looking at her. And no, she wasn't upset. And no, she wasn't crying.

Anna was sullen and resentful at dinner, sending murderous glances at her sister as they ate their Christmas Eve supper. Geraldine moved the mashed potato around on her plate and made a moat for the gravy but ate little. When Cathleen pulled her on to her lap to hug her one more time, Anna threw down her knife and fork.

'Leave her alone,' she snapped. 'She ruins everything.'

'Let the poor dote be,' Kitty scolded, wagging her finger. Anna jumped up with such force that her chair rammed into the Christmas tree, nearly knocking it over.

'I'm going to bed and I don't suppose Santa's coming for me. Only for good girls like her.'

The sitting-room door was yanked open and Cathleen closed her eyes as it shut. At least she didn't slam it, she thought. She must have wanted to slam it. Kitty swivelled to her feet, her own plate spinning meat and gravy as she leapt towards the door.

'Leave her, please.' Cathleen tugged at her mother's cardigan.
'That one needs telling.'

'I'll go to her in a minute.' Cathleen could hear Anna move
about in the room next door. It was really a slice of the sitting
room that had been partitioned off to make a space just large
enough for a single bed. Cathleen listened. The noises stopped.
Anna must have flung herself on to the bed: there wasn't much
else she could do.

Kitty's hand was still on the doorknob. 'You're too soft. Look
at you crying.'

Geraldine was still on her lap and Cathleen had to untangle
her arms before she could get to her feet. She hoped Anna was
crying too. I won't be able to reach her until she's ready to cry.
It's the tears that hold us together.

'God in heaven,' Kitty thundered, looking around the table at
her youngest daughter and two sons for confirmation. 'There's
not a bad thing happen but that girl doesn't make it worse.' Her
voice could easily be heard in the next room.

'Don't say that.' Cathleen surprised herself with the force of
her words. 'Don't ever say that again.' She pulled her mother away
from the door. 'Didn't you see Anna's face?' With an effort she
lowered her voice to a fierce whisper. 'When we were coming
up the stairs? Didn't you see that for a second – less than a second
– she believed? For a spit of a moment Daddy was back for both
of them.'

Cathleen released her grip on her mother's arm. 'You don't
always bleed when you're hurt.'

Later that night Cathleen fell asleep in the single bed, still fully
dressed, with a daughter curled on either side. Normally the girls
slept end to end and Anna, being oldest, was allowed the head-
board. Their feet once touched in the middle but now Anna's
long legs would tickle Geraldine's bottom whenever she turned
over.

Cathleen woke with a start at about three o'clock. Her neck
was stiff and her suspenders were cutting into her thighs. She sat
up gingerly and rolled down her stockings. Scared of waking her
daughters, she edged to the end of the bed inch by inch. When
she got up they tumbled together, still fast asleep, breathing warm
air into each other's faces, their hair fusing and flowing across the
pillow. Silently Cathleen filled the pair of knee-length socks that

hung on the bed post. A tangerine in each for a breakfast treat, a Brussels sprout to make them pull a face; a notebook and pencil for Anna and marbles for Geraldine because, although she had no interest in the game, she loved holding them up to the light. They would wake to find the big presents around the Christmas tree. Whatever had been said, Santa had come.

Cathleen was reluctant to leave. She wanted to creep back under the covers, but Christmas morning belonged to them. They needed to rush upstairs and surprise her with the wonders that had appeared overnight. When she tiptoed into her own room, the candlewick expanse of the double bed had never seemed quite so big or so empty.

Thirteen

Leytonstone was an old, sprawling cemetery. By memorizing landmarks Cathleen was able to work out her own route. She turned left after a pair of granite hearts, second right by the pencil-thin cypress dying from the top down, on past the Celtic cross that always had fresh flowers at its base whatever the weather, straight on to a T-junction of headstones. It was here that Cathleen paused. On every visit she spent a few seconds in front of a statue of a young woman. Around the next turning was the bare rectangle where she watched the contours of the newly dug soil soften and sink. The statue helped Cathleen draw breath.

When she first saw the slight figure, draped in folds like a nun or a medieval lady, she thought her lonely among the acres of crosses, but on Boxing Day Cathleen changed her mind. The gentle marble face turned to the sky seemed to be focusing on something that only she could see. Cathleen had a sudden urge to pull away the vegetation that obscured the lettering on the plinth. The leaves left her hands damp and gritty and she was scared to tug too hard, in case the stone and ivy were supporting each another, but she carried on until she could read two names: Emily and Lionel. Time and weather had blurred the dates but,

pulling off her gloves, Cathleen knelt down on the damp grass
to read with the tips of her fingers that Emily had died first, a
good eighteen years before her husband.

Cathleen struggled to her feet. So, it was his memorial to her.
He chose it, paid for it, and for years stood where she was standing
right now, looking up at a face turned away from him.

She held her breath as she walked towards Mick's grave. She
thought she knew what to expect but, even so, the white of the
newly carved limestone came as a shock. It cut through the landscape like a wound open to the bone. The stonemasons had
erected the headstone just before Christmas when they were satis-
fied that the ground was ready. The insurance money covered the
cost, and the mason eagerly suggested a range of traditional
phrases. Cathleen refused them all: even rejecting 'Dearly Beloved'
and 'In Loving Memory'.

'It'll look very plain without,' he had repeated, but Cathleen
was determined and she looked now at the words she had chosen:

Michael Aloysius Brogan
1930–1959

She was right. There was nothing wrong with plain.

You're named now, Mick. I couldn't leave you before, but now
I've got to. I'm keeping you alive, coming here every chance I
can, and that's hurting the girls.

She blessed herself and turned to go, pulling up the collar of
her raincoat against the damp air. But she allowed herself one
last look. I'll be back sometimes, she promised. I'll watch the ivy
grow.

The sky was a dull slate-grey. It would be dark before she got
to Islington and if she was unlucky with the connections the
girls might even be in bed before she got home.

As she walked through the cemetery she became aware that
she wasn't alone. She noticed an old man sitting on a bench
eating a sandwich and, as she passed, caught the tang of fish
paste and pickled onions. Nearer the east gate, she spotted a
couple hurrying as if they were late. The man was carrying a
wooden spinning top and the woman held a small bunch of
anemones close to her chest. In the distance a solitary figure
was standing motionless at the gate and, as she approached, his
stillness fixed her attention. Cathleen wondered who he was

waiting for, and why. As she drew closer, she noted a thin, straight nose and close-cropped hair. It was Tacit Donovan and he was waiting for her.

He fell in step beside her as if they'd planned it.

'How did you know . . .?'

'Your mother said.'

'But all this way!'

'It needed a run out.' Tacit shrugged in the direction of a maroon Humber. 'A Christmas present to myself.'

Cathleen put her hand on the glossy fat curves. Tacit opened the front passenger door and she sank into the brown leather interior. The inside smelt of polish.

The first raindrops fell as they pulled out into a deserted High Street. No one was out if they could help it, and Cathleen was grateful for the lift, but she felt self-conscious as she struggled to break the silence. She had thanked Tacit twice by the time they reached Dalston and felt she had said more about the weather than either of them needed to hear. She was startled when he spoke.

'Are you often at the cemetery?'

'No. Well, every week, I suppose.'

He didn't respond. Once a week sounded like very often, spoken aloud over the drone of the engine and the swoosh of the windscreen wipers.

'I don't drag the children with me and I don't go home all weepy.' That wasn't entirely true but he's not a priest, she thought, and this isn't confession. I don't have to be entirely truthful.

'But from now on,' she continued, 'I'll only come high days and holy days. I've decided.'

They were in Balls Pond Road before they spoke again.

'Can I ask you something?' Cathleen turned towards Tacit. *He's going to think I've gone strange, but I might as well.*

'Ask away.'

'What was Mick like? I mean to work with?'

Tacit whistled softly and for the first time took his eyes off the road: he looked at her and then away again.

'He wasn't in love with a shovel.' He shifted uncomfortably as they approached Highbury corner and for the first time met traffic. 'No better than all right, as a worker.'

Cathleen looked sideways at his sharp profile: it was a face that was hard to read.

'But as a man to work with, it was easier to have him beside you than not to have him.' Their eyes met in the car mirror. 'It doesn't sound much,' he added, 'but Mick helped carry the day.'

'It's enough.' Cathleen nodded. The masons should have suggested something like that, she thought.

When they pulled up outside Robert's Row, Cathleen was surprised that Tacit didn't cut the engine or make a move to get out.

'You'll come in? There's mince pies and Christmas cake and a supper of turkey if you have a mind for it.'

He shook his head.

'All those miles and not even a cup of tea?'

'It was a service to myself, killing an empty afternoon.' He glanced at his watch. 'But there's a pub in Kilburn open and a gang of wet throats wondering where I am.'

Kitty had been looking out of the window and now ran down the stairs to meet her. 'I wondered if he'd take the hint.'

'You didn't make him fetch me!' Cathleen coloured at the thought of what must have been said. Her mother's hints were more like commands.

'There's a fear of him,' Kitty snorted. 'I invited him indoors like a Christian but he wasn't having any of it. Which is just as well because I'd say he puts a fortnight between the beginning of a sentence and the end of it. I could talk a book in the time he takes to say it's raining. The long drink of water!' She sniffed. 'Go on, tell me I'm wrong. Tell me that you couldn't get a word in edgeways. Tell me he'd put legs under a chicken.'

'He's a quiet man, that's all.'

'Lord save us from the quiet men. When was there a tax put on words, that's what I want to know! And you can't tell what they're thinking or if there's a thought rattling around at all.' She paused and looked at her daughter narrowly. 'You better watch that Tacit fellow. You could lose your reputation over a man like that. You shouldn't encourage him.'

'You're the one sent him to get me.' Cathleen was angry. Her mother's words had destroyed the calm she'd felt in the cemetery.

'I was only thinking of you in that lonely place.' Kitty had her coat on and was now tying a scarf around her head. A few griz-zled strands of hair hung loose and she tucked them inside. 'All

I'm saying is that a widow's a target. I've been one long enough to know that.' She inspected herself in the mirror. 'Wouldn't the craw thumpers love a crumb of gossip to chew over? But it's the men you want to worry about. Watch the men.'

Fourteen

'I suppose this means the priest's not dead.' Thady threw a cream envelope on to the floor at his sister's feet, forcing her to bend over and pick it up. 'Go down on your knees. The great man has remembered you at last.' He had gone to the market on the horse and cart that morning and collected the post on his way home. A wad of other envelopes were thrust unopened into his back pocket.

'What a thing to say! Oh, but it's a blessing to have Father Jerry's Christmas card safe. I suppose it was stuck in some Eyetie mailbag but I said a prayer to St Anthony so I knew it would come.'

Although it was mid morning the farmhouse kitchen was dark; there were corners of the large room where only electric light could pierce the gloom, and Maeve moved towards the window.

'And there's a letter too.' Her voice rose with pleasure and she waved the crisp pages at her mother who was coming through the back door, cradling a clutch of eggs in her apron. Grandma Brogan moved slowly, her feet swollen inside the pair of unlaced men's boots she wore for outside work.

Maeve started to read aloud, but Thady snatched the letter from her, snorting with impatience. He scanned the pages quickly, his large red hands crumpling the paper.

'Says he's leaving Italy.'

'He's coming back to us! Are they going to give him a parish?' Maeve almost jumped at the thought. Her eyes, her hands and her whole body were animated and she reached over for the letter. 'I wouldn't wish any harm on our own parish priest but he's awful tired looking.'

'Arah, hold your whist.' Thady held the cream pages over his sister's head and she drew back. 'Could be Timbuktu that he's going to, for all you know.'

'The bishop wouldn't.'

'Why not? Aren't they in even greater need than ourselves? Don't the coloured fellas need a fine priest like Father Jerry?' Thady stood in front of the range and levered open the smoked black cover to reveal the turf fire beneath. He had the poker in one hand and the letter in the other. 'Or China, maybe. Arah, but don't they hang priests by their thumbs in China?'

'Enough.' The old woman held her hand out for the letter. She didn't raise her voice but the look she gave her son was unflinching.

'Hah!' Thady hunched his shoulders and spat into the fire, at the same time letting the crumpled pages slip from his fingers and into his mother's hand. He was a big man, carrying too much weight. His belly flopped over the belt of his trousers and where a button was missing on his shirt there was the pink of a fleshy and hairless chest. 'Youse women make a fuss about nothing.'

'Ah go on, don't pretend you wouldn't want to see him around the place.' His mother smiled as she smoothed the pages out. 'As lads you were always together.'

'What did he need me for? Wasn't there always a gang following after him. Any trouble though and I was the one flayed alive. You had him spoiled. The whole village had him spoiled.'

'He was an easy child to spoil, the poor motherless creature.'

'There was nothing poor about Jerry Brogan.' Thady almost collided with his mother as he brushed past. She frowned and glanced at the clock. It was just after ten in the morning and the old woman could smell whiskey.

'Read it,' Maeve urged her mother. 'I'm all goose gog with the thought that we'll have him back among us.' A smile creased her face as the soft, wispy curls that framed her forehead bobbed up and down. 'Does it say when? I suppose there'd be a party welcoming him home. At the bishop's house. Seamus will have to get a new suit.'

'He had a choice,' said her mother flatly, 'and he's chosen London.' She glanced at the calendar hanging next to the plastic holy water fount. 'And I'd say he's probably packing right now.'

Fifteen

It was the first day of term and Geraldine should have been starting school, but no letter had arrived to offer her a place. Cathleen grew nervous as she remembered the meeting with the headmistress.

There was nothing for it but to keep on asking, and Cathleen made sure that they arrived at the school gates in plenty of time. She'd even snatched a minute to apply a stroke of lipstick before leaving home. She felt better for it and, as she glanced in the hall mirror, she knew that she looked better too.

In the playground the headmistress was alone and the whistle around her neck silent. Cathleen walked over, smiled and opened her mouth.

'Not now, Mrs Brogan.'

The headmistress's eyes were small and dark. Cathleen felt them bore into her back as she walked back across the playground, her cheeks a blistering red. When she turned at the gate the headmistress was still staring.

'It wasn't so much what she said,' Cathleen confided later to Reg, 'but the way she looked at me.'

He nodded and offered a butterscotch in sympathy, but his next comment made Cathleen's face redden again. He had been thinking for some time that he needed help in the shop. Nothing much, just a few hours every day. He wasn't in a great tearing hurry to find someone. Getting the right person was the important thing.

Cathleen picked up her purchases and turned to leave, the hope contained in Reg's words drumming in her head. With a few hours a day here, and the pension I get, it would keep us safe. We could even have Ireland. Cathleen turned back.

'Do you think I could be the right person?' She had spoken so quietly she was afraid that Reg hadn't heard.

'I think you might be, Mrs Brogan. You just might be.'

★   ★   ★

Every morning Geraldine asked if she was going to school today. Soon, Cathleen told her, soon. She would learn to skip at school – learning anything else didn't seem to come into it – and make lots of friends. And she would go to their houses to play. And she would stay for tea.

But there was still no word from the school. Cathleen waited outside the secretary's office for over an hour to be told that a letter would be in the post. In due course. It was a phrase to put a chill down your spine, but it wasn't going to put her off. Every Monday morning wearing her best coat, a light touch of face powder and a careful application of lipstick, she found the courage to ask. For the last three Mondays the answer had been the same: 'Not now, Mrs Brogan. Not now.'

She wasn't going to let it cloud this special Monday. It was Geraldine's fifth birthday. It was also the day she had been persuaded to entertain her first visitor since the funeral.

'I'm not up for socializing,' she had told Mary when it was first suggested.

'A cup of tea, a biscuit, what's so social about that?' her sister wanted to know.

Cathleen had struggled to find an excuse. 'Making conversation . . .' She pulled a face at the thought.

'Oh, she has more than enough to say for herself.' Mary was dismissive.

'And meeting strangers . . .'

'Just the one girl. How scary can that be? An ordinary girl I've met at night school.'

But there was nothing ordinary about the young woman who walked up the stairs in the tallest stilettos Cathleen had ever seen. Kitty was already sitting in the best armchair when there was a knock on the door.

'I'm not missing this,' she had announced when she bustled in half an hour earlier. 'All I ever hear from your sister is "my friend says this, and my friend says that". So, I want a good look at this friend.'

A burst of high-pitched giggling followed the knock and then the sitting-room door burst open.

'I'm Aude—'

Kitty pursed her mouth, looking up at the young woman's carefully constructed bouffant, down at her sharply pointed shoes and then up again at the crimson lips.

'–drey. Aude-*drey.*'

Anna and Geraldine, sitting at the table, stared in amazement. The visitor turned her smile on them. 'But simply everyone calls me Aude.'

'Audrey Alibone. Actually.' Mary dropped the name like a stone and stood back.

'Alibone?' Kitty shrieked, then clamped a hand over her mouth. 'Not Alibone Corsets? Not the Alibone corsets that has the big neon sign near King's Cross?' Kitty's face contorted in pleasure. 'That's a lovely sign, that is. I know I'm nearly home when I see it.' She turned to Cathleen. 'Alibone Corsets in your front room, fancy that.'

'Alibone *Lingerie,*' Aude corrected, enunciating each syllable clearly.

'You do knickers as well?' Kitty was entranced.

'Mother,' Mary hissed and made small, agitated gestures with her hands.

'I had an Alibone corset once. All satin and bone. *Moatherajaysus,* it held back the flesh in places you wouldn't think needed holding.' Her grin widened as she glanced up at her daughter. Mary was still pulling faces. 'Your father, the Lord have mercy on his soul, said it was like scaffolding. So you're one of the corset people?'

'Uncle Bertie's firm.'

'She works in the office,' Mary interjected. 'We're learning shorthand together.'

'Uncle says I have a real head for business.' Aude spun around to see if everyone was listening and also, Cathleen guessed, because it showed off her swing coat. 'And Mary's so clever with all those squiggly lines perhaps she'll come and work for us one day.'

'I wouldn't know about that,' said Kitty slowly. 'I wouldn't know if Mr Crawford could run his old antique-ey emporium without her.'

'Yes, but isn't it funny he didn't want a strong boy to drag around that ugly furniture?' Aude wrinkled her nose. 'I guess Mary's looks clinched it. After all, Mr Crawford *is* a bit of a lech.'

'What's that you say?' Kitty half rose from her chair and Mary was blushing furiously.

'Oh, sorry.' Aude glanced at the children and dropped her voice to a theatrical whisper. 'But didn't you say he was a bottom pincher?'

'Once maybe,' Mary mumbled. 'But no, not really.'

'I'll lay into him with my broom.' Kitty was on her feet.

'Don't mind me, I get things mixed up. I'm always in a muddle.' Aude slipped her arm through Mary's. 'All I'm saying is that your daughter is wasted there. The laughs we'd have if she came and worked at Alibone's.'

Mary beamed and Kitty subsided into the chair, although the frown didn't leave her face.

'And is this the birthday girl?' A tumble of salmon pink ribbons fell out of the package she presented to Geraldine. 'Sweetly pretty,' she announced, looking up at Cathleen. 'You must be so proud.'

'She has a great welcome for herself,' Kitty remarked after they left. 'And that colour pink,' she added, looking at the bundle of ribbons strewn across the dinning table, 'puts me in mind of the corset I was telling you about. Puts me very strongly in mind of it.'

Cathleen looked up and saw the headmistress marching towards her.

'Nice to see you on time, Mrs Brogan.'

Cathleen bristled at the unfairness of the greeting. *I won't say anything; I won't let her rile me.*

'I thought I'd have a word now that Anna has recovered her intellectual capacity.' Cathleen realized that the headmistress was referring to Anna's recent promotion back to the top table. 'I wish her musical sensibilities would catch up.'

'You mean the dancing?'

It was Kitty who had persuaded her granddaughter to go to Irish dancing classes. It had been a fight and the two had hardly spoken to each other as they walked down Rosebery Avenue but, afterwards, Anna had rushed home to tell her all about it. Cathleen remembered the look on her face as she bounded through the door and she'd do anything to keep that look there.

'It's nothing but diddle-lee-dee music and silly girls in short skirts.' The headmistress sniffed. She sighed and glanced down at Geraldine's upturned face. 'I suppose you still want a place for this one. You might remind Anna that we have a very good church choir here, a much more spiritual outlet for her talents.' She started to walk away.

Cathleen followed. 'If I only knew one way or the other about Geraldine. The uncertainty is making things difficult.'

But the whistle was back in the headmistress's mouth and her cheeks ballooned as she started to blow.

Sixteen

'Milk Tray's always nice for a lady,' Reg volunteered. 'Right so, I'm not a good fist at this present buying.'

Reg looked the stranger up and down and noted the long black coat, the wool scarf wrapped around the neck, the soft hands and clean fingernails.

'Wrap it up, shall I?' One hand hovered over a square of brown paper as the other reached for a box of chocolates.

'Yes. And I need some sweets for the children. The Brogans. You know them?'

'I do.' Reg stiffened.

'It was this stuff I loved as a boy.' The man waved his hand over knotted liquorice laces, pink sugar mice and eight-for-a-penny chews. 'Let's have a shilling's worth.' His smiled broadened as he turned his attention to the tiers of glass jars in the window.

'And a quarter of aniseed balls, and the same of butterscotch. Isn't it great the way they catch the light?'

'They'll take a month to eat this lot.'

'Well, I might just have to help them out myself. Bung in a couple of gobstoppers, the big fellows, and I'll have some of those yellow ones, lemon sherbets, are they? Go on, we'll have quarter of pear drops as well.'

The scarf slipped and when Reg saw the white Roman collar he remembered he'd seen the man before. 'Very devout family, the Brogans,' he said casually, as he tipped out a shower of sweets. 'Going to church all the time.' Reg looked up from the scales to see what impression he was making. 'Twice on Sundays.'

'What on earth for?' The priest looked at him in mild surprise.

'They're a good sort, the Brogans.' Reg blushed. 'That's all I'm saying.'

'Oh sure,' the priest agreed warmly. 'Isn't that well known? Aren't I one myself?'

★　　★　　★

Father Jerry heard them before he saw them.

'There's a man outside our house.'

He turned around to find a child with wispy dark hair and large eyes running down Rosebery Avenue towards him.

'It's not a man,' the little girl corrected herself and called again to the woman hurrying towards them, 'it's a priest.'

'Cathleen.' He stepped forward to grasp her hand in both of his. Half an hour earlier he had been worried that they might pass each other in the street but watching her fumble for her keys he knew that couldn't happen. With her black hair and eyes as large as her daughter's, there was no forgetting Cathleen Brogan.

He followed her inside. He'd remembered the hallway from the funeral but had forgotten just how many flights of stairs there were and how many people lived in the house. Every door they passed had a lock on it.

'How long are you here for? Where are you staying? Isn't it great of you to call like this.'

He counted the questions off on his fingers. 'A few days. The diocesan house at Westminster. And yes, it is.'

Cathleen's laugh ended abruptly when she ushered him into the sitting room on the third floor. A wooden clothes horse draped in washing stood in the centre and he had to manoeuvre around it to get near to an armchair.

'Sorry, you must excuse the mess. Sorry.'

'Not at all.' He moved towards the mantelpiece and kept his back turned as he heard her attempts at tidying. Looking down, he realized a stocking had attached itself to his sleeve, the sheerness of the nylon standing out against his dark coat. He turned around in time to see Cathleen sweep all the other damp underwear into a cupboard full of glasses and bottles and he hastily tucked the stocking underneath a cushion.

'Right, tea it is.' Cathleen fled and he could hear her feet on the stairs but the little girl was still in the doorway. He smiled. She was as timid as a young calf, ready to rear up and run away at a false movement. He decided to ignore her and pat his pockets instead. There was a rustling. He patted them again and that produced more rustling. With exaggerated care, he pulled out paper bag after paper bag. Nothing was said but, as liquorice laces and pear drops slid across the polished surface of the table, Geraldine stepped forward.

Cathleen came downstairs with a tray heavy with her best china and a small plate of biscuits. She stopped at the door.

'I know.' Father Jerry smiled. 'I amaze myself sometimes.'

'I hope you bought all this from Reg.'

'Is that the man across the road?' Father Jerry handed her the box of chocolates with a grin. 'For yourself.'

'That came out wrong.' Cathleen coloured. 'What I should have said is that you shouldn't have.' Geraldine started to giggle and Father Jerry forced back a smile. 'That's what I had in mind to say. It's just I've never seen so many sweets outside the shop. And I'd want Reg to get the business.' She busied herself with the tea.

'He thinks well of you, I'd say. Although he has the idea you're some kind of religious fanatic.'

'Reg said that!'

'No, but I think he thought that would give me a good impression.'

'That's typical of him. But what am I thinking of?' Cathleen's hair fell in front of her face. 'We've no manners at all telling you where to shop and not thanking you properly. Thank you, Father. Thank you very much. This is generous.'

'I might have my own shop when I grow up and it will only ever sell sweets.' Geraldine moved forward. 'Or I might go riding with the Lone Ranger.'

'That sounds like a good plan but I have to tell you, I've absolutely no idea who the Lone Ranger is.'

Geraldine stood in the middle of the room with her mouth open in amazement. Father Jerry turned away with a grin, hoping to catch Cathleen's eye, but he found her preoccupied with the tea tray, frowning as if it had done something wrong. His own smile faded as he watched her.

I'm a nuisance here, he decided as he glanced around the room. The windows, sweeping almost from ceiling to floor, were of the kind you'd see in a big house made for high living, but the curtains told a different story. The unlined red brocade hadn't taken kindly to being washed too many times and he could see that the embroidered antimacassars on the armchairs were hiding worn cloth.

He smiled ruefully at Geraldine. *And I turn up out of the blue with six months' worth of sweets. What was I thinking of? A few holy pictures would have been more appropriate. Or perhaps something worldlier, something actually needed. I should have realized there wasn't much money coming in.*

He was silent for a moment, uncertain what to say until he noticed the Papal blessing displayed in a gilt frame between the windows.

'I see you have it in pride of place.'

'We have indeed.'

It had been his wedding present and he wondered if there was any small anecdote attached to it that would fill the silence.

He suspected Cathleen was also searching for something to say. This poor girl doesn't need me getting in the way, he thought. I'll make my excuses and go: duty done on both sides. He turned around to find Cathleen looking at him thoughtfully.

'You're going to think me awful rude.'

'You're busy, of course.' He looked around for his coat. She must have put it away somewhere. 'I just popped in on the off chance. Lovely drop of tea.' He had hardly touched it.

'Oh no,' the stunned look on Cathleen's face made him hesitate. 'Please don't go. Really you mustn't. There's so much I want to talk to you about. And tonight's a special night . . .'

Hurried footsteps on the stairs interrupted what she was going to say and the sitting-room door was suddenly flung open to reveal Cathleen's mother. Kitty's hair was wild and her coat undone, but there was something triumphant about her entrance. Anna was behind her.

'The shoes are bought! Although we're half dead from the journey. How many buses were we on?' She turned to her grand-daughter but didn't wait for a reply. 'And I was afraid there'd be none in her size but we have them, we have.'

She paused for breath and then noticed Father Jerry who had retreated to the fireplace. 'Cathleen! Why didn't you tell me you had company?' Her eyes widened in surprise. 'Oh it's yourself! Father Brogan!' She strode forward, her hand outstretched in greeting. 'You'll remember me, of course. Kitty Cooney. Cathleen never told me you were coming.'

'Well, I never told her myself. A flying visit only, although I should be back for good in the autumn.'

'Won't that be lovely! I haven't seen spit of you since the funeral but sure wouldn't I know you anywhere. There's something of Mick about you. And what a day to come! It was meant. It surely was.'

Cathleen stepped towards the door. 'I was just about to say the same thing myself.'

Kitty turned back to Father Jerry. 'Oho and there will be plenty of entertainment for you tonight down in the church hall. Irish dancing. Only a little local competition but it's her first one.' She looked sternly at Anna. 'Sit down and rest those legs.' It was then that she noticed the table. 'Who bought all this rubbish?'

'I did,' admitted Father Jerry.

'Very nice too. But, hear me, girls, not one bite till after the competition.'

'But I'm not dancing!' Geraldine was outraged.

'But your sister is and she can't be seeing you gee-jawing your way through this lot when her mind should be on her feet.' Kitty delved into her shopping bag and produced the new shoes. 'A good soft pair of ghillies. Feel the soft leather on them, go on, Father, feel it.' He did as he was told. 'You'll come, Father?'

'Is it a Feis?'

'No, nothing so grand. Or so long.'

'It's to see who gets a dress.' It was the first thing Anna had said and Father Jerry was pretty sure that there was something in her mouth. Glancing down, he saw her hand move steadily towards the cough candy. Not those, he thought, they're too big. You'll be found out with those. He noted with satisfaction the supple fingers change direction and move towards the Black Jack chews. He caught Anna's eye and they smiled at each other.

'Well, Father, are you coming? The parish priest will be there. You'll have company.'

'Will you, Father?' said Cathleen.

He was gratified by the look on her face. The children seemed pleased too. The sweets were a good investment, after all. Yes, he would.

He smiled to himself. Really, the diocesan house just couldn't compete.

Seventeen

'Is it yourself?' The parish priest bounded across the hall. 'Is it yourself back with us?' He stared up at Father Jerry, a grin spreading across his face.

With bony elbows at right angles, he cleared a path through parents and children, steering Father Jerry towards the front row, stopping every few feet to tap someone on the back.

'Here's a man you'll want to meet. All the way from Italy!' Hands were shaken and introductions made. 'He's going to put a good word in for me with the Holy Father,' he said with a broad wink and whoop of laughter as they moved through the hall.

Kitty followed behind in the wake they created. 'That's *our* Father Jerry, that is. Just popped in on a family visit.' Cathleen squirmed as her mother mouthed the word family as if she was speaking in capital letters. 'Wanted to see our Anna dance, of course.'

Our Anna had been forgotten by her grandmother and Cathleen was left to work out the new shoes on her own.

'I think I've got it right,' she said, standing up to inspect them. The soft leather moulded itself to Anna's feet and the black laces stood out against the new white socks, criss-crossing from ankle to shin. 'They look good any way. Do they feel good?'

Anna shrugged.

'You look like a proper dancer,' said Geraldine.

'I *am* a proper dancer.' Anna shook her mane of curls, but reached out for her sister's hand. Cathleen bent to kiss her forehead, half expecting her daughter to pull away, but she didn't.

The dancing teacher led her pupils backstage. Cathleen followed them with her eyes. *Never mind what the headmistress says, Anna needs this. She doesn't have to be the best; she doesn't have to win prizes, she just has to come away smiling.*

Cathleen and Geraldine found space in the second row, almost directly behind Kitty. She'd already claimed a chair on Father Jerry's left-hand side while the parish priest was on his right. As the hall started to fill up, Cathleen felt a tightness growing inside. She imagined an old-fashioned clothes wringer in the pit of her stomach, like the one her mother had back in Dublin when she was a child. It was pulling at her, stretching her, squeezing. Oh Lord, she prayed, don't let Anna feel any of this. Let me be nervous for her.

School dinners had been served in the hall earlier in the day and Cathleen caught sight of a small dollop of grey mashed potato underneath the parish priest's chair. He was tilting it in Father Jerry's direction. Her mother was doing the same on the other side. Two bookends, she thought, trapping the father in the middle. Although he doesn't look trapped. I suppose he's used to the attention.

Cathleen sat back. Was he like Mick? There was something about the hair, although Father Jerry didn't use Brylcreem. She noticed the way the fine cloth of his jacket stretched across his shoulders: hod carrier shoulders. Mick would have approved.

'Cooo-ee!'

Cathleen had forgotten that Mary and Aude said they might come. They looked out of place in a hall of headscarves and gaberdine. Aude was in a tailored two-piece and, although Mary's dress was old, the starched white collar and cuffs were new. Both had more make-up on than any of the other women in the hall, Cathleen noticed, as they exchanged a few words with Kitty and Father Jerry. Cathleen could smell the hair lacquer even before her sister sat down. She seemed ill at ease. Cathleen looked more closely: she was blushing.

'What's wrong?'

'Nothing, it's just that Aude doesn't understand.'

'Darling,' Aude smiled. 'I know an attractive man when I see one.'

Mary leant closer to Cathleen. 'She just asked Mum – our Mum! – where she got her handsome hero from. Isn't he the priest from the funeral?' Cathleen nodded. 'Thought so.'

'What did Mum say?'

'Just looked, with that eyebrow of hers. And then blessed herself.'

'So I'm well and truly punished.' Aude smiled again.

She's nothing but smiles thought Cathleen, turning away.

The sound of a fiddle made them start. The mangle inside Cathleen gave a lurch as she realized the dancing was about to begin. She was surprised to see the headmistress take her seat next to the parish priest.

A fair-haired child with blazing cheeks was pushed to the centre of the stage. Cathleen craned her neck but couldn't see Anna in the wings. She could, however, hear her mother above the music.

'The legs are very good but I don't know where she got the arms.' Kitty was providing Father Jerry with a commentary and Cathleen watched in sympathy as the child performed a jig. Her upper body was stiff, just as it should be, but her hands fluttered up, as if they had been caught in a breeze.

'Too much yip-e-dee-do-dah,' Kitty snorted. If Cathleen had been closer she would have poked her mother in the back, priest or no priest. She prayed that the child's mother was out of earshot.

More girls performed, most in their Sunday best. They're all so earnest, thought Cathleen. A podgy four-year-old in pink flounces, her tongue licking the corner of her mouth, skipped a few steps and then fled in tears. The next girl had red-gold hair in shoulder-length ringlets. The stiff fan of her skirt fitted so well it was obviously made to measure. A gold sash hung in graceful folds across her back.

'There were tears cried for that hair and big money paid for that dress,' Kitty muttered. 'But she has a leg,' she conceded when the girl started to dance. The clapping was spontaneous when the last notes of the reel faded away. The girl bowed stiffly from the waist to the audience, turned and made the same bow to the fiddle player.

'Some beginner!' Kitty exclaimed before turning to give an exaggerated thumbs up sign to Cathleen.

In her white school blouse and pleated tartan skirt, Anna walked to the front of the stage. She was the last dancer in the section and the audience was getting restless.

Anna's eyes were fixed on the floor and she swallowed nervously, but her heels were together and toes turned out. Her head snapped up with the first notes and her right foot glided in front of the left. Cathleen guessed she was counting the bars when she saw Anna's mouth move and then suddenly she was off, jumping on her back foot and bringing her right up so high it was almost level with the waistband of her skirt. Cathleen held her breath. She could feel Geraldine beside her, feel the hall around her, but she was with Anna. With every turn of her head and kick of her foot.

Cathleen remembered the steps from her own dance classes as a child and Anna repeated them, effortlessly in time with the music. She was sidestepping now, almost counting aloud but that didn't matter, as her feet crossed in front of each other, over and over again.

'Like a cat running to milk,' Kitty marvelled.

Then Anna frowned and her step faltered. She carried on, still frowning, lifting her leg to meet the sweep of the note. Another hopping kick. And another. But the frown stayed. She bit her lip as she tried to sidestep again, but the rhythm was swirling away from her. She was lost. The music drifted into silence as Anna came to a halt and begged for rescue with her eyes.

Cathleen scrambled to her feet and pushed her way down the row of chairs.

'Nervy little thing, but sweetly pretty,' Aude whispered as she passed, but she hadn't seen what Cathleen had seen. She ran to her daughter.

'It's your shoes.' It wasn't a question: she had seen a streak of blood on her daughter's left foot.

'Do you want to carry on?'

Anna nodded. Holding on to her mother, she tore off first one shoe and then the other. Next came the socks and with a tiny smile, so small only Cathleen saw it, Anna flexed her toes.

'Get her off! She's had her go.'

Cathleen turned to see the headmistress gesturing violently and realized that she must be one of the judges. It was hopeless. She swung back to lead her daughter off the stage. Soothing words of comfort began to form in her mind, although she knew they couldn't do a bit of good. There was agitation in the audience and she turned to find Father Jerry on his feet, talking to the parish priest. Together they turned to the judges. All she could see was a cluster of heads and the glow radiating from the headmistress's face. Then Father Jerry was beside Cathleen, smiling.

'She deserves a proper chance,' he whispered, a reassuring hand on her shoulder. He turned to the fiddle player and motioned for him to begin another reel. On the sixth bar Anna pointed her bare toes. On the ninth she flew.

The redhead won the medal for the beginner's heat.

'The unfairness of it,' moaned Kitty, feeling the sharp seam that had lacerated her granddaughter's foot.

Father Jerry looked down at Anna. 'Do you mind not winning?'

'She was always better than me.' The child glanced across at her mother. 'Can I still get the dress?'

Kitty was there before Cathleen could speak. 'Oh, you'll get a dress, I'll make sure of that. Even if I have to sweat blood and hang all the rotten, robbing shoemakers in Kilburn.'

Anna looked at her mother for confirmation.

'Yes,' said Cathleen quietly. 'You'll get your dress.'

The headmistress bustled over. 'Well done everyone, a superb night.' Her remarks were supposed to be for the dancers but she was only looking at Father Jerry. 'We're in *desperate* need of your expertise, Father. You'll find us quite the ignoramuses when it comes to the traditional splendours of our Gaelic heritage.' She laughed. 'And we must talk about Italy. I expect you've been to many audiences with the Holy Father. I envy you. Truly I do. I've only managed five myself. But they live with me, Father, they live with me.' She trembled slightly. 'So, we will see you again, won't we?'

'Sure to. Of course, I'll be visiting my cousins anyway.' He nodded in the direction of Anna and Geraldine and the headmistress followed his gaze.

'My two favourite pupils! What a coincidence.'

'Geraldine's not a pupil.' Cathleen stepped forward. She couldn't let her get away with that. 'If you remember we've been waiting for a place. She's getting very old to be starting school.' She held her breath and wondered if she had said too much, not daring to look at the priest.

The headmistress was making small flapping movements with her fingers as if to shoo away something disagreeable.

'Tell me more.' That was all Father Jerry said and it was all he had to say. They moved to one side, excluding Cathleen; but she could still hear the odd word. He was using all the authority of the priesthood but there was something else too, something that was just him.

They turned back and the headmistress, putting her head to one side, as if she was still considering her decision, looked at

Cathleen. 'As an extra special favour I suppose we could squeeze one more into reception.'

'You can pay me back.'

Cathleen was waiting with Father Jerry as the others saun-tered ahead. He was getting a taxi to Westminster and she was still breathless with gratitude. There weren't enough thank yous for the look on Anna's face or the knowledge that Geraldine had a school place at last. And she would always relish the memory of the headmistress's pursed lips.

She glanced up to find him studying her and she felt herself blush. She was glad it was dark.

'I mean it. I'm starting a new venture. In a new city. I'm going to need a lot of help.' He grinned. 'My chaplaincy is to serve men like Mick . . .' He paused and corrected himself. 'No, not like Mick. It's more for the men who've never made a real home here, the drifting, single men. Those are the ones I want to reach. I want to make things happen.'

'What could I do?' Cathleen asked.

'Haven't a clue, but I'll think of something.' He spotted a taxi and stepped into the street to hail it. As it slowed down, Father Jerry loosened the scarf around his neck to reveal his clerical collar. 'It always works in Italy and Ireland – do you think it will do any good here?' He didn't wait for an answer and climbed into the back but, before closing the door, he looked up. 'Will you help me make things happen, Cathleen?'

'Did you see that neighbour of mine in the back of the hall last night? Did you, with her face all screwed up like a lemon?' Kitty stood in the shop doorway. She had seen Cathleen from across the road and had dashed across to talk to her. 'She's always breaking your ear about *her* priest, some old uncle, Father Pius Pity-face in Patagonia. Oho, but she was very quiet this morning.'

'Mum, it's her brother – Father Tom and he's in Ghana.'

'All I know is that it's the Missions, the Missions. All the time we have to be giving to the Missions.' Kitty rolled her eyes. 'Now we have one of our own. And he's only going to be on the other side of town, not the other side of the world.'

The back-room door swung open and Reg emerged with two mugs of tea.

'You don't want to hear me rattling on, you not being a religious man, but what did you think of our Father Jerry?'

'I saw him.' Reg put the mugs down on the shelf underneath the counter. He and Cathleen were about to agree her hours over a cup of tea and a digestive.

'Of course, you did. The whole place saw him. When he's over here proper I expect he'll be in and out and we won't even give him a second glance.'

Eighteen

The next Monday Geraldine was a schoolgirl.
When she trooped off with the rest of her class into the hall with a bright, brave smile it didn't seem to Cathleen like such a great victory and she had to resist the urge to grab her back. She watched the hours pass, trying to imagine what she might be doing, and picturing her behind a desk.

Cathleen stopped asking if Geraldine had made any friends by the end of the second week. It was the brave little smile that hurt and the hopeful comment that went with it: 'I expect I will tomorrow.'

If Cathleen was anxious to find out what had happened at school, Geraldine fretted about her mother's new job. She was convinced it would not last. Every evening she wanted to know if Reg was going to let her go back the next day.

Reg was determined to set her mind at rest. He took Geraldine to one side and presented her with a dog-eared invoice, which he signed in front of her.

'Your mother has a job forever. That's what I've written on this paper.' He stamped the invoice with a date stamp and found another that said 'paid in full'. 'Now it's official. And if you go to school you can have a job here too.'

'I'm not very good at being at school.' The whisper was so small a sound that Reg picked up the sense of it rather than the words. He crouched down to Geraldine's level.

'That's all right. You don't have to be any good. You just have to go.'

He was rewarded by a hug that nearly knocked him off his feet.

With Cathleen helping out behind the counter, Reg announced he could get on with his paperwork and would retire frequently to the dingy, windowless back office that was separated from the shop by an ill-fitting hardboard door. The only comforts were an old horsehair sofa and a small Belling cooker. He would brew strong tea there at eleven o'clock and at five minutes past they would drink it together.

If Cathleen went into the office she usually found Reg asleep on the sofa, the morning newspapers a pillow for his head. Sometimes he would come back into the shop with part of the day's headlines printed on his forehead.

The office also housed the telephone. Reg treated it with respect, polishing it regularly and ringing the speaking clock once a week to check that the shop clock was still working. It was the only call Cathleen ever heard him make.

He was on the phone when the bell on the door jangled. Cathleen looked around and registered a tall man with broad shoulders before she realized she was staring at Father Jerry. The bundle of magazines she was holding scattered across the floor, making a path to his feet.

'Sorry, sorry.' She knew her face was red with embarrassment. 'Only I didn't know. I wasn't expecting you . . .'

'I was hoping it might be a surprise, not a shock.' He grinned and crouched down to help her pick up the magazines. Cathleen wasn't sure why she felt so flustered, although she had assumed that he was now back in Italy.

She looked across at the face that was suddenly very close. He has the same mouth as Mick she thought, and for a moment wondered if she was looking at the man Mick would have become if he had been given more time. Father Jerry straightened up, blocking out the light from the side window.

No, how could she even think it. The priest was altogether bigger, taller. They didn't even look very alike, except sometimes – like now – when the smile seemed the same. She swallowed and looked away. He was saying something and she'd missed it. Today she was being a complete idiot; he'd never come visiting again.

'A neighbour said I'd find you among all the sweets!' Father Jerry surveyed the shop with obvious pleasure. 'I just came to say goodbye. I've a plane to catch and a taxi waiting outside.'

A croaky sound came from Reg who was leaning in the doorway between the shop and the office, the telephone receiver still in his hand.

'Ah, I know what you're thinking.' Father Jerry turned his smile on him. 'But I'm not throwing money away. The taxi driver's an old altar boy with a day off.'

Cathleen tugged at Father Jerry's sleeve. She was surprised at herself. Interrupting a priest! But he hadn't seen what she had seen: Reg's face was turning the colour of dough and the phone was swinging loose, knocking on the hardboard door.

'Are you in pain?'

Reg closed his eyes and made an attempt to shrug. He managed to wring out a few words. 'Bit of gyp.'

Suddenly everything changed. The smiling, genial priest vanished: Father Jerry was taking charge.

'Where does it hurt?' He was beside Reg now, forcing him to sit down. 'Show me.' Reg made a weak circling motion with his hand.

Father Jerry looked across at Cathleen. 'We need to get him to hospital.' He lowered his voice. 'I'm no doctor but I think he's having a heart attack. Can you lock up the shop?'

Cathleen nodded and put the telephone back in its cradle. 'Shall I ring for an ambulance?'

'Yes.' He frowned. 'No, hold on, I have the taxi outside. That has to be quicker. Is there a hospital near by?' Cathleen nodded. She knew only too well that it was a short, straight road to Barts.

Father Jerry tore off his jacket and thrust it at Cathleen, pushing up the sleeves of his shirt. Reg was now drifting in and out of consciousness. Very slowly, as carefully as a mother with a newborn, Father Jerry leant over, flexed his knees and stood up with the old man in his arms.

Reg would be mortified at the indignity, thought Cathleen. Lucky he doesn't know what's going on, thought Cathleen.

Lucky Father Jerry has such strong arms.

Lucky Father Jerry came to say goodbye at the right time. Keep lucky Reg, she prayed, following behind.

'Is he Catholic?'

'No.' Cathleen was certain of that. 'I don't know what he is.
We've never talked about it.'

'Ah, a few prayers wouldn't hurt.' Every step he took was punc-
tuated with the *Our Father*, spoken softly as if he was chatting
with Reg.

> forgive us our trespasses
> as we forgive those
> who trespass against us

After a brief, urgent conversation with the taxi driver Father Jerry
settled Reg in the back seat.

'I'll go on my own,' Cathleen insisted. 'He knows me and you
have your plane to catch.'

Father Jerry looked at his watch and nodded.

Cathleen held Reg's hand as the taxi began to pull away. She
looked back at Father Jerry and wished she hadn't sounded so
brave. Not again, she thought. I don't want to do this again.

The taxi slowed to a stop at the zebra crossing a few yards
from the shop and the passenger door suddenly flew open.

'I couldn't leave you.' Father Jerry climbed in and took Reg's
other hand in his. As the taxi roared down St John's Street,
Cathleen realized he was feeling for a pulse.

Nineteen

Cathleen visited Reg as often as she could. She hated it.
Hated the smell of the wards and the sight of the long
line of beds, but she couldn't not go. A few people gave her
cards to put on Reg's bedside locker but she was his only
visitor.

By the end of Reg's second week in hospital, Cathleen felt
able to bring the girls with her. She thought Geraldine needed
to see for herself that ill people could get better.

★   ★   ★

That Friday night Cathleen discovered the first bruise.

Fridays were bath night. Cathleen would lay newspaper down on the kitchen floor to sop up the water from the galvanized iron tub that spent the rest of the week on top of the dresser. It took kettle after kettle of boiling water, topped up with saucepans of cold to get the right temperature. She didn't begrudge the work and enjoyed the steamy warmth of the kitchen on Fridays and the way her girls were turned into puppies by the water.

Geraldine was struggling into a nightdress when Cathleen noticed small smudges just above her hip bone: rich purple to sludge green. Cathleen touched them gently with her fingers.

'How did this happen?' Her tone was deliberately light but the little girl's shoulder blade jerked up.

'Don't know,' she said, disappearing into the pink brushed nylon nightie.

'Did you bang into anything?'

'Don't know.'

'Or did someone bang into you?'

'No.'

'You would tell me if anyone hurt you.' Cathleen struggled for the right phrase. 'Or if anyone was unkind.' She glanced over at Anna who was curled up in the opposite armchair. 'Anyone at all, grown up or child. You'd tell me?'

'Yes, Mummy.' Geraldine joined Anna, folding her body into the gap left by her sister. The bruises look very like marks made by small fingers, Cathleen thought.

'And people sometimes hurt people they love. And they don't always realize they're doing it.'

Anna and Geraldine exchanged a look that Cathleen couldn't read.

Reg was going to convalesce by the sea. Thrilled by the prospect, he gave Cathleen five pounds to buy him new shirts and pyjamas. He'd be away a month at least. There was no word about what would happen to the shop.

'You should never have promised.'

Kitty picked up a blue envelope with the blurred postmark of the Irish postal service and stared at her daughter.

Cathleen said nothing. She knew Maeve and Grandma Brogan

would be wondering why she hadn't written. She still had Father Jerry's Christmas money, but that's all she had.

'You shouldn't even think about squandering your pittance just because his family make all the right noises. Oh please come, they'll say. But do they give a tinker's how you're managing in the meantime? What do the Brogans know about hard times? Didn't I bring youse lot over without so much as an iota of help from anyone?' She sniffed loudly. 'And if I hadn't done that we'd all still be in Dublin, with no work and no hope of getting any.'

Cathleen had heard it all before. After a couple of sherries her mother would belt out 'A Nation Once Again', but when she got off the boat eleven years earlier she had sworn never to return. She hadn't kept to it, of course, and had raised no objections when Cathleen announced she wanted to get married back in Dublin. Indeed, she had relished showing Mick off to their old neighbours for the fine young farmer's son he was, and Mick had enjoyed it too, because he didn't mind a bit of showing off himself.

Kitty still maintained that when she had taken the gamble of turning up – unannounced – at her husband's lodging house in Holloway Road she had said goodbye to Ireland forever.

Cathleen remembered their arrival. Remembered the frosted glass of the front door and how her mother had muttered a prayer before ringing the doorbell. She had rung it again and again, too jumpy to wait, careless of the fact that it was seven o'clock on a Sunday morning and that Fergus Cooney wasn't the only sleeping man behind the peeling paint. And miracles upon miracles there he was: with the beer of the night before gummed to his lips, braces hanging loose over trousers that he must have just put on, the glue of sleep sticking to his eyes. Poor Dad. Cathleen could still see him opening and shutting his mouth before the wife and children that he thought were still in Ireland.

Kitty's voice softened. 'You're a great manager, girl, I'll give you that. None better! But you can't work miracles. You'll pick up another job somewhere and you can go another year.'

Twenty

Cathleen couldn't sleep. Geraldine's pinched face worried her and there had been more bruises. And, although Anna's position on the top table now seemed secure, she was no easier to live with. She did though have two passions: reading – they had to change her library books at least once a week – and dancing. Kitty reported that her granddaughter had inherited her legs. Anna wasn't entirely sure if that was a good thing, but never missed a class and practised at home, bare feet on lino, with Geraldine as her audience, clapping whenever she was told.

There was noise on the street far below. A clanging, metallic noise. Dustbins, Cathleen thought turning over. But it was the wrong day for dustbins and the wrong kind of noise. She sat up. She'd heard that sound before.

Pulling back the curtains, she saw at once what had woken her. The shutters were up on the corner shop. And Reg was squinting through the jars of barley twist.

'You were supposed to be away a month.' Cathleen was breathless from running.

'A lot of old fogies.' Reg grimaced. 'And the place! What do we want from the seaside? Fish and chips. A stick of rock. A bit of life. Not where we were. It was all bracing cliff-top walks and cream teas. If I never see a horse brass again it won't be too long.'

'It's good to have you back. Only . . .' Cathleen hesitated. She hadn't asked while he was in hospital, but now he was looking so well, so much like the old Reg, she felt she could. 'Are you back for good? Some people thought that you might retire.'

'No.' His vigorous answer seemed to close off all discussion but after a few moments he continued, 'I'm grateful to you, Cathleen, but if it ever happens again, well, I'd rather you left it a bit before ringing the hospital. I've been thinking about this and the shop . . .' He stopped. 'I'd rather wear out than rust away, that's all.' He straightened his tie. 'Enough gloomy talk. I've got suppliers to ring. Newspapers to order. You'll do some extra hours, won't you? And there's a couple of sticks of rock for the girls, somewhere. I got them at the train station while I was making my escape.'

He was leaning on the door frame between the shop and the back office and his hand touched the telephone. 'Funny thing, I have this memory of coming over all strange. Not even a memory really, more a feeling. I was falling, falling and then someone caught me. It was like being a nipper again.' He shook his head and smiled. 'If it wasn't for the pain, a heart attack wouldn't be too bad at all.'

When Cathleen increased her hours, Reg increased her hourly rate. Every week more money was going into the jam jars than was being taken out. She wasn't certain, but she thought that maybe it would be Farran this year after all.

Aude's visits were becoming more frequent and she would sit on the sofa with Mary, eating fondant fancies, watching television and flipping through the out-of-date women's magazines that Cathleen brought back from the shop. Together they planned their futures and every conversation seemed to start with the words: 'When you work at Alibone's . . .'

Cathleen often woke up to the reassuring sound of Reg opening the shutters: one morning she realized that the impossible had happened. The days had grown longer and acid drop marigolds and dahlias the colour of boiled sweets had replaced the daffodils in the park. The girls had eaten their first ice cream of the year. And all without Mick seeing it, or feeling it. She got out of bed to find their wedding album and turned to the picture of their first waltz together as man and wife.

'Somehow I'm going on without you,' she told the handsome young man in a hired suit. 'I'm sorry.'

Twenty-One

'Can't you be pleased for us? Just a bit?'

After counting the jam-jar money three times, Cathleen had marched down to Euston Station. The tickets were bought. There wasn't much left over but they were going to Farran.

Kitty's mouth went in and out, as if she were chewing something she didn't like.

'Here.' She shoved a roll of notes at Cathleen. They were held together by a dozen elastic bands. 'It's your spending money. Your brothers put in most of it, so don't be thanking me.

'And Mary says she'll be over on Saturday to take the girls down the market. She's going to treat them to a new dress each. I suppose Aude will be in tow. That pair can't go to the toilet without each other these days.' She turned away. 'Don't be looking at me! You're sorted now and that's that. For pity's sake have a holiday. Have a bloody good holiday!'

Cathleen and the two girls climbed down carefully from the train with their heavy suitcases, including the one Mick had carried on the day he left Farran. Cathleen was bringing it home. They had caught the eight o'clock Irish Mail the night before from Euston.

Doors slammed, a flag waved, smoke belched from the engine and the train roared up the line to Tralee. The station was deserted. Impressive grey stone buildings with blank windows lined the wide platform and somewhere a gate creaked. It was mid afternoon, it was July and they were alone.

'Is this Ireland?' Geraldine whispered. Cathleen nodded. She was wearing her best coat and her best dress underneath. Back in London she'd decided that she should arrive looking smart, but standing on Farran platform, looking down at the faint watermark on her skirt, Cathleen wondered how she could have been so foolish. Sometime during the night, somewhere between

Holyhead and Dun Laoghaire, Anna had been sick. Cathleen wasn't sure if the swell of the Irish Sea or the smell of grease and Guinness from the boat's bar had been responsible, but the poor child had spent the rest of the journey over a toilet bowl that would not stay still.

Cathleen had been warned that the boat would be crowded, but she hadn't realized she would have to stand for three rolling, pitching hours, propped against a wall, with the girls wedged on to a step, its metal edge cutting into their legs. She hadn't understood how many children there would be, how many mothers on their own, husbands left behind to work while they made the annual pilgrimage. They were all going to the same place. They were all going home.

She was the outsider, like an English tourist in the countryside beyond Dublin. Where had she ever been except on a day trip to Powerscourt to admire the ornamental gardens or walking on the strand at Sandymount? Cathleen felt alone among women whose homesickness she could sense in the fetid air below deck.

Standing on Farran's deserted platform, she looked at the girls' tired, anxious faces. There was a translucent quality to Geraldine's skin that worried her, and, although there had been no more bruises, on the last day of school three ugly scratches had appeared on her shoulder.

The girls were looking at her as if she should know what to do and she didn't. She didn't have a clue.

Then Geraldine tugged at her sleeve and pointed. Cathleen turned to see a loose-limbed man with a slow, easy smile amble up the platform. He took off his cap to reveal silver, crew cut hair.

'Thady?' She stepped forward with her hand outstretched. 'It's good to see you.'

'Good God, you have the wrong fella.' The man looked startled. 'But would I be right in saying you're Mrs Mick? Mrs Mick Brogan?' He grabbed the suitcases and started to walk backwards. 'I am what passes for a taxi service in these parts and I've been sent to fetch you.' The girls nudged each other and watched his progress with fascination, convinced that he was about to collide with the doorpost. 'Malachi Murphy it says on my passport but my mother needn't have gone to the trouble of naming me.' With an agile side step, he navigated his way back into the ticket hall.

'Why's that?' Cathleen laughed. Never mind what his name

was, he was nice and he was funny and he was taking charge. This was better. This was what being on holiday felt like. The girls were grinning too.

'Because hardly a beggar would recognize it but everyone knows the Yank.' He held a car door open. 'That's me,' he added.

'And why are you called that?' asked Anna.

'Five years in Britain. Five years in America. All the time saving to come back. Fifty years I've lived in Farran and only ten away but that's me. The Yank, a foreigner in my own country.'

He pulled out on to the road. Cathleen and the children craned to catch a glimpse of the hills and fields.

'I saw a cow!' exclaimed Geraldine.

'So did I, and a horse.'

Cathleen was grateful for the children's excitement. She hoped that they could keep it up for a little while longer, although she knew they must be hungry. Early that morning they had shared a cheese sandwich that tasted of plasticine. *It's probably no bad thing. The hunger is keeping us going.*

As the road climbed higher they could see that they were skirting a saucer-shaped valley. Below them were soft green fields with patches of dull gold, the colour of tarnish, held together with a stitch of dark hedgerows. At the top of a hill the Yank pulled over and urged them to take a look. Cathleen would have paid good money to stay just where she was, but she smiled obediently and pulled open the door. There was a smell of hay in the air and turf smoke; the verge was purple with wild fuchsia. To the west was bogland and for every shade of green in the landscape there was a brown to match it.

'No one will try to sell you a postcard of that,' said the Yank relishing a Woodbine. 'But look over there.' He jerked with his thumb towards the west. 'That is something that would never tire a man's eyes.' They gazed past him to a range of softly curved mountains the colour of rain. 'Those are the Reeks. The MacGillycuddy Reeks.'

'Mick never said . . .'

'Well, Mrs Mick, when I was hanging over Brooklyn Bridge I didn't talk much about the mountains of home either. That was for the songwriting fellas. Didn't mean they weren't in here.' He touched his chest firmly and got back into the car.

'You were in New York, Mr Murphy?'

'I was indeed, but the Yank, if you please. There's no good

bucking the trend. I'm Mr Murphy to the taxman, bad cess on him, and the Yank to you.'

They turned on to the road for Farran village and they were soon in a world of filtered green sunlight. Whitethorn hedges brushed the side of the car and grass grew in the middle of the narrow track.

'I hope we don't meet anything coming the other way.'

'Bless you, don't we all hope that!' The Yank grinned.

They stopped briefly at the crossroads in the centre of Farran. A church stood on one corner, built of the same grey stone as the railway station. Almost directly opposite, a couple of yards back from the road, was Patsy Mulligan's Bar.

'That's the residence of the most important man in the village.' The Yank pointed at the squat brown building. 'Easy-going fella, Patsy. You're unlikely to get on the wrong side of him unless you commit a mortal sin, like ordering a pint without money in your pocket.'

They passed a pebble-dashed hall. The windows were black with dirt and a rusty padlock held the doors in place.

'That was a dance hall when I was a young lad,' the Yank sighed. 'There's no one left to dance in Farran. They're all dancing in Chicago and Camden Town. In Brooklyn and Birmingham. We all went the same road.'

'Do you ever regret coming back?'

The Yank considered the question carefully. 'To tell the truth, Mrs Mick, I regret going. I regret us all going. As old as I am, I'd love to hear a band strike up in that dance hall again.'

They had taken a right turn at the crossroads and Cathleen was relieved to see that the road up to the Brogan farm was wide enough to allow two cars to pass, although it still had its own hazards. The Yank braked suddenly as a large grey cow emerged from the shadows. The girls squealed in delight.

'A Kerry blue,' announced their driver. 'Too good an animal to be living off the side of the road but if you have no land and a taste for milk what can you do? Land is everything.' He turned around to the girls. 'Do you remember the name of this village?'

'Farran,' they shouted, pleased with themselves.

'And do you know what it means?' They shook their head. 'It means land. Plain and simple. Not land halfway up a mountain or land with a river running through it. Farran is what every Irish man wants.'

He slowed down as they passed a tiny, pink-washed cottage with a corrugated iron roof.

'Your Auntie Maeve's house. But she will be waiting for you above at Brogan's.' He pointed to a track that led past the cottage and Cathleen could see trees, stout fencing and a smoking chimney. 'Now down there is an oddity: Jehovah's Witnesses. Would you credit it? I mean in big cities you can get away with all sorts, but in Farran? A man coughs in a field and everyone has him buried.' He turned around his seat again in a way that made Cathleen nervous. 'I mean who do they think they're going to convert in Farran?'

Twenty-Two

'Are you shy of me?' Grandma Brogan sat at the kitchen table, her square, mannish hands clenching together as she waited for an answer. The house smelt of wet dogs and slow cooked stew.

Cathleen swallowed nervously and willed her daughters to smile. Anna scowled at the floor but Geraldine stepped forward.

'I'm not shy of this house,' she announced, fascinated by the side of bacon that was swinging from a hook in the ceiling. The adults laughed and an awkward stiffness fell off them. Maeve held out her fleshy arms and Geraldine ran to breathe in the smell of flour and sour milk from bread making.

It's going to be all right, thought Cathleen. Her neck muscles were rigid and there was a headache beginning to form behind her eyes, but all that would go once they had something to eat. She could smell lamb and she knew it didn't get to smell like that unless the meat was falling off the bones and the onions and potatoes were melting into each other. She looked across at Maeve and her smile grew wider. She had only seen her once before but she was just as she remembered: pink, round and welcoming. It was good to feel wanted.

And then there was Thady. The brother-in-law she had never met. How could she have mistaken the Yank for Thady Brogan? Thady was much younger, about the same age as Father Jerry, although that was where the similarity ended. Here was a lumpy man, slouching at the table, who had only looked up once or twice since they arrived, taking no part in the conversation. A shy man, guessed Cathleen. Perhaps lonely too. He'd never married and by the looks of him he'd never set a girl's heart alight.

The Yank was going. He put his cap back on his head to signal his leaving. 'They'll be a comfort to you.'

Grandma Brogan acknowledged his remark with a dignified nod and with less dignity jerked her head at her son. The old woman flushed with embarrassment as she whispered across to Thady. It was only when she repeated her request that he slowly heaved himself to his feet.

'Here's something to keep you quiet.' Cathleen looked up with a start. There was nothing shy about the way Thady was pawing a handful of coins. The Yank coughed but said nothing. 'Is it more you're wanting? These girls could have walked it quicker. And so could their mother if she wasn't afeared of spoiling her fancy shoes.'

Cathleen regretted that she hadn't insisted on paying the taxi fare herself, but she had been told to put her purse away. She leapt up now, her face burning. 'Don't, please. There's no need.' She was scrabbling around in her handbag when she felt Thady's breath on the back of her neck.

'A bit of codding! That's all.' He was very close to her. 'You'd think Mick would have chosen a wife with a sense of humour.' He thrust his hand into his trouser pocket and drew out a cluster of coins. 'Here's a shilling and a tuppence. Another tuppence. You surely won't be wanting any more?'

Cathleen turned away and neither Grandma Brogan nor Maeve would meet her eye. Perched on the edge of a chair, she could feel bands of pain tighten across her forehead as she listened to the Yank start his car.

'Is Seamus around?' She had to break the silence and there was, after all, another Brogan she had never met, although his mother's letters were so detailed, she felt she almost knew him.

'Oh yes.' Maeve beamed. 'He knew the time of the train.' She glanced at Thady who was back slumped in his chair, head bent over *The Irish Independent*. 'I thought he'd be here now . . .' Her voice trailed away, but at that moment the latch on the back door jerked up and Cathleen prepared a smile. It was an effort. She looked up and the smile froze on her lips. It was Mick who walked through the door: Mick shorter than he had been in life.

Mick at seventeen. Of all the things that Maeve had told her about her son, she had never mentioned that one detail.

'I'm very glad you've come.' His hand was outstretched and she was reminded of Mick when they first met. Cathleen could almost feel her headache ease as he turned to Anna and Geraldine. They were aching to be noticed. 'And I'm very pleased to meet you two.'

They giggled at his insistence on shaking hands. No one had ever asked them to do that before.

'You're so late. I wondered where you'd got to.' Maeve's eyes darted between her son and her brother.

'I had to mend the gate in the top field.'

'Holy Joseph! The bull's field.' Maeve shuddered. 'You didn't get near that devil, tell me you didn't?'

'It's all right, Mammy.' Seamus patted his mother on the arm. 'I kept well away from the mad thing.'

'Listen to the pair of you.' Thady was contemptuous. 'Bad mouthing the finest animal we have. Every time I go to the mart, it's "are you selling him Thady? Are you selling?" The calves will be worth a fortune next spring.'

'Maybe.' Although Seamus' voice was mild, his face was flushed. 'But there's a mean spirit in that animal that makes him more trouble than he's worth.'

'Sez you. When you've a big farm of your own you can make the big decisions.'

Grandma Brogan made a shushing sign with her hands, and started to ladle out carrots, onions and great hunks of meat from a large soot-blackened pot.

The door to the next room was ajar and Cathleen caught sight of a large sink. It was just what they needed.

'We'll wash our hands before we eat. We're so grubby from travelling.' She pushed the door open to reveal a small square room built under the stairs and smiled, glad to see that there were clean towels on the draining board. She was aware though, that the ladling had stopped.

'I should have thought,' Maeve called after them in anguish. 'But Seamus hasn't been around all morning and we were boiling potatoes. And the stew, of course, that took the rest of it.'

Cathleen nodded as if she understood; she carried on nodding as she turned the tap. It spun easily but no water came out.

'Seamus can get a bucket. Only the well's a couple of fields away and the dinner . . . but it's no trouble at all.' The boy was on his feet.

'Please don't.' Cathleen's face was red as she ushered the children back to the table. 'We're fine the way we are. Is there a problem? I mean the taps . . .' Her voice trailed off. 'I didn't think.'

'You didn't think a place could be so backward?' Thady snorted. 'Everywhere has to be like Dublin or London or it's no place at all. Isn't that it?' He emphasized every point with his knife. 'Brogan water is better than anything a Dublin jackeen ever tasted.'

'That's enough.' Grandma Brogan passed brimming bowls of stew down the table. 'Anyone would think a tap meant water. Sure, isn't the plumbing all there for it. It's the last thing your father did, the very last bill he paid. He'd have loved to see water piped into the house.'

The first and the largest bowl went to Thady who started eating at once.

'We have visitors,' Maeve pleaded. 'Won't you say grace?'

'Ah, go on with you, as if we do it every day. As if we're the Holy Family.' One hand was mopping up the gravy with a wad of bread while the other spooned up mouthfuls of meat.

'Oh, I forgot to tell you.' Maeve's pink face shone as if Thady hadn't spoken. The warm food was making Cathleen feel human again and she nodded at her sister-in-law, encouraging her to say more. Blow Thady, she thought. I'm not going to let him spoil anything.

'There's to be a mission with sermons and novenas and all sorts. Isn't that darling news?' Cathleen nodded again, her heart sinking. 'And the best part . . .' Maeve took a breath and Cathleen managed another smile, although she couldn't think of anything that would put a gloss on it. 'The very best part is that our Father Jerry will be doing it.'

'Here?' Cathleen sat up.

'The bishop said he could have a holiday before his new job and, of course, where would he choose but Kerry.'

Cathleen looked across the table to see Thady studying her. She pulled her cardigan around her. It suddenly felt cold.

'You can't be calling him "our" Father Jerry anymore. He belongs to London now.' Thady pointed with his knife in Cathleen's direction. 'And London will claim him. Wait and see.'

Twenty-Three

Lying in an iron bedstead that creaked every time she moved, Cathleen listened to the sounds of the farmhouse waking up. After Thady thumped downstairs, the wireless in the kitchen blared into life. The front door was opened and there was a yelp as a dog was let in. She recognized Seamus' voice and the sound and smell of cows in the yard below.

Cathleen and the girls had been given a large room at the front of the house. She guessed that Mick had once shared it with his brother. She wanted to picture him here but it was hard. Thinking of Thady and Mick as brothers was even harder.

The children slept late and woke to the sound of their uncle rattling down the boreen on a horse and cart loaded with two large milk urns. It was a gentle introduction to the steady rhythm of the farm and they quickly learnt that every morning the herd of black and white Friesians were milked in the low shed beside the farmhouse.

In the middle of the day a dinner of boiled bacon and cabbage appeared on the table. Breakfast occurred between these two main events, a leisurely meal of boiled eggs and thick slices of toasted day-old bread. It had the added attraction of being eaten while Thady was at the creamery, a chore that usually took him two hours or more, although he only had to go to the other side of Farran church. Maeve would join them after she had eaten her own breakfast, the hem of her skirt wet with dew from walking across the fields.

Cathleen found it impossible to make herself useful in a kitchen dominated by two other women. You're on holiday, they said, you don't want to be bothered with that, even if she just picked up a tea towel. For the first time in years Cathleen wondered how to fill the day.

The children didn't have to wonder. They fed the hens and helped to bake bread. They splashed in puddles with their new

Wellingtons and helped Seamus bring water from the well, spilling more than they carried. They rode with him on the horse and cart, visiting other farms and villages, learning the geography of the fields and the neighbours' names. In the evenings they would herd the cows back to their pasture and after supper all three would race a bicycle wheel up and down the boreen, hitting it with a big stick, their whoops and cries bouncing off the farmhouse walls.

The farm was theirs and so was the village. With few cars on the road, they were able to saunter to Farran every day. And the cars that did pass usually stopped to give a sixpence to Mick Brogan's girls.

Cathleen was feeling the pressure of empty, wasted hours and when Seamus mentioned that he needed a new roll of binder twine she eagerly volunteered to go with the girls to Mulligan's. The shop was an odd, makeshift affair, a corrugated iron lean-to bolted on to the walls of the pub. The door handle was a greasy loop of rope and inside reels of chicken wire surrounded a counter littered with children's plimsolls, packets of Daz, tubes of ointment and a selection of *Superman* comics.

Anna and Geraldine had already made friends with the girl who served in the shop.

'She says she loves our accents,' Anna whispered. 'She doesn't know that she's the one with the accent.'

The girls were choosing sweets when Patsy Mulligan poked his head around the heavy curtain that separated the shop extension from the bar. Before the curtain swung shut, Cathleen caught sight of a dark interior with walls covered in a jumble of oil paintings and ancient posters advertising local dances. Although it was too early for the bar to be open, a solitary drinker was perched on a bar stool. The man's hand covered the side of his face, but Cathleen felt sure she recognized the way the squares on the checked shirt were stretched into oblongs. It was Thady.

She turned away to find Patsy solemnly handing Anna and Geraldine two packets of Tayto crisps.

'I heard you were over.' The girls giggled and nudged each other. They were famous. 'And a little drink for yourself.'

'Oh no, I couldn't.' Cathleen smiled politely.

'You will in memory of Mick. There's no more to be said.' He produced a glass with an inch of treacle coloured fluid that clung to the sides. Anna and Geraldine giggled again and the shop girl grinned as Cathleen reluctantly edged towards it. Her nose twitched at the smoky vanilla smell and under Patsy's silent scrutiny she made herself gulp it down, longing to get back and wash the taste away with a cup of tea.

Thady was outside waiting with the horse and cart.

Without a word he made room and the girls scrambled up, sliding in between the empty milk churns, leaving a space at the front. Cathleen wasn't so keen on being close to Thady, but this was the first friendly gesture he'd made since she'd arrived. It would be wrong to turn it down and she decided not to mention seeing him in the bar.

'Can you help me up?' She held out her hand smiling. Thady looked at it and then looked away again as if he hadn't heard.

'It's easy, Mum. Come on!'

She started to pull herself up, her right foot using the spokes of the front wheel as a step, when Thady twitched the reins. The horse moved forward and Cathleen's foot slipped, jarring her ankle. That was deliberate, she thought, I'm sure that was deliberate. She was irritated now and drew herself up in one, strong push. Thady flicked the reins and the horse moved forward in a slow trot.

'Faster, girls?'

'Yes!' yelled Anna and Geraldine and he gave the horse two sharp blows on its flank. The girls were laughing and holding on to each other, but Cathleen was grimly aware that her skirt had ridden up and that it was impossible to pull it down without standing up. The horse broke into a canter: standing up wasn't an option.

'Are you keeping busy, Cathleen?'

'Not as busy as at home.' She was on one side of the horse and Thady on the other but she could smell him from where she was sitting. It was strong, like meat sweating.

'I could keep you busy. I could keep you very busy in the hay shed.' She looked at him sharply.

'What could Mummy do?'

'I could have her look for eggs.'

'We do that!'

'I could have her . . .' he paused. 'Do lots of things.'

One more word, Cathleen thought, and I'll say something, even in front of the girls. She felt his eyes on her legs and, although it was useless, she kept tugging at the hem of her skirt.

She was glad when the farmhouse came in sight and even gladder when the horse stopped and Thady jumped down.

'Come on, girleen, I'll catch you!' Geraldine squealed in delight and before Cathleen could say a word she flew off the cart and into Thady's arms. Anna was next and Thady caught her neatly and swung her around.

'Again,' pleaded Geraldine.

'Ah now, it's your Mammy's turn.'

'Oh I'm too old for this game.' Cathleen looked at her daughters and smiled, avoiding Thady's eyes. As she twisted around to make her own way down, the horse moved and knocked her off balance. Thady was holding the reins tight to the horse's head. She knew if she attempted to get down by herself Thady would make the horse buck. He held his arms out.

'Come on.'

If he touches me I'll knee him, she promised herself. If he makes a grab I'll slap him so hard he'll be sorry.

Cathleen managed an inelegant slide rather than a jump, and Thady stayed where he was, his arms stretched wide. There was no attempt to hold her, but at the last moment he jerked forward forcing them to collide. Just as she felt his flabby flesh, she knew that he'd felt her breasts press into the soft walls of his chest.

'I bet Mick kept you busy, you hussy,' he whispered, grinning.

Twenty-Four

The men of Farran weren't happy about the Mission. Cathleen met the Yank coming out of Mulligan's shop and he told her that complaints were aired every time two met along the road.

'Crazy they're calling it. But they wouldn't dare not go.'

'And yourself? Are you going?'

The Yank gave her a slow wink.

'I'm a businessman, Mrs Mick. Where else would I be but with the people? And I'm a poor sinner so what else can I do but follow the priests, even if they're leading us by the nose.'

The Brogan women were in good time for the first night. Grandma Brogan had rested all day to make sure her legs would allow her to kneel at all the right times and Maeve had splashed out on a shampoo and set. Cathleen lagged a little behind mother and daughter, as they walked arm in arm along the road. If they were men, people would say that they were swaggering. There was a lot to be said for having a priest in the family.

As they passed the cottage that Seamus and Maeve shared, Anna spotted the blue-grey cow that they had seen on their first day tied up at the back. Cathleen remembered the Yank's words: 'if you haven't got land'. Yet Seamus worked hard on his uncle's farm and Maeve baked Thady's bread and made his bed. Why did their cow have to forage by the side of the road?

Cathleen looked across at her mother-in-law and felt a stab of pity for the old woman. There's nowhere for you to go. When Thady inherited the farm and the house, your life disappeared. And Maeve could never break away. But Seamus? She thought of the small suitcase Mick had carried when he'd left Farran with a few pounds in his back pocket. Perhaps she'd leave it behind for him.

The church was packed. The women sat in the pews while the men took up their traditional positions kneeling and standing by the door. A bell rang and a sullen, sniffing altar boy sidled out of the sacristy. Oh, blow your nose and get on with it, thought Cathleen, who longed to run up to the altar with a handkerchief.

When the bell rang again two priests emerged from the doorway at the back of the altar.

'God love him, doesn't Father Jerry look like a missionary with that tan.' Cathleen could feel Maeve grow taller as she threw her shoulders back, lifting a radiant smile to the altar.

'It's good to be back.' Father Jerry strode to the pulpit to read the gospel, but before picking up the text he took time to look around. 'And it's good to see so many friends.' There was a warm murmur of approval.

He has the storyteller's knack, thought Cathleen. We all think he sees us, but we must look like daisies in the field from up there. Then, with a soft smile, Father Jerry turned to where the

Brogan women were sitting. Their eyes met and she could feel colour flood her face. It was as if he knew what she'd been thinking.

In contrast, Father Jerry's companion twitched with nervous energy. With his slush-coloured hair, shorn tight to a square skull, he looked like a drill sergeant.

'They say Father Phelan's a ferocious preacher.' There was a tremor of excitement in Maeve's voice as she settled back for the performance.

'I can see into your hearts.'

Not mine, thought Cathleen, folding her arms. Father Phelan's grating bark reminded her of Thady. She wasn't impressed, but it soon became clear that he wasn't talking to her, or any of the women in the church. It was the men who mattered.

'I know you farmers resent spending time on your knees. After all, you're busy men. Am I right? Am I right?' There was a reluctant drone of agreement. 'But this is the very place you should be! And the very moment! The devil is alive and well in Farran.' People glanced at each other uneasily. 'There are Jehovah's Witnesses in this village.' The words were spat out as if they were contaminating his mouth. 'If there were only women in Farran it could be forgiven. If there were only children I could under- stand. But you fine, strong men let heathens stay among you. That is *your* sin.'

Cathleen looked at Maeve. Her mouth was moving. 'Oh dear, Oh dear,' she was saying over and over again.

'These heathens rob the weak of their faith,' continued the priest, his forefinger jabbing the air. 'They trap the unwary. That is *their* mission. That's why we need our own. There can be no home for sin in Farran.'

Cathleen searched Father Jerry's impassive face. He was sitting at the back of the altar and it was only at the end of the sermon, while the last rasping syllable was resonating around the plain walls of the country church, that she saw a flicker of emotion. She followed his gaze and noticed Thady for the first time, kneeling beside the baptismal font. His eyes were shining and he was grinning again.

Twenty-Five

A knot of men had gathered on the other side of the road, outside Mulligan's. Voices were raised but Cathleen couldn't make out what was being said. She noticed Thady prowling on the edge of the group

Cathleen was surprised at how agitated she felt. A hand touched her elbow and she spun around.

It was Father Jerry. Their gaze held for a moment: he seemed about to say something, then shook his head and smiled.

'All priests have different styles and some take a bit of getting used to.'

The tone was light and Cathleen was disappointed. For a moment she'd thought that they'd understood each other and agreed. But he was a priest. He was that before anything else.

'It's good to see you again. How's the shopkeeper?' It only took a few sentences to fill him in on Reg's progress. Father Jerry had stayed with her in hospital long enough for a doctor to make a decision and Reg to be wheeled away on a trolley. She would always be grateful to him for that.

Father Jerry glanced down at Geraldine. 'Still dancing?'

'I'm the one who doesn't dance.'

'Of course, you are.' He winced at his mistake and straightened up. 'You're the one who's going to school.' He turned to Cathleen. 'I have to stay here awhile.' He glanced over her shoulder at Mulligan's. The men had disappeared inside. 'And I think I'll visit Maeve and Seamus later – see how things are.'

Cathleen nodded and watched Father Jerry rush away. It was a good plan. Even as an outsider she could feel a strange, tense atmosphere and any troublemakers would be deterred by the sight of the priest's car on the lane leading to the Jehovah's Witnesses. All the same, she felt a stab of jealousy. Maeve and Seamus would have Father Jerry's company while she and Grandma Brogan would be back at the farmhouse, kneeling on the floor, reciting a decade of the rosary with a mug of cocoa to look forward to as a treat before bed. Only tonight they might not pay quite so much attention to their prayers as they should. They'd both have an ear out for Thady.

She sighed and related the conversation to Maeve. Her sister-in-law's face flushed in anticipation

'The dear man. The dear, dear darling man.' She gave Cathleen a little pinch on the cheek. 'Ah, don't look so glum. You'll see enough of him this week.'

'On the altar.'

'Well, yes there too, of course, but I was thinking of Thursday at our place. It's Farran Fair Day.' She looked as though Cathleen should know what she was talking about. 'Fair Day was always big in Farran. Games and races. Things to buy. Things to eat. They'd come from miles around.'

'Oh great, that sounds just like our kind of thing.' Cathleen beamed at Anna and Geraldine.

Maeve was frowning. 'Ah no, there hasn't been a whiff of that kind of gaiety for years. Never mind, though, my husband, God rest him, always marked Fair Day at our house. And Seamus and I keep up the tradition.'

'What with?' Don't let it be more decades of the rosary, thought Cathleen.

'A hooley! And that's something Father Jerry would never miss.'

That night Thady came home long after the church service finished. Cathleen woke up as he climbed the stairs unsteadily. He seemed to be bouncing off the walls and she caught snatches of a hymn.

' . . . we WILL be TRUE to thee till DEATH . . . we WILL be . . .'

He was on the landing but she hadn't heard him go into his bedroom. The singing stopped. Cathleen imagined Thady shifting his weight from one foot to another as he stood outside her door. The floorboards creaked. She held her breath and glanced over at the children. They were asleep in the other bed and in the moonlight she could see that Geraldine had her arm curled around Anna's neck. The creaking stopped. Cathleen felt able to breath again.

'Are you cold Cath-leeeen?' The throaty whisper came from the keyhole.

There was nothing to bar the door. The wardrobe and dressing table were too heavy to drag across.

'Wouldn't you like a cover?' The voice was even lower now and she imagined his mouth touching the lock, bubbles of saliva bursting against cold metal.

'You need a man to cover you.'

She grabbed something from the dressing table and stood in front of the door, waiting for it to fly open. Instead the landing light flashed on. Cathleen stood still and heard shuffling and the voice of Grandma Brogan. The words were hard to make out, although she thought she caught her own name. The door to Thady's room opened and closed.

Cathleen looked down and realized that she was clutching a long-handled mirror. She put it next to her on the pillow and tried to sleep.

Twenty-Six

Strolling across the fields the next day, while the girls were in town with Seamus and Grandma Brogan, Cathleen heard a noise that she didn't recognize. The loudest sound came from the rooks circling overhead but underneath there was a low, irregular murmur. It was only when she reached the last stile that she realized what it was.

Coming from both directions, it was the sound of men. On bikes. On foot. In cars. One even on horseback. And all of them praying, the words sewed together in an expressionless drone.

Cathleen guessed that there were about fifteen or sixteen in total. Not many, if they had been sauntering along Rosebery Avenue, or browsing the stalls of Chapel Market, but in a narrow lane scarcely the width of one man lying down, this was a crowd. Cathleen shook her head. No, in the lane leading to the house of the Jehovah's Witnesses, this was a mob.

There was a seediness about them and guilt hung in the air. Most weren't looking at each other. If this was at night, Cathleen thought, they'd be terrifying, but even in the daylight they made her uncomfortable.

Maeve's white face was at the tiny window of her cottage. Cathleen ran over and pushed at the door and for a moment she thought someone was pushing against her. She could hear her sister-in-law inside, panting with effort and then the door swung open. She'd wedged a high-backed chair against the doorknob.

'The poor people,' Maeve repeated again and again. She was staring about her, as if her own home was strange. 'The Jehovah's brought me a barmbrack when I was ill. Wasn't that good of them? A brother and sister, you know. The poor people.'

'We've got to get help.' Cathleen shook Maeve gently. 'Where shall I go? Who has a phone?' Maeve didn't seem able to concentrate. Her wispy hair looked uncombed and she started to rub her hands as if they needed washing. 'Why did he have to go and preach against them? They weren't harming a soul.'

'Tell me what to do,' pleaded Cathleen, but Maeve kept shaking her head in bewilderment. Then, glancing up at the clock that hung on the whitewashed wall, she grabbed Cathleen's shoulder.

'Holy Hour! The Exposition of the Blessed Sacrament. Father Jerry might still be at the church. Run to him, Cathleen. Run. God bless him, he'll do the right thing.'

Cathleen ran. Looking back over her shoulder, she saw more men approaching and that made her run harder. Stumbling on a pothole, she broke the heel of her slingback and, with furious impatience, she shook off both shoes, holding them high as she sprinted into the empty church. She stopped. Every instinct, everything she'd learnt since childhood, told her to slow down. The smoky spice of incense and the smell of rising damp demanded hushed respect. Cathleen shook her head. Not today. He might still be here, somewhere. She darted up the aisle, slipped behind the communion rails and crossed the thickly carpeted floor. Twisting the gilt handle, she opened the door to the sacristy.

Father Jerry was standing with his back to her, framed by the arch of a narrow window in the afternoon sun. Afterwards she remembered that there was a swathe of green brocade lying across a chair but, at the time, all she could see was him and the muscles of his bare back as he changed his shirt; that and his brown hair, turned wine-red where it was caught by the sunlight through the stained glass.

'It's all right, Cathleen.'

He was on the other side of the room but his voice was like the lightest of touches, calming her breathing and giving her back her voice. As she stammered out a few phrases, they both pretended that this was normal; that she hadn't invaded a priestly sanctum and that he wasn't dressing in front of her, although she noticed that his fingers slipped as he tried to button his shirt.

Cathleen was running again, this time to keep up with him, but he frowned when she got into the front passenger seat of his car.

'I don't know about this.' He paused, looking at her and she looked back just as frankly. He turned the key in the ignition. 'Yes, better if you're with me. Look, if it turns nasty, if I say go, you will go? No arguments?'

'Yes.'

'Good. If I give the word run back to Pasty Mulligan's. Tell him I sent you, be sure to say that, and get him to call the Garda.'

Father Jerry drove to Maeve's cottage and grimaced when he saw the men. 'I didn't expect so many.' He faced Cathleen. 'Are you sure you're all right about this?' She nodded again. She didn't think he had noticed her shoeless feet and torn stockings, but he reached in the back of the car for a pair of Wellingtons. 'These will be as big as boats on you but it'll save you from being torn to pieces.' He studied the scene from behind the driver's wheel. 'This was set up and not a word to me, not a whisper.'

When they climbed out of their car, Cathleen was surprised to see the Yank lolling by the side of the road looking sheepish. He raised his hand in salute.

'I'm only here in a business capacity.' He took the Woodbine out of his mouth and nodded in the direction of his own car parked further along the road.

'It's a bad business,' said Father Jerry shortly, as he strode towards the lane.

Twenty-Seven

Father Jerry tried to make his way through the crowd, but few would look him in the eye and most turned their backs.

'I'm going to push our way to the front.' He clasped Cathleen's hand. 'You stay behind me and hold on.' The men might not have wanted him there, but Father Jerry was taller and stronger than most. He used his shoulder like a chisel, prising his way through, forging a path for himself and Cathleen.

'How you doing there, lads? All right?' His tone was affable, easy-going, at odds with the pressure of his hand. He was holding her with a grip that hurt.

'We don't want no trouble, Father.' A sullen voice called out from somewhere in front and Cathleen heard the hint of a threat in it.

'I'm glad to hear it,' Father Jerry called back, still struggling forward. 'That's right, lads. No trouble here.'

'We don't want no trouble with you.' The same voice spoke again but the threat was more than a hint this time. 'We've to do the right thing.'

'No heathens in Farran,' someone called out from behind them and there was a general mumble of agreement. The lane widened out at this point allowing Cathleen and Father Jerry to see the front of the crowd. A circle of men stood by the fence that skirted the Jehovah's house.

'Is that Mossie Lynch in front? It's a good many years since I saw you last.' Cathleen heard warmth in Father Jerry's voice. At the mention of his name a large man turned around slowly, nodded, and turned away again.

'It's a good many more years since we stood next to each other.'

Cathleen had never seen a priest talking to a man's back before.

'But perhaps you've forgotten.' It sounded as though he was simply chatting to Mossie Lynch. His voice was quiet, untroubled, but everyone in the clearing could hear and everyone was listening.

'It's not a day any man could forget.' Mossie Lynch's rich, earthy voice suited his frame, but he still hadn't turned around.

Father Jerry turned back to Cathleen and spoke in an urgent whisper. 'When I go like that –' he pressed her hand hard – 'you ask questions, pretend you've no idea what we're on about.' Cathleen nodded and he loosened his grip.

'What were we to each other back in the old days, Mossie?' Silence. A few men shifted their feet but no one spoke. 'I thought we were friends back then when the world was young. What was I to you, Mossie, tell me that?'

Mossie Lynch turned and faced Father Jerry. The two men seemed to be sizing each other up. 'You were my captain.'

Cathleen looked up in surprise and Father Jerry pressed her hand. Somehow she managed to speak. 'Were you in the army together, Father?' She hoped that was the sort of question he wanted, that she sounded ignorant enough. There was laughter from behind.

'Do you hear that?' Father Jerry was smiling and addressing the whole crowd now, turning around so everyone could see him. 'I'm not sure any army would have Mossie and myself, but here we have the girl Mick Brogan married. Aren't we glad she's come to visit? But aren't we sad to see her here a widow? God help us, though, Mick should have given her a few history lessons.' He paused and sighed dramatically. 'Ah, but then I don't suppose any of you remember when Mossie Lynch and I stood next to each other to clash the ash.'

'May 30th 1942.' A boy younger than Seamus spoke up. 'Farran Junior hurling team won the county championship.'

'He knows right enough,' Father Jerry laughed, playing to the gallery now, knowing that every eye was on him. 'And he wasn't even born when Mossie Lynch thundered down the pitch.'

'And Jerry Brogan was captain. No man could stand against you. If you hadn't deserted hurling for the priesthood there's no telling how far you'd have risen. You were the star among us.' Mossie Lynch took a step forward. 'You were golden.'

Father Jerry dropped Cathleen's hand and shouldered his way to the front. There were no backs turned to him now and he grasped Mossie Lynch's arm. 'What a team, Mossie, what a team we had.'

Cathleen clambered on to an embankment to get a better view. From her vantage point she could see him clapping men on the back, greeting anyone who met his eye. He's very good at this, she thought. She hoped he would be good enough.

'What's going on here at all?' He shook his head in gentle amusement. 'You're not the kind of men who'd torment an old couple.'

'There's no place in Farran for Jehovah's.'

'Whose against the Constitution?' Father Jerry frowned as he scrutinized the crowd and then focused on the man who'd called out. 'That's a strange sentiment coming from you. I always had you down as a De Valera man.'

'I am, and he wrote a Catholic constitution for a Catholic country.'

'He did, and wasn't the Church by his side when he wrote it? It was a bad time when the whole world was getting ready to tear itself apart and he put it down in black and white: Catholics were free to worship. And Jews. And all those different brands of Protestants whatever flavour they came in. And in black and white it still is. What other country ever dared do that?'

'Dev never said anything about auld Jehovah's.'

'He didn't because he never thought that the eejits would turn up in a place like Farran.'

There was laughter at this and the men looked at each other and began to relax. 'Fair play to Dev, he thought of a lot of things but don't blame him for missing that. All the same, they're covered by the Constitution.'

Father Jerry's voice had a gentle, teasing quality to it. 'Ah come now, you didn't think Dev was going to pop down from Dublin and say, "Well done lads"? Or that the bishop would be on the next train from Killarney?'

'We're only praying.'

'Then where's the women?'

There were ripples of laugher and the remark was repeated for the benefit of those who hadn't heard.

'If that's all this was about then you'd be outnumbered three to one and you know it. There's praying in church or kneeling by your bed at night. There's praying in front of the Blessed Sacrament, which you could have done this very afternoon, but there was only one man there and that was myself. And then . . .' Under a leafy canopy created by the overhanging branches of an alder, his voice suddenly became loud and defiant. ' . . . there's praying to intimidate. To scare old foolish folk who should be left in peace. There's praying as a weapon and that is no prayer at all.'

'Father Phelan said—'

Cathleen sensed that this was the moment Father Jerry had been waiting for and he jumped at it.

'Is he not here to speak for himself?' He looked around as if he expected his colleague to appear from behind a hedge. 'Well, Father Phelan *preaches* the Church Militant.' Father Jerry lingered over the word and Cathleen saw that the implication was not lost on the men around her. 'But I see he leaves it to you to carry it out. Well, I was once a Farran hurler so I've felt a few blows in my time.'

'And given them!' The mood of the men was transformed. They were a mob no longer: they belonged to him.

'Lies given out by the opposition,' laughed Father Jerry. 'But it can't be right to make a stand against old folk who know no better than to go knocking on doors.' He grinned. 'Have they knocked on any of your doors?' Men shook their heads and some put their caps on, sensing that the show was nearly over. 'No? Maybe we've converted them.' There was more laughter and he stood back, weighing up the reaction.

He sent them on their way as if he had been the one who had called them together in the first place. 'You're busy men and too much of your time has been wasted with this business. But tomorrow you can come back. Not here, mind, but next door. It's open house with good music and good company and all here are welcome.'

'That was an education.' Cathleen was following Father Jerry back up the lane to report to Maeve. It was hard walking in his boots.

'I suppose.' He started to smile. 'Politics. A bit of history and sport, of course. Sport most of all and . . .' He stopped in his tracks and turned to face her. 'Cathleen, I'm sorry. Mentioning Mick like that was a bit of cod psychology. He was well liked. I did it and only thought about how you might feel afterwards.'

She nodded. 'I like hearing his name and it was a good way to hear it.' She looked up. 'All the same, I think this afternoon was an education in Father Jerry Brogan. You were . . .' She stopped, trying to think of the right word. 'You had them in your hand. I've never seen anyone do that. If you said let's march to Tralee, I bet they'd have followed you.'

Father Jerry laughed. 'Only as far as Mulligan's. Anyway, you're a bit of a revelation yourself.'

She wondered what he was thinking. Watching a slow smile spread across his face, she remembered how he'd looked when she burst into the sacristy. The thought made her blush.

They reached the road in time to see the Yank's car speed off. In the back was Thady, glowering. He saw them and wound up his window with a snarl. Wherever he was going it wasn't home. The Yank was driving in the opposite direction.

'I never saw him there.'

'No.' Father Jerry was thoughtful. 'At the back somewhere, I suppose. I used to think it was shyness kept him on the edge of things but now . . .' He shrugged. 'That's too soft a word for the way Thady is now.'

Maeve's door was open: the chair gone. She was out to greet them, her face ecstatic. 'But look at the pair of you! Cathleen those horrible old boots are spoiling your fine dress and you, Father, what were you thinking of going out like that!' Father Jerry was mystified and Maeve had to explain. 'You forgot to put on your priest's collar. Someone might see you and think you're just a man.'

Twenty-Eight

An angry sunset poured over the sky as Cathleen walked across the fields with the girls and Grandma Brogan. They were almost on top of Maeve's cottage before they could see it, but they heard it long before that.

'Is that a wireless?' asked Anna.

'No, I don't think it can be.'

Grandma Brogan smiled, but said nothing.

Music was playing. There was a fiddle and something else, something sweet that rolled fast and high and then doubled back on itself. Cathleen didn't know what that could be but she was able to pick out the rich rhythms of an accordion in the river of sound.

Anna grabbed her grandmother's hand and without thinking began to twirl the old lady around. Geraldine joined in and all three of them held hands as they hurried in the direction of the music. It was calling to them and making them laugh. Cathleen followed behind and she couldn't stop grinning herself.

They helped each other over the stile, crossed the road and charged into the cottage. Yesterday Maeve had sat there trembling as men congregated outside, today many of the same faces were sitting around the hearth where an enormous soot-blackened kettle hung over the turf fire. Cathleen had to wait for her eyes to adjust to the gloom before she could make out a huddle of musicians sitting on stools in the corner. The Yank held a fiddle. It looked small in his large hands until he started to play and then it seemed a part of him. Seamus was playing a tin whistle and it was his music that Cathleen hadn't been able to identify. The girls gazed up at him, mesmerized by his dancing fingers.

Cathleen was surprised to see Patsy Mulligan by the hearth in what looked like the best chair but as she looked around she understood. There was no point in opening the bar tonight. The whole village was here except Thady.

Anna kicked off her shoes and stood in the middle of the flag-stone floor. For the moment she had it all to herself and she frowned in concentration as she positioned her feet: heels together and toes turned out. The Yank stood up and started to play a reel just for her. People turned around and conversations were hushed as Anna's legs followed the rhythm of the music. Jigs and reels tumbled together as the music became faster and wilder. Cathleen glanced around the circle of flushed, laughing faces. This was better than the church hall.

'Does she get her feet from you?' Cathleen turned to find Father Jerry standing behind her.

Cathleen shook her head. It was hard to make herself heard. 'From her father, I guess. Mick waltzed and foxtrotted around the Irish dance halls of North London. I met him during a Ladies Excuse Me at the Galtymore.' She grinned at the memory. 'I had to fight off the competition.'

The Yank broke into another swirling reel as Anna pulled Grandma Brogan to her feet and Seamus held out his hand to his

mother. Others were pairing up and tumbling out of the cottage
to dance in the thin strip of yard at the back. Doors and windows
were flung open so that the music could soar around them.

Although it was getting late, Farran was far enough west for
the sky to still radiate with light. The clouds were now wisps of
white in an electric blue that seemed deep enough to drown in.
Cathleen followed her daughters outside and took a deep breath.
It was a magical evening.

The musicians joined the dancers outside and nearly everyone
was on their feet now, Anna in the middle of it all. Grandma
Brogan's face was glowing in the dim light and Seamus had taken
up his whistle again.

Cathleen stood on the edge with her youngest daughter, almost
hidden in the shadows. 'Shall we?'

Geraldine held back, shaking her head, and looking longingly
at her sister.

'I'm stocious.' Mossie Lynch careered into them, almost
knocking Cathleen over. She lost her balance and clutched at the
nearest arm. It was Father Jerry's and she found herself looking
up into his face as he gripped her elbow. She remembered how
his hand felt the day before, remembered the pressure of his
fingertips and was aware of how close they now were. This is
ridiculous, she thought. But she didn't feel ridiculous. She felt as
though she'd woken up.

'Look after yourself, Mossie.' Father Jerry called out, as his old
friend rejoined the dancers. He turned to Cathleen. 'I haven't
thanked you enough for yesterday. Walking into all that, well, you
didn't know what you were walking into, but you kept your head.
I hope you won't think badly of us. It's time you saw another
side to Kerry.' He turned back to watch the dancers without
explaining what he meant.

'I never knew you were a famous hurler.' She could barely see
his smile in the dark.

'Famous in Farran.' He laughed softly and then his voice
dropped, it was almost as though he was talking to himself. 'I
wasn't born a priest.' She looked up: his face was in silhouette
and she thought again of the way his hand had held hers.

The dancing had come to a natural lull and Maeve shooed
everyone back inside, making sure that Father Jerry was seated
first at the head of the table.

'It's nothing at all, just a bite to eat. You'd hardly notice it going down.' Cathleen was the last to go inside, reluctant to leave the velvety darkness that smelt of grass and whiskey. She looked up to the sky. *Now I'm breathing again.*

The kitchen table was covered in white oilcloth and steam was rising gently from a mound of boiled potatoes on a tray in the centre. They were flanked by slabs of butter and small glass bowls of salt.

'A floury spud is God's own food,' said Mossie, leaning over Grandma Brogan in his eagerness to spear one.

Anna was fighting sleep as she nuzzled into her mother's hip. We better go back, Cathleen thought, looking around for Geraldine.

'What's this?' Mossie peered at the potato with a strange expression on his face. 'It's not blight — that I do know. Is it a worm, do you think?'

He held up a single strand of black thread. Seamus pushed forward and snatched the man's knife. He grabbed another potato from the tray and slashed it down the centre, exposing another black thread. Another potato; another thread. The gathering of dancers and drinkers fell silent, as they looked at the potatoes already split open and those that remained in the centre of the table.

'Begrudging a few spuds!' Seamus slammed down the knife and strode angrily to the back door, flinging the contents of the tray outside. 'They're only fit for the hens.'

'Shh.' Maeve made vague fluttering movements with her hands as tears welled in her eyes. People started to drift away in ones or twos; a few called out goodnight but most left in subdued silence. Maeve stood at the table, looking down at the empty tray.

'It was a great party.' Cathleen put her arm around her sister-in-law. 'Don't let this spoil it.'

'Was it?' Maeve looked down at the tray again. 'That brother of mine . . . he's not a man you can cross.'

There was no light from any of the farmhouse windows when they got back. The house seemed empty, but when Grandma Brogan opened the front door they both saw Thady squatting in the kitchen, stirring the embers of the fire with a poker. He didn't move. He didn't turn his head. But before Cathleen could close the door he kicked the empty whiskey bottle at his feet.

'I don't need any of you. I can ceilidh by myself.'

Twenty-Nine

'I never preached violence and no violence was offered.' Father Phelan stood in front of the desk, his nostrils flaring. 'If a God-fearing Irishman cannot pray against unChristian abominations the country is in a poor way.'

'The abominations are an old couple, I think.' The bishop looked down at the paperwork on his desk. His tone was dry. 'Both Irish, both with as much right to live unmolested as you or I.'

'Irish!' Father Phelan spun around, as though he had been insulted. 'Joan and Eric Jackson! Their names tell the whole story. My people were princes on the banks of the Barrow when the Jacksons were grubbing in an English sewer.'

The bishop's horn-rimmed glasses had slipped down his nose and he glared at Father Phelan with eyes that were a strong blue. 'I have the facts of the matter now, thank you, Father Phelan. You may leave.'

The polished oak doors closed behind him as Father Jerry was ushered into the bishop's study. He waited until the priest's footsteps died away before turning to the bishop.

'Will you deal with it?'

'In my own way, yes.' The bishop took off his glasses and sighed. 'Don't look at me like that, Jerry, as though I were one of Father Phelan's abominations. I'll give the eejit a parish, probably the one I was trying to palm off on you.'

'Pity his parishioners.'

'They're few enough. You did right to clamp down on this nonsense, but let's not get it out of perspective. Even without Phelan, there would have been trouble. Some hothead burning hayricks. Perhaps your own cousin.' The bishop put his glasses back on. 'You're not my only informant. Have this strange couple bought the house they're living in?'

'I'm pretty sure it's rented.'

The bishop smiled for the first time that afternoon.

'Well, the way ahead is clear then. When the Jacksons are moved on the matter will be closed.' He held up his hand as Father Jerry started to speak. 'Closed. There's no more to be said. I want to talk to you about London. I expect you to make a name for yourself reaching out to our drifting population of young men. Reel them in for me, Jerry. Get them back in touch with Mother Ireland and Mother Church. I'm expecting great things from you in London.'

Thirty

Anna stole into the kitchen just as Cathleen pinned the last curler in place. Maeve's head was covered in tight pink and blue sausages of plastic.

'I'm a sight! You mustn't look at me until I have the head-scarf on.'

'I don't want to look at you.'

Cathleen looked up sharply. A telling off was on her tongue, but her daughter's face stopped her.

'What's happened?' Cathleen was on her feet, knocking over a box of hair grips. 'Where's Geraldine?'

'I don't know.' Anna pushed her mother away and started to cry. 'She climbed over the gate. I told her not to but she wanted to meet Uncle Thady so she can have a ride back on the horse.'

Cathleen didn't wait to hear any more. Seamus was outside cutting back a hedge and she ran to him, repeating Anna's message.

'It's going to be all right.' Seamus jumped down from the step ladder. 'The bull's in the top field. She won't go up that far.'

Cathleen followed him to the gate of the three-acre field that the children were told they should never go beyond. She'll be there on the other side, Cathleen told herself. She'll be hiding and so glad to see us that I won't tell her off.

'What's she wearing?' Seamus was standing on top of the five-bar gate.

'Her pale blue dress. The one with daisies on it. Can't you see her?'

She joined Seamus and realized for the first time how large the field was, edged on three sides by thick hedges of gorse and bramble, on the fourth was a bank of earth and stone, a little over four-foot high with barbed wire running along the top.

'I see her. She's down the other end. Good girl, she's climbed up.' Seamus pointed towards a splash of blue and, as the wind picked up, Cathleen could see that Geraldine's skirt was a flag, whipping around the child's legs. She was far away from them, clinging on to something, and waving hysterically.

'Oh God, the cows are coming.' Seamus was looking at the gap in the hedge that linked one field with another. It was a couple of football pitches away, almost directly opposite them. 'And the bull's with them!'

There was no mistaking the wide barrel chest, the heavy legs and the horns. With iron muscles he was leading his harem. But it was all right. He hadn't noticed Geraldine and he was making straight for the gate. Cathleen closed her eyes and willed him on: all Geraldine had to do was stay where she was.

A twitchy heifer stopped in front of Geraldine and lowered its head to make a long, low complaint. Other cows stopped and those that had gone on ahead twisted around to see what the fuss was about. The bull stood still and slowly turned its head. Cathleen thought she could hear Geraldine crying above the wind.

Cathleen started to shout and scream. She called out all the bad words she could think of; throwing every bad name she had ever heard at the bull, anything to get its attention. Seamus looked at her as if she'd gone mad, and then, realizing what she was doing, joined in. Together they yelled, but the bull continued to turn, focusing his wild, red-veined eyes on Geraldine.

'Oh God,' cried Seamus jumping down into the field. 'He's seen her.'

Cathleen cursed her skirt for getting in the way as she climbed over the gate. It was hard to move fast. What looked like an even field from a distance had been churned by hooves into mounds of grass and potholes of soft earth. Cathleen flung herself into the wind, her black hair streaming behind her. Seamus was jumping up and down on the other side of the bull, waving his arms and calling. But the powerful animal wasn't paying attention. He was moving back towards Geraldine.

★　★　★

Seamus and Cathleen looked up at the sound of a horse. Thady
had appeared in the opening of the hedge as it started to rain:
summer rain, hard, heavy and sudden. They couldn't tell if Thady
had understood the danger but the old carthorse suddenly broke
into a gallop, making for Geraldine. And so did the bull.

The horse slowed and started to sidestep. It lost its footing and
lurched, throwing Thady forward, but rider and horse righted
themselves as the bull pounded forward.

Thady stretched towards the embankment, leaning over in the
saddle at a treacherous angle. The horse edged sideways again and
Cathleen caught a flash of blue and saw her daughter's thin legs
dangle between the safety of the saddle and the ground. He had
her.

The bull stopped and snorted. Thady stood up in the stirrups
and it seemed to Cathleen that he was taller and wider than he
had ever been before. The wind caught his old Mac and it billowed
around him like a cape, polished by the rain.

The bull stepped forward and lowered his head.

A thunder of sound escaped from Thady, a raging fury poured
into one word.

'No!'

The bull stopped, not even raising its head, as Thady hit the
horse's flanks and cantered past.

Geraldine tumbled from the horse into Cathleen's arms. Sobs
wracked the thin body, and Cathleen was shaking too. Looking
down she saw a row of serrated holes on her daughter's palms
and arms. Geraldine had been clinging to the barbed wire.

When Cathleen went down for breakfast the next morning
Seamus pulled her aside.

'He's sold the bull,' he whispered, a delighted grin spreading
across his face.

Thady was at his usual place at the head of the table, a hunk
of thickly buttered soda bread in his hand. He motioned for the
girls to come near. Geraldine's eyes were brimming with tears
even before he spoke.

'Youse two.' He took a bite of bread. 'Youse two can go
anywhere. Do you hear? There's nothing to be afeared any more.'
He looked up at Cathleen, staring steadily into her eyes. 'And
you should look after your children better.'

Thirty-One

Cathleen gazed open-mouthed at the mountains circling the bay.

On their last full day in Farran, Father Jerry had turned up unannounced and told Cathleen and the girls they had half an hour to get ready: he was taking them to the beach.

She hadn't expected such clear, sharp beauty. She drank in the salt air as she looked across the wide sweep of sand. A wind was blowing off the ocean, whisking her hair away from her face and the words from her mouth. It was the most glorious place she'd ever seen.

That morning Cathleen had resented his assumption that they would fall in with his plans. For a moment, she had imagined saying thank you very much, but it's not convenient. But now, standing on the strand, she understood why he had wanted them to come.

The four of them were the only people in sight. It felt as though they were the only people left in the world.

They had parked on a headland that jutted out over the Atlantic, waves crashing on the rocks below in a white rage. The girls had raced on ahead to the beach, marvelling at the different textures of sand beneath their feet, and returned, laughing and shrieking. Anna held the bony skeleton of a crab high above her head.

'It's for school.'

Cathleen backed away laughing, but Father Jerry took it in his hands.

'I was here once with a whole gang from the seminary. There's nothing better than crab roasted over a turf fire.'

The girls raced inland, playing hide and seek among the dunes. Cathleen followed, but it was hard to make progress and the girls were always ahead, darting from dune to dune. Retracing her steps to the beach, she lost her footing. This was sand you could drown in, she thought, when she reached for a tussock of grass to steady herself and felt it come away in her hand.

'Grab on to me.' Father Jerry was just below. Cathleen had no choice. She tumbled down, rushing into him, holding on and dragging him backward. Father Jerry staggered a few steps but held her firm. They stopped moving when they were at eye level. Here in between the dunes the air was still and the surf sounded like faraway thunder. Cathleen was close enough to see the grains of sand stuck to his eyelashes. She could feel the warmth of his body and the pressure of his hands. They had stopped moving but he was still holding her.

'We're hungry.'

Anna and Geraldine threw themselves down at their feet. Father Jerry relaxed his grip slowly and turned away to look out to sea.

Anna squinted up at him, shading her eyes against the glare of the sun.

'Are you going to see me dance again in London.'

He turned around and smiled.

'Oh yes, we'll see a lot of each other when I'm in London.'

Thirty-Two

'And did you hear what she said to Reg this morning? Awe-fully sorry I don't have the right change. Awe-fully sorry.'

Cathleen spluttered. Kitty's imitation of Mary's new vowels was perfect. Kitty smiled. 'It's good to have you back, girl.' She patted Cathleen's hand. 'And I've got other news.' Kitty's voice fell to a whisper. 'I'm on the change. I wasn't 100 per cent sure until I had my first flush.'

'What's it like?'

A slow smile spread over Kitty's face. 'It's worth half a crown a go. There was I standing outside the fishmongers while you were away, chilly, drizzly old day it was, and suddenly a lovely glow washed over me. I won't be spending as much on coal next winter that's for sure. Ach, but I'm fed up with Aude all the time. Even when's she not around I still hear her.'

Cathleen pulled out the photographs she had picked up that morning and passed them over.

'That Box Brownie takes a very good picture.' Kitty held each photograph up to the light. 'Mick's mother is looking a bit saggy, the poor creature. And the sister is no better. But this fella –' she put the photograph down and tapped it with her nail – 'this fella.'

Anna snatched it up. 'It's not a fellow. It's Seamus and he's lovely.'

'He is.' Geraldine's head bobbed in agreement as she craned over her sister's shoulder. 'Anna's going to marry him when she grows up.'

'I only said I might.'

Kitty inspected the photograph again.

'He's very like, isn't he?' Cathleen murmured quietly.

'I wasn't going to say anything if you hadn't seen it yourself, but he's the spit. In ways too?'

'No.' Cathleen put her head on one side, considering. 'Seamus is a lovely lad but I'd say there's something inside him that was never in Mick. The uncle won't be able to push him around forever.'

'Oh Lord, what happened there?' Kitty wasn't paying attention and had moved on to the next photograph. 'It's ghosts, you are. I can see right through you.'

Cathleen laughed. 'It's called a double exposure.'

'It's a queer looking thing, whatever you call it.' Kitty peered more closely. 'For all the world, it looks as though you and the priest are holding hands. Better tear it up, you wouldn't want anyone having a gander at that.'

'If anyone believed that, they'd also have to believe I can walk on water. Look at it, I'm floating . . .'

'People would believe anything if it was bad enough,' Kitty snapped.

As they approached the school gates Cathleen noticed the parish priest pacing in front of a huddle of mothers and children. With each step the hem of his cassock rose to reveal his thin, hairy shins. Cathleen urged the children to speed up. He's back, she thought and felt a shiver of anticipation. The priest's waiting to tell me that Father Jerry is back.

'I wondered if the children were going to school at all. There's places where I'm needed.' The parish priest pulled a face.

'I'm sure there are, Father.'

'Only I've been waiting here to give you the message. There's all kinds of excitement going on. Only a week back in London and Father Brogan's up to all sorts. He has a ton of meetings organized and he's promised a powerhouse of help. Whenever you need a Mass, says he. I'm your man, says he.' The parish priest spun on his heel as the first urgent note of the whistle floated over the tarmac. 'Well, now you know.'

'But, Father, the message?' Geraldine was tugging at Cathleen's sleeve.

'Didn't I say? Dinner on Sunday.'

'He's coming to us?' The priest nodded. 'What time?' Geraldine was tugging at her urgently now.

'How should I know? Dinner time, I suppose. The questions women ask!'

Cathleen turned to watch as Geraldine ran to join her class. It was the first week back at school and she insisted on bringing one of her sister's books with her every day. Now Cathleen understood why. Geraldine stood a few feet away from the other children, her forehead wrinkled in concentration, the book open a few inches from her face as though she was absorbed in the story. Cathleen wondered how many times she had seen Anna stand just like that, lost in another world.

There was a big difference though. Anna could read.

Cathleen saw one of the girls glance in Geraldine's direction and with a flounce of ponytail nudge the others. Cathleen wanted to snatch the book from her daughter's hands. It didn't give her the protection she was seeking; instead it was making her a bigger target. Miss Ponytail and her pals probably couldn't read either, were probably still sounding out the same simple words from *Janet and John* that Geraldine struggled with every night. Was it one of them with pinching fingers? She turned away in case Geraldine looked back and saw the expression on her face. She had discovered another scratch the night before. The red thread-like line on Geraldine's neck, almost hidden by her hair, looked as though it had been made with something sharper than a fingernail.

Thirty-Three

Father Jerry was standing outside Number 3 Robert's Row. He glanced at the corner shop and noticed Reg staring at him through the rows of jars. He lifted his hand in a wave but the face disappeared abruptly.

Turning back, he saw that the drab front door was opening slowly. Inch by inch cooking smells escaped from within. There was basil and tomato – from the Italian family who lived downstairs – and the richness of roasting meat from Cathleen's rooms at the top of the house. He smiled. It was the smell of all his Sundays in Ireland and Italy rolled into one. He wasn't sure what home was supposed to smell like, but yes, perhaps it was something like this. He looked down and found himself staring into Anna's frank, grey eyes. Behind her he could just make out the giggling, wriggling shape of Geraldine and his smile broadened.

'We saw you from the window. Mummy made us look. We've been looking for ages and ages.'

The girls had already caught sight of the pink, brown and cream cardboard box he was carrying in the crook of his elbow. They left him in the hall, racing up the stairs to be first with the news. 'He's here. He's here. And he's brought ice cream.'

A lot of work's gone into this dinner, Father Jerry thought as he took his place between Cathleen's mother and sister. There were fresh flowers on the table and he could feel that the damask tablecloth was stiff with starch.

'I met him once.' Father Jerry picked up one of the holy pictures he had given Kitty.

'Not Padre Pio himself?' Kitty peered at the photograph of the bearded monk. 'And did you see the what-do-you-call-it?'

'The stigmata. No, I didn't.'

'Ah, was he wearing gloves? They say you can put your finger right though the hole where the nails went in.'

'That may be a bit of an exaggeration but it does cause him a lot of pain and they bleed from time to time.'

'The poor fella. Not all roses being a holy man, is it?'

He glanced up and caught Cathleen's eye. It was a mistake: they both had to look away. Mary pushed her plate to one side and yawned.

'That was lovely, darling.'

'Darling!' Kitty glared. 'It's far from darlings you were reared.'

Father Jerry glanced across at mother and daughter and allowed himself a smile as he speared the last roast potato. He liked the way his knife broke through the mahogany veneer to release the steam from the fluffy interior. He was more used to being catered for than cooked for. Real cooking was done at home, and it was a long time since he been part of a family. Even as a child he was only a weekend member, cadging a ride to the farm in Farran as soon as school finished on Friday. However good those weekends were, Monday morning always came around. He could still remember the dull, leaden feeling that descended at the sight of his father waiting to take him back to their rooms above the town pharmacy.

He looked up and realized that Cathleen was struggling to get through the door with a tray full of plates. Mary and Kitty were bickering again and hadn't noticed. He jumped to his feet and hurried across, held the door wide and then followed behind with a tureen of cold carrots. As the door swung shut he had the satisfaction of hearing Kitty's exclamation: 'That's not bad for a priest. What am I saying? That's not bad for a man!'

Father Jerry grinned and Cathleen must have heard, but she didn't turn around. She was a few steps above him on the stairs and it meant – for the moment – that they were the same height. He stopped grinning when he realized how close they were. The knowledge was like a punch to the head and he heard a sharp intake of breath. He couldn't be sure, but thought it was his own.

In the dunes, with the taste of sand in his mouth, and here, on the brown linoleum stairs, he felt himself reeling from the nearness of Cathleen. Even with his eyes closed he could see the waves of black hair, the pale skin that blushed so easily, and the small, almost invisible scar just above her right eyebrow. He'd first noticed it outside the Jehovah's house when she was telling him how great he'd been and electricity was still buzzing through his veins. He wondered what it felt like to kiss that scar.

Thirty-Four

'Gangway!'

Kitty kicked open the sitting-room door. 'Let's get the washing up done. We can have afters later with a cup of tea and a ciggy.' She led the way up the stairs to the kitchen where they found the ice cream melting into a multicoloured puddle on the kitchen table.

'Ruined.' Kitty was furious. 'Wasted.'

Cathleen ignored her mother and carefully tipped the contents of the soggy cardboard into tumblers. 'Milkshakes for the girls. They'll love them.'

Father Jerry watched her light, deft movements. There was nothing to show that she had felt any of the tension that had threatened to overwhelm him on the stairs. Good. It was an aberration: he was himself again and Cathleen was what she always was, an attractive woman and a good mother.

Kitty was taking charge at the sink and was already up to her elbows in washing up. He watched as she and her two daughters moved around each other. It's like choreography, he thought. It was the same with the way they spoke. Words and phrases flowed together in a continuous stream of conversation and for whole minutes they forgot he was there. It was a novel sensation and he liked it. Real food and a real family: he grinned at the thought. He wouldn't allow anything to spoil it.

This is the time to ask, he thought, he needed something else to focus on and what better subject than the campaign. He needed a way of getting under the surface of the building industry in London. He had been introduced to a few men in the Irish Club at Eaton Square, well-dressed contractors with soft handshakes, but he knew that he would never be able to reach the building sites through them. How could he reach men like Mick? He smiled at the pun: one subby with a Cork accent and beery breath had put his arm around him one night to confide that really they were all the same. Weren't they both just Micks on the Make?

But it was Mick Brogan that Father Jerry wanted to keep at the forefront of his mind. His mission was in memory of Mick and all the other men who left home to endure hard labour and sleep in lodging houses. His Mick had escaped through marriage, but not everyone was so lucky. He started tentatively; it wasn't so much an introduction he was seeking as a suggestion, a name perhaps.

'Tacit Donovan.' Cathleen cut across him.

'He would be helpful, you think?'

Kitty turned from the sink. 'You won't get many smiles from that one, but everyone knows he's the best ganger in North London. Hasn't he built most of it!' She plunged back into the washing up. 'Well, that's one thing sorted. What else do you need?'

Father Jerry grinned. 'A base away from the chaplaincy, somewhere men can come in.'

'A pub!' Kitty was jubilant.

'Perhaps. It would have to be the right sort of pub and I'm not sure the right sort exists. I'd have to be able to run a committee from it – start a campaign. A place where—' He was interrupted again.

'Well, if that isn't The Sleeping Dog I don't know what is.' Kitty's hands were on her hips, her face creased in childish delight. 'Sure Pat and Christy would love it. Go on, what else do you need? Aren't we able to sort any problem here!'

Kitty was facing him now, splattering his jacket with droplets of soapy water and then she faltered, as if she was looking at him for the first time.

'Oh Father, you sitting here with the dirty dishes. You must think us dreadful heathens. Cathleen, let the poor man go downstairs and sit in a comfortable chair, why don't you?'

The doorbell rang just as Father Jerry was putting his coat on to leave and Cathleen felt a sting of irritation when she heard the clatter of high heels on the stairs.

'Only me,' Aude called out. In full make-up and a mustard suit, she was overdressed for a night in front of the television. For the first time, Cathleen saw the orange peel quality of her skin underneath the thick foundation and noticed that the hem of her skirt had been let down. These were things that might have recommended her to Cathleen – the girl was only making

the best of herself – if she hadn't held on to Father Jerry's arm
for so long.

'Really you must get a car. It's not a luxury for a man in your
line of work.'

When Aude squealed with delight at the news that he expected
to buy a car sometime soon, Cathleen felt compelled to say something. Aude and Mary shouldn't think that they had found a
chauffeur.

'But darling, I wouldn't dream of taking him away from *you*.'

The cerise-lipped 'you' seemed to echo around the landing. It
flamed Cathleen's cheeks and followed her upstairs as she ran to
the kitchen, saying she thought she'd left something on the stove
although she knew she hadn't.

Thirty-Five

'Tacit Donovan?'

Father Jerry wondered if he could be heard over the din
of Friday night banter. The Cricklewood pub was packed with
men straight from a building site. Every pore and crease in the
raw faces was marked by their twelve hours of labour. Steam rose
from damp donkey jackets and tables were black with Guinness,
each pint accompanied by a small amber chaser – whiskey to
burn away the taste of a hard week.

Father Jerry raised his voice. Several men had pointed to the
slim figure sitting at the bar but he began to lose confidence.
From the way people talked about him, somehow he had expected
Tacit to be an altogether bigger man.

'Are you Tacit?'

The shoulders turned slowly. Father Jerry could see the top
of a handsome, well-proportioned head and the priest grinned
when he realized that he was being inspected feet first.

There was a pause and Donovan's eyes were still firmly fixed
on Father Jerry's polished Oxfords. 'To those that don't know
me, it's *Mister* Donovan.'

Father Jerry's grin widened. It was as neat a put down as he'd ever received and he saw with regret the man's embarrassment when his eyes at last reached his collar.

'Ach, I meant no disrespect, Father.'

'None taken. My fault entirely, Mr Donovan.' Father Jerry held out his hand. 'I presumed an acquaintanceship we've yet to make. But your reputation goes before you.'

'What reputation would that be?'

'As a ganger and a fair man.' Father Jerry wished he could think of a third item for the list.

'He is that!' A watery-eyed youngster with shaggy, unruly eyebrows, was tipping back and forth on a stool next to Donovan. 'You won't get a man in here that'll say different.'

'Are you collecting?' Donovan's hand was already moving towards his wallet.

'No.'

'But if it was money you were after, if it was, this man would be the first to put his hand in his pocket.' Back and forth the stool went and the boy's head nodded in time. 'And he wouldn't look to see what came out.'

Father Jerry decided to ignore the interruption. 'We have someone in common. My name is Father Jerry Brogan.'

'Cathleen?'

'No. Well, yes, I suppose. Mick Brogan was my cousin.'

'Of course, you're the priest that said the Requiem. I should have recognized you. God have mercy on him.' Tacit took a sip of Guinness.

'I knew him. I did!' The boy bounced off his stool in excitement. 'A Monagahan muck shifter, wasn't he? With a foxy moustache. We worked together a ton of times until consumption got him.' He plucked at the priest's sleeve. 'Or am I thinking of Mickey from Carlow, who was after getting a crane dropped on his head?'

'Whist, man.' Donovan turned towards him. 'Me and the priest have business to discuss. Here.' He pulled ten shillings off a roll of notes. 'Get a round in and bring it over to that table there.' He glanced at Father Jerry's lapels. 'I don't see a pioneer badge, so a pint, is it Father?' The priest nodded.

Donovan led the way. The pub was even fuller than when Father Jerry first arrived and great platefuls of egg, sausage, mashed potato and cabbage were being ferried from hand to hand at head height from a dark doorway at the side of the bar. Two men were already sitting at the table Donovan had selected but they moved away without a word when they realized Tacit wanted it.

'How is Cathleen?'

'Bearing up.' Father Jerry winced at the cliché. The truth is I don't know, he thought. Aloud he added, 'It's been tough on her.'

'I know.' Tacit nodded, as the drinks arrived.

'It's your help I'm after.' Father Jerry took a sip from his pint. It was good Guinness. 'I'm part of the Irish Chaplaincy and we're setting up a project to find new ways of reaching out to the lads.' He looked up wondering if this would get a reaction. It didn't. 'You know the chaplains in Wales live cheek by jowl with the men where they're building the power stations?'

'Rough conditions down there.' Donovan spoke slowly.

'Yes, that can't be denied, but the priests are doing a great job, keeping the men's spirits up.' Donovan looked at him steadily but said nothing. 'I've been talking to another colleague who's a chaplain on the motorway and he moves along with the work, same as the men, saying Mass on site.'

'Is that what you're after?'

'Something similar.' Father Jerry decided to change strategy. The lean face in front of him was giving nothing away. 'Listen, Ireland's bleeding. Every year the youngest and the best leave to break their backs over here. And their hearts.' Father Jerry leant forward in his seat as he continued, 'The Church can't stop that. That's a job for the politicians but we can be with you. Irish priests should be with our own wherever they are – whether it's making the M1 or building a block of flats in Vauxhall.'

'The motorway men lodge in villages with no Catholic church in miles.' Donovan's voice was low. 'In Wales they live in camps that are a world in themselves. It's a different story for my men. They can get to Mass if they have a mind for it. Ever heard of Penguin Island?' Father Jerry shook his head. 'It's what the locals call a traffic island in Camden Town. On Sundays it's where the Irish gather, after Mass and before the pubs open.'

'Penguin?'

Tacit smiled for the first time. 'Even the worst of us can manage a dark suit and a decent white shirt for Sunday. My point is, Father, here in London we've become part of the geography. There's a church and a priest around every corner. You don't have to seek us out. We can find you.'

'Maybe it would bring the lads closer to the Church.'

Donovan lifted the glass of Guinness and siphoned off a third of a pint in one fluid ripple. He wiped his mouth with the back of his hand. 'The lads might think that the Church was close enough already.'

'Come now, we're not a Sunday-only religion.'

Donovan sighed. 'From birth to death you have us, as kids in school you have us, in the marriage bed you have us. Wouldn't you leave a man his work?' It was Father Jerry's turn to keep quiet. 'What exactly are you wanting?'

'To be on site often enough to make it seem ordinary: saying Mass, hearing confession if need be. It will work hand in hand with another campaign I'm launching to encourage the lads to keep in contact with home.'

Tacit leaned back in his chair. 'You know I can't say no, although I might not like it.' He shrugged. 'If my church asks there's only one answer I can give. But you need to understand different rules apply on site. Forgive me, Father, but nothing gets in the way of the work. Nothing.'

'I understand. I might not like it, but I understand.'

Tacit acknowledged the remark with a slight jerk of the head. All his movements were economical, as if a terrible force of energy was being held back. Getting up to leave, Father Jerry held out his hand and he wasn't surprised that Tacit's grip was a band of iron-hard muscle.

'Cathleen Brogan.'

'Yes-s?'

'Tell her I was asking after her.'

Their meeting was over.

Thirty-Six

Father Jerry was feeling pleased with himself. The fund-raising dance was a sell out and his campaign was about to establish its headquarters at The Sleeping Dog. And here he was in his new car, an Austin A40 that the man in the showroom had called peacock green. He was rather glad to own something that wasn't clerical black. He turned up on Cathleen's doorstep with an itch to drive her somewhere.

The bulb had gone out in the hall and he couldn't see Cathleen clearly when she came to the door. She didn't invite him in and that was strange in itself.

'What's wrong? Are you ill?'

She moved and for a few seconds her face was illuminated by the street light. Her hair was hanging in dull, limp curls and there was something hollow and bruised looking about her eyes. After she murmured something about a headache, he was left staring at the front door, convinced that something or someone had made her cry. He was surprised how angry he felt.

One glance at his list of appointments when he got back to his car told him everything he needed to know. He was scheduled to say one Mass in the morning. Months ago, in his own hand, he had noted down the dedication. It was the anniversary of Mick's death and he had forgotten.

He glanced up at the sitting-room window. The light was off and he imagined Cathleen sitting in the dark. He thought of going back, slipping quietly up the stairs and holding her. She could cry for as long as she wanted and he would hold her.

The car's engine growled as he drove away.

Father Jerry was sure she wasn't going to come. He'd kept looking out, glancing towards the door whenever he got a chance and questioning Pat Brady who had taken charge of the tea urn in the school hall, rolling up her sleeves as if she was preparing for a fight. But she knew as little as he did.

'Ah, she'd never miss your first fund-raiser.'

Yes, but the Cathleen who had answered the door on Wednesday night didn't look as if she would be going to go to a dance on the Saturday.

But here she was, with Kitty and Mary and that friend who was all nail polish and big hair. He strode towards her but the parish priest ambushed him after a few steps. He turned around. Cathleen had disappeared. Never mind, she was here somewhere and after the speech making, he'd find her and make her glad she'd come.

'Ladies and gentlemen.' The pianist was on his feet. He coughed. People ignored him. The crowd seemed to be talking louder on purpose. The poor lad, thought Father Jerry bounding on to the stage next to him. He's no talent for this kind of thing.

'Thank you for coming tonight.' Father Jerry's voice carried easily to the back of the hall. 'This is a special night for me and not just because we've all been entertained by great music from . . .' He spotted Cathleen sitting at a crowded table and was sure there was a smile playing around her lips. She thinks I've forgotten the name of the band and she's right. '. . . from these talented young men.'

Cathleen was grinning at him now and he was starting to enjoy himself. As a young priest he'd been told to preach to a congregation of one. Imagine one man sitting in the church waiting for the word of God. Tonight Cathleen would be his congregation. There would only be Cathleen.

'This is a special night because this is the very first dance in aid of a cause that I hope you will all support. Ireland has sent her young people across the world. Every generation has gone. To America, to faraway Australia and New Zealand, but most of all to this country. And some would say she sends her bravest and her best.'

'Isn't that the truth!' There was a whiskey-wet laugh from somewhere near the exit.

'But the world isn't always kind no matter how brave you might be. So the Irish Chaplaincy in London is setting up a new scheme to help our own when they need it. Because the building site can be a lonely place, am I right?'

There was a polite swell of agreement: not as much as he had hoped for. He searched for Cathleen's face. Kitty was in the way again and not paying attention.

'It's easy to lose touch with home. How many lads have got on the boat at Dun Laoghaire meaning to write every week? And at first they do. But if there's no work they don't write. And if there is work, the days melt into one another and they don't write. The lucky ones might find the right girl and she'll take over the letter writing. But if the right girl doesn't come along, doesn't make a move at a Ladies' Excuse Me dance . . .'

He saw Cathleen's head jerk up and, although she was still partly obscured by Kitty, she would know that he'd remembered. It was a way of saying sorry, he thought.

'. . . the mother is left at home watching out everyday for the post van and everyday it drives past the door.'

Father Jerry paused. He had them now. He was sure of it. He could feel Cathleen's eyes on him.

'And then the letter writing is left so long it's hard to write anything at all. There's too much to tell.' He looked up. There was movement by the door. Had he misjudged it and bored the very men he was trying to reach? No. Tacit Donovan had arrived.

'All we're trying to do is give a helping hand to those who are scared that they *have* left it too long. And when I say "we", I don't just mean myself, and the priests in this parish who have already done so much, but you as well. Looking around I can see many faces who have already helped and more who have promised to help. And a few who don't know it yet, but will be helping by the end of the evening.' A wave of smiles broke across the hall, one or two laughed out loud. 'It's important work because if our young men lose touch with home, won't they also lose touch with the Church? Adrift without faith or family. Lost entirely. And they deserve better than that.'

He looked around. Did they believe him? Did they care? Most of the people gathered here had come over in the last ten years. Most said they were going back some time – I won't die here, Father. They of all people would understand the importance of keeping the idea of home alive.

'You've heard enough from me. The Letter Home Campaign needs you, spread the word and dance away.'

The band struck up a new tune as Father Jerry jumped off the stage. People were still applauding as he made straight for Cathleen's table, wanting to be reassured that he had got it right. Here he was in a new country, new job and, for the first time since his youth, living outside the embrace of an institution. He was lucky to have a new family. Father Jerry smiled to himself. He was still smiling when he heard Aude announce that it was all very amusing.

'But Father, do Irish men really need help to write to their mummies?' Aude patted his hand. 'Aren't you in danger of being a tiny bit patronizing?' She didn't wait for an answer. 'I do believe the band's trying to play "Apache". Aren't they priceless?' She pulled a reluctant Mary to her feet and brushed past Father Jerry. 'We're going to get near the stage – Mary has a thing about piano players.'

'Ah, go on with you.' Mary's accent slipped in embarrassment. 'Anyway, you were the one making eyes at Donovan.'

'The man by the door? I simply recognize a good suit when it walks in. You didn't say you knew him.'

'Ah, we all know him. He used to be Mick's boss but he's awful old.'

Father Jerry grinned. Tacit must be a lot nearer thirty than forty, he thought, as he made his way to the trestle table where tea was being served. He'd volunteered to get a cup for Kitty but a large plump hand gripped his shoulder before he reached the urn.

'You're doing God's own work, Father.' A man with a ruddy, fleshy face was looking up at him. 'That's a cracking article on that table. Is she free, do you think?' He nodded in Cathleen's direction. 'Sorry, Father, you're above all that yourself. You wouldn't have an idea what I'm on about.' He turned away, his fat hand groping for a flask in his trouser pocket. 'Not an idea.'

Father Jerry was about to make his way back when he spotted Tacit, leaning against a pillar. Other young men had gravitated towards him but were keeping a respectful distance. There was something uncompromising about the way he was standing that made him an odd figure at a dance. It wasn't surprising that Aude had spotted the ganger from the other side of the hall. And it was more than just the good suit he was wearing. The priest wondered what was going on beneath the stern exterior: Tacit seemed to be focusing on someone or something at the other end of the hall. Father Jerry followed his line of vision. Tacit was watching Cathleen.

Thirty-Seven

The sight of Pat Brady striding towards the stage, the diamanté in her red glasses glinting in the glare of the overhead lights, distracted Father Jerry. She grabbed the mike and announced that the Siege of Ennis was about to start. The band started to play a tune that sounded faintly like a polka and dancers filled the floor.

Father Jerry had no intention of joining them, but when he saw both the parish priest and the curate take their places, he knew he would be given little choice. He could, however, choose his partner. Possibly. He made his way back to Cathleen's table. The red-faced man had got there first.

'A bit of a dance?'

'No, thank you.' Cathleen's head was down, studying the floor.

'Go on, a bit of an old shuffle. I don't bite, honest I don't. Ah go on, yer mother is dancing with the priest!' Cathleen looked up, frowning. Sure enough, Kitty was standing next to the parish priest. 'And he gargles with vinegar.'

Father Jerry stepped in. 'Sorry, my fault. I made her promise.' He took her hand and guided Cathleen to the floor. 'Would you rather not? Only they were bound to make me dance and . . .' His voice trailed off.

Cathleen flicked the fringe from her face. 'No, I'm fine. Really, it's easier this way.'

Father Jerry nodded and, glancing back at the Brogan table, realized that Aude was the only one still sitting down. Mary was calling over to her now, urging her on to the floor with the pianist who had jumped down from the stage. Aude's haughty expression wasn't fooling anyone and he'd noticed the resentful look she gave Cathleen as she brushed past.

It was time to take their places and he grabbed Cathleen's hand to join Kitty and the parish priest who were already arguing.

'I'll have you know, I cut a fine step at ceilidhs in Monasterevin forty years ago.' The parish priest was whining.

'We'll see if your feet have a good memory,' chirped Kitty, swinging into a two-step, two-step, make-up-a new-step as she waited for other dancers to form a set.

'That's some kind of heathen jazz thing you're doing,' the priest said, his Adam's apple bobbing up and down above his clerical collar.

'Go on, Father! It's a fine mover, you are! Swing the lady.' Father Jerry didn't know who said it, but it was all the permission he needed.

Cathleen crossed her hands and held them out. He knew she was expecting to be pulled and pushed in a jokey version of the real thing, both of them falling over their feet. A polite smile was already forming on her face.

He held Cathleen's hands tight and, with heels planted, he slowly made her spin, savouring the sensation. The speed picked up, his eyes never leaving her face and, for a moment, he saw panic as her feet flew over the parquet and the room flashed past. Then she relaxed into the pulse of his strong grip: they were circling round together. There was the parish priest tripping over his cassock. There was the drinks table, the band, Aude sitting on her own, Tacit still in the shadows. There was Cathleen holding tight.

Then the whirl of feet slowed to a stop. Father Jerry dropped Cathleen's hands as the last bar of the dance faded away. It was over.

Cathleen was gasping for breath and laughing. 'It was . . . a tonic.' He was self-conscious as they walked off the dance floor together and embarrassed by Aude's compliments.

'You know how to treat a lady, Father.'

He brushed away the remark as he brushed away Cathleen's hand. Her court shoe had slipped off and she needed to steady herself but he removed her hand from his arm. He was aware of her puzzled frown as he moved away to check on something at the back of the stage that didn't need checking. He could feel Aude's eyes following him and noticed that Tacit had left.

Most of all he was aware of himself. It felt as though his every nerve was stretched. He was electric. Dancing was dangerous. He wouldn't do that again.

Thirty-Eight

A s Father Jerry slipped the chasuble over his head he said a short, silent prayer. Under a slate grey sky he was ready to say his first Mass on a building site. His altar was a table carried out from the office, its surface patterned with white circles from a generation of tea mugs. He wedged a square of cardboard under one leg to keep it steady.

Father Jerry shivered. Looking out across the warren of trenches, ramps and scaffolding, he could see that most men had discarded their jackets and were working in their shirtsleeves. He felt cold in his vestments and wouldn't have minded ten minutes of ditch digging to send the blood coursing through his veins.

He looked up into the sky. There was water up there, just waiting to fall. He sent a swift prayer to St Francis for a quarter of an hour of dry. Don't let the men get wet hearing Mass, not on the first day.

The midday bell rang and, as Father Jerry intoned the words of the opening blessing, he felt the first raindrop on the back of his neck. Right, he decided. This is going to be my first ten-minute Mass.

Afterwards a young, soft-skinned lad who blushed to the roots of his blond hair every time he spoke, brewed a large pot of tea and splashed it into the mugs the men held out. Father Jerry joined them.

'Watch out, Father, that'll strip the enamel off your teeth,' someone called out. There was laughter as the men huddled around, each one clutching a brown paper bag of bread and butter and the odd bit of cheese. The boy's face flushed crimson as he handed Father Jerry a mug. The priest wanted to tell him that he had never tasted better, but the dark liquid seared his throat with tannin. He hoped the lad didn't notice when he poured most of it into a nearby trench.

It was Pat who suggested that Cathleen should be on the Letter Home Committee. Cathleen refused. She had no skills to speak of, what good would she be?

'Go on, Father, tell her.'

The pair of them, sitting at Cathleen's kitchen table, had looked across at him, waiting for an answer. Behind her glasses Pat's eyes were bird-like, small and fierce, protective of her friend. He avoided looking at Cathleen. He could have talked about some airy time in the future when the children were older. He could have said that what they needed was hard-nosed businessmen with connections, or hard-handed working men who knew what it felt like to dig a ditch. He could even have said the committee was full up. Instead he'd looked out the window across the roofs and bare tree tops towards the dome of St Paul's Cathedral and shrugged. He hoped that it would appear as if he hadn't given the matter much thought.

'Join us, Cathleen. We'd be better with you than without you.'

When he turned around both women warmed him with their smiles and he was convinced that he had made the right choice.

Back in Verona he would have advised seminarians to remove themselves from temptation, but he was no naive youth. Yes, Cathleen was a constant reminder of the vows he'd taken and the promises he'd made, but celibacy was even more precious if it was hard won.

And hard kept.

Thirty-Nine

Cathleen was thinking about her first committee meeting. The air had been blue with smoke and the talk littered with phrases she'd never heard before. The men were impatient when Pat spoke and greedy when it came to their turn, but she left feeling more vital than she had for a long time. It felt good to do new things. Perhaps next time she'd even try speaking herself.

Cathleen stood in the middle of the bedroom lost in thought. She only realized that her youngest daughter was crouching on the bed when she moved. Geraldine was bending over, her back to the door, oblivious to her mother's footsteps. There was a glint of silver and Cathleen made a grab for the little girl's hand. Her fingers closed around the cold blades of the nail scissors.

'I didn't mean it. It was an accident.' The child's mouth wobbled as her eyes filled with tears. A small streak of blood trickled down the inside of her arm where the skin was translucent.

'I'm going to kiss this better,' Cathleen said, forcing her voice to sound ordinary. She sat on the bed next to her daughter, not sure what else to do. Geraldine was crying properly now and burrowing into her mother's lap, trying to make herself even smaller.

Cathleen counted to ten. *I mustn't shout and I mustn't cry myself. I'll try telling her the truth; see how she reacts to that.*

'I thought Anna was hurting you.'

The little girl pulled away in surprise. 'Anna would never do that.'

★　　★　　★

'Letter home?' The man scoffed. 'Errah, what do they want that for? It's the remittance they want. It's the wire they want. Think they want Dear Mammy? Dear Daddy? Not on your life, not unless it comes with a nice bit of folding stuff.' He was angry and shouting.

Father Jerry stepped forward but Cathleen was ahead of him.

'How old were you when you came over?' She softened her voice. If the man wanted to hear what she said he would have to stop pacing up and down. It worked with children. Sometimes. It had worked with Geraldine who told her at last, after more hot tears, that pressing hard until it hurt made her feel squishy inside. And squishy was what she wanted to feel when she was sad.

The man turned and looked at her. He had a glass in his hand and the beer sloshed over the rim as he waved it around.

'Seventeen and as green as they come. God, when I think how raw we all were.' He stopped and seemed to see Cathleen for the first time. 'I went home after a few months but there was no encouragement to stay.'

Cathleen nodded. She guessed he was now in his thirties. 'How long since you've been back?'

'I don't know. How can a man remember a thing like that?' His voice rose and his lips twisted, as if a sour taste had suddenly flooded his mouth. Cathleen was aware that Father Jerry was edging towards her and that Christy, behind the bar, was glancing over his shoulder every few seconds.

The man tried to haul himself up and she wondered if she had misjudged the situation: would it end in broken glass and blows? His shoulders shot up to his ears and just as suddenly slumped. When he spoke again his voice was as soft as Cathleen's.

'I never went home again.'

She led him away to a corner of the bar where they wouldn't be disturbed and together they sat talking. When he left half an hour later, as Christy called last orders, he shook her hand.

'You'll write for me, Mrs Brogan? You'll smooth the way with my sister? The old folk are dead but I have a mind to see her and the old place again.'

Pat was jubilant when she saw a completed form in Cathleen's hand.

'Is that our first letter home? It is, isn't it? You were wonderful, ignoring all his blather. I'd have given him a load back with bells on. And you looking so nervous before tonight started, there's a fear of you.' She squeezed Cathleen's arm.

'He was shy, that's all, and scared that he's left it too long.'

'I don't think anyone else had any kind of success.'

Father Jerry glanced at his watch. 'Well, we never planned on our first session lasting so long. And I'd say we can count this as a good start. Five men in.'

Cathleen started to button up her coat. She couldn't remember the last time she'd been out this late. Not since Ireland.

'You're not walking! Sure, you'll give the girl a lift, won't you, Father? In your grand new car.' Cathleen looked up. She hadn't realized that he'd bought the car. They hadn't seen much of each other since the dance.

'Ah, it's nothing much.' Father Jerry shrugged casually. 'An old Austin.'

'A car's a car,' said Pat. 'And that will do you fine. The limo will have to wait until they make you a bishop.'

'Pat Brady! Will you listen to yourself.' Her husband pretended to be scandalized, as he gave the bar a quick wipe with the small towel that had been flung over his shoulder all evening. Father Jerry was laughing at both of them and, for a moment, Cathleen was reminded of the wedding photograph that used to be in the kitchen. It was tucked away now, face down, in a drawer behind the rubber bands. Cathleen smiled. It was a nice picture: it deserved to be out on display again.

The Austin was parked around the corner, about a foot away from the kerb.

'Was it easier with the big car you had in Ireland?' she asked, as Father Jerry crunched the gears and shuffled backwards and forwards before driving out of the side street.

'It was easier when I had a wide road to myself and all I had to do was point it.'

Father Jerry was frowning. It was a dry night but the wipers started to scrape across the windscreen. Cathleen glanced over and wondered if she could talk to him about Geraldine. She needed to confide in someone, but would he understand? She didn't herself. All she could do was watch and not let Geraldine know she was watching.

No, his mind was elsewhere. She was pretty sure that they were in the wrong lane of traffic and he seemed to be having trouble reading the road signs. Cathleen realized that they were now travelling west along Pentonville Road. 'I think we've come a long way round.'

'I was just thinking that myself,' said Father Jerry.

'When I said long way, I really meant completely opposite direction. This is Kings Cross. Look, there's the Alibone lady.'

The curvy neon figure glowed in the dark night above Bravington's, the jewellers.

'Left here, or we'll be in Euston.'

'Are we that far away from the Angel?'

'We'll be in Marylebone at this rate. Jerry, left!' She called out as they reached the junction. 'And left again.'

I called him Jerry, she thought, and he hasn't noticed. Jerry Brogan. It sounds like a poem.

'Ah, I recognize this! I can find anywhere as long as I start from Rosebery Avenue. I can't go wrong now.'

No, Jerry, she thought. You can't go wrong.

Forty

Cathleen wasn't sure she could solve Geraldine's problems, but she could put a smile on Anna's face. Anna needed a dress. And not just any dress, but one that conformed to her dancing school's strict regulations. It could be a certain kind of blue, or green, or the cream that Anna had set her heart on. It didn't matter what colour it was, thought Cathleen, as she looked at the few coppers saved in the jam jar at the back of the cupboard. She didn't know how the pile was going to grow any bigger.

She'd passed the shop on the corner of Chapel Market almost every day since she moved to London. Glancing up at the three gold balls prominently displayed over the entrance, she was convinced it was the solution to at least one family problem.

In the window two cuckoo clocks, both frozen in mid coo, were displayed on a heavy lace tablecloth that was jaundiced from the sunlight. There's a story behind everything here, she thought, noticing a dusty canteen of cutlery in the corner. After one quick look to check if anyone was watching, she pushed open the door.

It was dark inside, with an old man serving behind the counter. The bald dome of his head glistened in the light from a lamp. Cathleen took a step forward, swallowed and, without saying anything, undid her marquisate watch and laid it on the counter. The pawnbroker picked it up and turned it over in his hands before placing it to one side.

He named the figure and explained how the calculation was worked out.

She had been a fool; it wasn't nearly enough.

'Think about it,' said the man handing it back. 'We've been here since 1873. We're not going anywhere.'

Cathleen, conscious of his eyes on her, felt her cheeks burn. Finally she made up her mind. With a short, savage twist she took off her wedding ring and laid it down on the counter.

The man didn't say anything. He checked the hallmark and placed the plain gold band on a small scale. Cathleen nodded as he named the amount she could borrow.

Cathleen hurried out. She had to go home to put a bandage on her finger. It wasn't a very good lie and it wouldn't last long but it would do for now.

She'd order the cream dress. It was done and she wasn't going to cry about it. She had another committee meeting to look forward to and an outing with Father Jerry. The future was bright and she wouldn't let herself cry.

Forty-One

Cathleen looked at her reflection in the wardrobe mirror. Best coat and best shoes too. It was good to have a reason to get dressed up.

Anna and Geraldine were lying on the bed.

'Mary puts on more lipstick.' Anna frowned as she inspected her mother. 'And you should have your hair up like Aude's.'

'It would never stay up.' She kissed both daughters on the cheek, automatically checking Geraldine's legs and all the exposed flesh she could see. Nothing. It was a fortnight since she discovered the truth about Geraldine's injuries and since then there had been no more bruises or scratches. Perhaps the craving to feel squishy had passed.

It was a strange time to go out, just after school had finished, and a strange thing to do: attend a special showing of a film. The girls had been very impressed.

'Will you see someone famous?'

'Will you get autographs?'

This was Islington Green, she reminded them, not Leicester Square, and she was going to see a film no one had heard of and the really special part was that it was free, but only for local businesses. Pat and Christy had received their invitations as landlords of The Sleeping Dog but they were expecting a visit from the brewery that day. They had pressed the tickets on Father Jerry.

'Talk to people, be seen around. Someone might be glad to make a donation,' Pat argued. 'There's little enough money coming into this campaign. We can't turn up our noses at anything.'

Cathleen was not given a choice.

'Of course, you have to go.' Pat was adamant. 'You're the only one free and we can't send the father on his own.'

He was waiting outside the box office when she got off the bus. 'You're looking very swish.'

'I haven't overdone it, have I? Only I wasn't sure what to wear.'

'Ah, no,' he reassured her. 'I'm the one who looks out of place here.' He glanced around at the others milling in the foyer as he fingered his collar. Not that many people had taken up the free offer.

'So much for Pat and her contacts.' Father Jerry grinned. 'Let's see the film anyway.'

They chose seats in the middle of the central section. No one else was near: above their heads the gallery was in darkness.

From the opening scene Cathleen knew it was going to be bad. The actress' lips were tomato soup red and the beach looked more like custard than sand. It was a bright, shiny story about teenage love in America where every boy had a car and every girl had just been to the hairdresser. Cathleen could sense that Father Jerry was bored from the way he shifted in his seat. Somewhere to their right there was a sudden flare of light as a cigarette was lit, and from behind came an occasional cough and shuffling of feet, but she could almost imagine that they were on their own. She closed her eyes.

'You can't go to sleep on me, Cathleen Brogan! I'm not suffering on my own.'

'Shh, I'm trying to . . .' She stifled a giggle and turned around quickly. Too quickly. She hadn't realized that he was looking at her. They were almost touching and they froze for a second, less than a second.

Cathleen tried to follow the story but there was a low sound from somewhere behind that distracted her. She turned around: a couple were sound asleep. The credits rolled and Father Jerry suggested they leave.

'Coo-eee!'

From across the other side of the auditorium came a shrill, penetrating call. It was Aude.

'My goodness! Aren't you a pair of dark horses!' She had dodged through the rows of empty seats so quickly that she arrived in their aisle panting for breath. 'I got here late – the office is so busy and they can't do without little old me. I really wish Uncle Bertie would hire Mary. It would be such a weight off my shoulders. But what brings you two here?'

'Same as yourself, I imagine,' said Father Jerry, putting his own coat on. 'Free seats.'

'You poppet! What a lovely, lovely not-very religious thing to do. And Cathleen!' Aude stood back to look at her as the house lights went up. 'You've made a real effort today. Good for you. In fact, the pair of you make an awfully attractive couple . . .'

'We are not a couple,' said Father Jerry firmly, as he brushed past her in the aisle.

'That's not what it looked like from where I was sitting.'

Forty-Two

'I think it must be a sex thing.' Cathleen looked up startled. Kitty was standing by the kitchen window, blowing smoke rings at the ceiling.

'Your father could blow lovely ones but I've never met a woman who could,' continued Kitty. 'Have men and women different lips, is that it?'

Cathleen finished the washing up and reached over for a tea towel.

'Jaysus! Your finger.'

The plaster had floated away in the water exposing a thin band of white flesh.

'I've ordered the dress.' Cathleen turned back to the sink as her mother sucked in air through her false teeth.

'But your wedding ring! Don't you know what people will say?'

'I don't care.'

'Why should you? Aren't you as good as any of them but, all the same, awful cruelty can come out of mouths and words can hurt as much as fists.'

Kitty started to pull at her own hand, screwing her face into a grimace in the effort.

'Mum, what are you doing? Stop it.'

Kitty sighed. 'It's no good any road. It would have to be cut off.' She held up her hand. It was clear that her wedding ring would not pass over her swollen knuckles. 'God love you, they'll say you're thinking of another man. That Mick's forgot and you have another man in your head even if they can't put him in your bed.'

Cathleen stared down at her ringless hand. It looked naked in the afternoon light. If people were saying that it will only be the truth, she thought. I didn't mean it to happen but it's true, every word of it.

Kitty put an arm around her daughter. 'Girl, you'd better buy another pack of them plasters.'

Forty-Three

Father Jerry held the phone away from his ear.

'The curate's hawking catarrh and now he's gone and lost his voice.' The parish priest's own voice dropped to a wheedle. 'Would you ever give me a hand with tonight's confession? Would you?' He took a heartbeat of silence for assent. 'Good man yourself and you might as well stay the night. There's two early Masses you could do that would save a lot of bother.'

Father Jerry opened the lounge door to find the diocesan housekeeper waiting outside.

'I suppose you're going out again.' She was a small woman in her sixties with an obvious moustache.

'I'm afraid that I won't be back tonight.'

'It's hard to run a regular house with all these comings and goings.'

'I know, but you make a grand job of it.'

'Breakfast?'

He shook his head.

'Dinner?'

Father Jerry hesitated. He could easily be back for the formal dinner gong but he didn't relish the watery cabbage, chewy brisket and thick gravy. He'd throw himself on Cathleen's mercies and the thought cheered him.

'Supper?'

'Oh yes. No danger. I'll be back for that.' He was rather proud of the way he had managed to sound so enthusiastic about a couple of inches of dry Cheddar and a few cream crackers.

The highly polished baroque confessional boxes stood to the left and right of the baptismal font at the back of the church. They had been made for a smaller man than Father Jerry. The dark interior smelt of old incense and furniture polish. For a moment he was back in the church of San Lorenzo in Verona. There the priest was hidden by a purple curtain but poor penitents were exposed to public curiosity as they confessed through a pierced copper screen. He smiled at the memory.

The parish priest scuttled into his own box with a wave and what looked like a packet of biscuits. A steady stream of young and old were taking their places in the pews: men in gaberdine and galoshes, women in damp headscarves, grumpy children shushed to silence. A reasonable turnout for a damp Saturday. Father Jerry closed the door again, flicking a switch to illuminate the curate's name board.

When the stout doors closed all that could be seen were the motes of dust floating in the feeble light that shone from the priest's side of the cubicle. A short curtain drawn across the double meshed grill added to the seclusion.

'Bless me, Father.' It was a tired woman's voice. 'I've done something very wrong.'

'Was it something you did?' Father Jerry asked gently. 'Or something you didn't do?'

'Oh, how did you guess? I haven't honoured my mother.'

'Go on.'

'It was her anniversary and I didn't have a Mass said.'

'And why was that?'

'I couldn't afford it.'

Father Jerry sighed. 'Go now to the presbytery and say Father Brogan sent you. Leave your mother's details and I'll say one tomorrow.'

'Yes, Father.'

He could tell from her voice that there would be no slip of paper waiting for him. 'What's wrong?'

'It wouldn't be the same. Me not paying for it.'

'It would be in God's eyes.' There was no answer. 'Tell me her name, tell me now. I'll keep it in mind for tomorrow. Your mother will have her Mass.'

Her whisper was so soft, so little above a breath, that Father Jerry caught a rhythm, but no syllables. He knew he couldn't ask again. It doesn't matter, he thought, God knows his own. 'I can't give you penance for this. It's not a sin to be without money.'

There was silence in the dark. A musty smell of dandruff and sweat drifted from the other side of the grill and Father Jerry flinched at the sudden intimacy. The woman was raking her hair with her fingers again and again, and he realized that she wouldn't leave without being ordered to atone in some way.

'Is there anything else you want to tell me?'

'I was cross with the children. They're always after me for something. And I say no. And then they get upset and shout and I start shouting. And it's all, "why can't I?" Then we make up until the next time.' Her voice dropped and Father Jerry leant forward to put his ear to the grill.

'My husband's left me,' she whispered.

He sat back wondering if there was anything he could say that would make her feel better. He wanted to tell her that the sin she was confessing belonged to someone else but he didn't. Instead, he gave her the three Hail Mary's she needed.

Next came a cigarette growl of a voice. Father Jerry could smell whiskey.

'To tell the truth I wouldn't know how long it was since my last confession. I'm an old altar boy, I am. My poor mammy would weep if she could see me now. I'm a thoroughly bad lot but where to start? It's my life story you're wanting.'

No, thought Father Jerry with a grin, that's what I don't want. 'You're here now. That's what matters. You're back home and it won't be so hard again.'

The man stumbled out of the confessional five minutes later. He had asked for money, after announcing that he was so hungry he could eat the fleece off the Blessed Lamb of God, but came away with the address of a homeless hostel instead. Other parishioners came and knelt on the other side of the screen and left again, usually with three Hail Mary's as penance, although he instructed one young man smelling of cheap aftershave to say one, properly, and write a letter home.

Father Jerry looked down at his watch but it was too dark to tell the time. He guessed it must be well after seven. Not much longer and he could have a fry up back at the presbytery. Rashers and black pudding, and he promised himself a good big mug of tea. His mind was elsewhere and he didn't take much notice of the next occupant. Would he have a couple of eggs as well? His supper was already forming in his mind when he became aware of damp wool and the rustle of a skirt.

A woman; Father Jerry closed his eyes. They always outnumbered the men. It was a mystery why God hadn't made the priesthood female. Then he became aware of another smell, something delicate with a touch of sweetness to it, something he associated with his childhood. He struggled for the memory and then it came to him: his mother's dressing table. On one side there had been a green glass dish holding hairgrips and on the other a pot-bellied bowl of face powder. It was a long time since he'd thought of his mother.

'Bless me, Father.'

Cathleen.

He sat up suddenly. It was her voice. He would know it anywhere.

'For I have sinned. It's three weeks since my last confession.'

It happens all the time, Father Jerry told himself. If I was settled in a parish it would be strange when I didn't know the person in the confessional. But that wasn't good enough and he knew it. Another name was illuminated outside and Cathleen had come here expecting someone else. I must say something, Father Jerry told himself; let her know it's me. But it was Cathleen who spoke first.

'I've lost patience with my children, several times,' she began. 'With my sister several times, and with my mother all the time.'

Father Jerry smiled. This wouldn't be so bad after all; less than his own sins, so much less. It was an account of everyday failings, of hopes and expectations disappointed. It was a woman whispering in the dark.

His job was to hear and not to listen because the message wasn't for him. He had the power to forgive but not to withhold forgiveness. Surely, it would be an intrusion if he were to make his presence known.

'I was late for Mass last Sunday.'

Father Jerry sat further back in the shadows, imagining Cathleen marching her daughters down the road; Anna's hair electric with brushing, little Geraldine dragging behind, both faces shiny from washing.

There was a pause and he wondered if Cathleen had finished. Her voice, when it came again, was muffled.

'There's been times when I thought I would give way to the sin of despair but that's behind me now. Not that I've gotten over my husband's death because I haven't, but I've got used to going on without him, like someone gets used to only having one leg. But you never forget that you're a one-legged man.' She paused and he imagined her frowning. 'That wasn't what I wanted to say.'

Another pause.

'What I wanted to say was that sometimes my thoughts run away with me.'

Father Jerry held his breath.

'I sometimes think things I shouldn't. I miss being married.'

He sensed her shift position and knew that she was waiting for him to say something. This was too close, he thought, too near something raw and private in her heart. If he could have spoken he would have begged Cathleen not to; that he didn't deserve this confidence. But he could not speak.

'There's a friendship that's helped me through this hard time but I don't want to be friends any more.' He was conscious of his own shallow breathing now. 'I love him and I shouldn't.'

'Ah.'

Father Jerry despised the sound he made, hated Cathleen hearing it, scared that it would give him away. He put his hand up to the thin partition and felt the chipped veneer beneath his fingers. They were only inches apart.

'He's not free. But I think, I don't know, but I think that maybe he feels . . . maybe.'

He wanted to put an end to all this and dry the tears that were just a shadow's width away, but when she spoke again the strength of her voice surprised him.

'No, I'm wrong. I'm sorry, Father. I shouldn't have said anything. I'm wrong.'

She was on her feet now; he could hear her damp raincoat swish against the wooden walls as she rushed away.

Outside Cathleen cooled her face against the rendered wall of the church. She saw Father Jerry everywhere, heard him every-where: he was in a certain broadness of shoulder she noticed on a teacher taking young boys for football, in a laugh overheard at the market. Cathleen had scanned the stalls, walking up as far as the pie and mash shop but she couldn't find him. And now her mind had betrayed her again, imagining him in the confessional.

Why did I come? She was angry with herself.

A large cross was mounted on the church wall and the nailed feet of the crucified Christ were smoothed from the kisses of children. Geraldine had to be lifted up to reach but Anna was tall enough now. Cathleen traced the painted plaster with her finger.

Did I really think something would change, that I would stop feeling? That would be a miracle worth having. She tried to imagine waking up just the same as always, that bit of her gone. That was her problem. *Take what I feel for Father Jerry away and I'm gone too.*

Forty-Four

Cathleen climbed the narrow stairs with a tray piled with letters. She had popped into The Sleeping Dog after her morning shift at the shop. When she walked into the tiny pub kitchen Pat seemed to be drowning in committee work. Boxes of headed notepaper were stacked on top of the cooker and Pat was furiously addressing envelopes in a bold, sloping hand that barely left enough room for a stamp. Cathleen had never been so warmly welcomed.

Cathleen liked the way the days had become crowded; being busy suited her. The shops were full of Christmas and the children had already written their list for Santa. This year there was no talk about where they would have dinner. It would be back home where it belonged and there would be guests. Reg and Father Jerry had already said yes, and she would ask Aude, although surely she would be going home. And Pat and Christy could come around in the evening.

Father Jerry had breezed into the kitchen an hour earlier, refusing even a mouthful of tea. Within minutes he would be away again, after signing a few letters and reading a few documents. Away, away, he had laughed, backing out the door, and she and Pat listened to the clatter of his feet on the stairs as he dashed up to the room above their heads.

He knows about busy, Cathleen thought, as she began to turn the handle of the room that was set aside for meetings. She had hardly seen him in weeks. Gone were the days when he would pop in for a meal or cup of tea. Now he hardly had time to chat. She missed him. She missed the easy way that they used to have with one another. At times it seemed as if they had gone back to being strangers.

She stepped back puzzled when the door resisted her pressure. Something was forcing the handle on the other side. Slowly the door opened. There was no natural light in the narrow passageway and the panelling that lined the walls made it a place of brown shadows. She could see the shape of a man standing in the doorway. Father Jerry hadn't left.

She was about to say something, had opened her mouth to speak, but the look on his face robbed her of words. She could see past him into the room, see the green tablecloth and the minute book lying open. It all seemed ordinary. She looked up at him again and knew it wasn't.

His face was stern, almost angry. All either of them had to do was step back and allow the other person to pass, but neither moved. They were locked in the doorway, inches apart. And she couldn't stop looking up at him any more than he could stop looking down at her.

Very slowly he leant forward. There was dust on his cheek and she longed to brush it away. He was so near she could smell him: the clean cutting edge of soap and something faint and faraway and rich like the smell of cinnamon in a kitchen cupboard.

The pressure of his lips scorched her mouth. They were a branding iron that burnt long after he had gone. She stood for a moment in the dark listening to the sound of his footsteps fade away.

Nothing had changed. Cars were still passing outside. Christy was still humming downstairs and Pat was still stuffing envelopes. Nothing had changed and that was a wonder because everything had changed.

Stepping into the committee room, Cathleen studied her reflection in the mirror that hung over the mantelpiece. She touched her mouth lightly, as if it was bruised.

He kissed me. The thought circled her mind. *He kissed me and he's run away.*

Forty-Five

'Those ladies are demons!'

'What?' Father Jerry's head shot up. He had been charging through the public bar with his shoulders hunched and his hands thrust into his pockets.

'The way they work. Your Cathleen and my Pat are a pair of wonders.' Christy frowned. 'Are you all right, Father? Can I get you something?'

'No, I'm late. I forgot how late I was.' He stood for a moment as if lost in thought. 'I don't need anything.' The bar door swung shut.

His car was outside and it started after the second attempt. He grabbed the gear stick with such aggression that heads jerked at the noise. Lurching towards Rosebery Avenue he made a sudden right-hand turn into a side street that earned him a blast of abuse from a lorry driver.

Father Jerry hadn't intended to stop, but there was a parking space and he pulled over to take several slow, deep breaths. His right hand was still gripping the driving wheel as his left searched for the breviary in his jacket. He stroked the maroon leather before opening the prayer book and touching the tissue thin paper. As he whispered the familiar phrases something fluttered on the edge of his vision and looking up, he gradually became aware of his surroundings. He recognized the ugly red-brick block of police flats and knew that he was only yards away from the school and church. Across the street a trickle of children were emerging from Merlin Street baths, wet swimming costumes dripping on to the pavement, damp towels draped in childish togas over their school uniforms, looking cold and miserable.

'I just need a few minutes,' he muttered to himself, as he turned back to the breviary and traced lines of text with a finger. 'Nothing has changed. Nothing.'

A towel fluttered and flapped again. He looked up and this

time noticed a hand raised in greeting. It belonged to a girl with long wet hair as sleek as an otter. He frowned and was about to return to his prayers when he registered the broad band of freckles and frank, grey eyes. Anna Brogan.

Father Jerry turned the key in the ignition and drove off.

Forty-Six

Everyone else knew he had gone.

The chaplaincy had been informed. He'd telephoned the presbytery. He had taken the time to ring The Sleeping Dog and talk to Christy. Committee members had been contacted and appointments cancelled. Messages had been left all over North London.

Cathleen found out at the school gate.

It was the Monday before Christmas and Geraldine had just come out of her class when Anna dashed towards them with an angel in her hands. The body was the cardboard tube from a toilet roll painted white, the head a ping pong ball and the wings a paper doily that had been crayoned yellow. Cathleen was crouching down to admire it when she felt a firm tap on her shoulder. The parish priest blew his nose loudly.

'Will he be back for the Epiphany, do you think? I wouldn't mind an extra pair of hands then.'

She stared at him blankly. For a moment it was as if he were talking a language she didn't understand and then the words fitted together like jigsaw pieces. Father Jerry had gone.

Every night for the last week she'd rehearsed what she was going to say when they met again. She would lie awake for hours and go over the scene in tiny detail.

She'd begin with something that would ease the frown from his forehead. *We'll only talk about this once, Jerry.* (She would allow herself to call him Jerry because she never would again.) *It happened, but it doesn't have to be a shadow between us. You're still a good priest and I'm still me. We won't hurt each other or ourselves. We'll manage.*

And they would too. She would show him how. In the past year hadn't she learnt enough about managing?

Father Jerry must have had other ideas.

'What's wrong?' Cathleen's eyes were shut. She couldn't see Anna's face but she felt her daughter's hand on her cheek.

'Are we going to have a sad Christmas again?' Geraldine's voice was brittle.

Cathleen stood up. 'No, we're not. We're going to have a lovely time. And Reg is coming for his first proper family Christmas in years. So we can't be sad, can we?' Cathleen put her arm around Anna's shoulder. 'And you didn't make a sad angel. She's going on top of the Christmas tree and we'll smile whenever we look at her.'

'Mrs Brogan!' The parish priest was following her up the road, and it felt as though he was snapping at her heels. 'You never answered me! When is he coming back?'

'I haven't an idea.' Cathleen held her daughters' hands tightly, and didn't turn around. 'He might never come back.'

Forty-Seven

The idea came to Cathleen when her mother remarked that at least it was one less sitting down to eat. A full house and people fighting for elbow room at the table had been exactly what she wanted.

The telephone number was in an address book kept at the committee room, and Christy let her ring from The Sleeping Dog. An elderly woman told her to hang on and she heard shuffling feet and banging doors. It took so long Cathleen was almost tempted to hang up and she panicked when eventually she heard a voice on the other end of the line. This is foolish, she thought. He will have forgotten who I am, but he cut across her faltering introduction.

'It's all right, Cathleen,' said Tacit Donovan. 'I recognize your voice. Is there something wrong?'

It took less than a minute to arrange: Tacit was coming for Christmas.

At one o'clock on Christmas Day Cathleen wondered if she had made a mistake. Reg stood by the fireplace, reluctant to let go of his brown paper bag that contained a tin of Quality Street, two bottles of cream soda and a bumper set of colouring pencils. He was finally persuaded to have a sherry.

'A small one. I'm not much of a drinker.'

Her brothers Dermot and Dessie, with red-rimmed eyes, hooded with sleep, helped themselves and stood on the other side of the fireplace. They woke up when Tacit Donovan walked in. Shock registered on both faces and then another reaction that they made no attempt to hide. The brothers knew Tacit and they didn't like him. Cathleen watched in horror as together they turned their backs and started to talk to a surprised Reg.

Tacit gave no sign that he had noticed while Cathleen struggled between cooking the dinner and her duty to smooth over her brothers' rudeness. She took refuge in small talk and Tacit wasn't the kind of man to make it easy. Yes, he did drive over and, after a pause, he agreed that there wasn't much traffic on the road.

When he accepted a small whiskey, she decided that the turkey needed her more. She made her apologies and ordered Dermot to come with her. Once she got him on the landing she demanded to know what was going on.

'It's him.' Dermot shifted uncomfortably. 'A couple year back he wouldn't keep Dessie on.'

'Tacit sacked him?'

'Laid him off with some of the others. Said he didn't need them any more.'

'So? That happens all the time.'

'But then he went and laid me off when I said I wouldn't work without Dessie.'

Cathleen stood back considering. It was taken for granted by the family that the brothers always worked together. Until that moment she hadn't realized that it was something that had to be planned. Dermot was a chippie, able to fit windows, doors and skirting boards. Dessie was only a pair of strong shoulders and there were plenty of those in London.

'Talk to Tacit,' she begged. 'It'll spoil Christmas if you don't.'

'Ah, I can't.' Dermot shifted from one foot to another.

'I wouldn't have invited him had I known.' She stroked his arm. 'But he's here and we have to make the best of it. Please.'

His ears went red as she sent him back in. *Poor Dermot and probably poor Tacit, as well.*

Cathleen's courtesy invitation to Aude had been accepted. She was visiting her widowed father on Boxing Day and no, Aunt and Uncle Alibone wouldn't miss her a bit.

'I bet they wouldn't,' Kitty had muttered darkly.

She arrived shortly before dinner was served and Cathleen felt that she'd earned her place at the table because she and Mary had enough talk between them to kill any silence. Aude recognized Tacit from the dance and perched on the edge of the sofa next to him. 'I do admire your taste in tailoring,' she purred. 'Tell me, what lucky lady helped you choose it?'

As Cathleen was about to go through the door, holding the turkey on a carving dish, she paused and allowed herself a moment to breath in the herb and onion steam from the stuffing. *Where are you Jerry Brogan? And why aren't you here?*

Tacit volunteered to carve and he did it with sure, deft movements. Aude clapped when thin slices of meat landed on her plate.

'You're such a darling.'

Tacit's face remained impassive but Cathleen noticed that the back of his neck went pink each time she spoke. Attraction or embarrassment, she wondered. He paused before serving Dermot.

'Until today I never made the connection between Cathleen and the Cooney brothers.'

A small slice of white meat slid on to the plate. Dermot looked at it anxiously.

'You have a good name as workers.' A drumstick appeared and Dermot began to relax. 'I know I'd be happy to have you on site again. In fact I may have an opening coming up.'

'Together?' Dessie's lower lip quivered. 'I don't go nowhere without my brother.'

'It would be madness to split up a good partnership.'

The brothers smiled at each other and then down at the generous load of meat in front of them.

After the pudding was served Cathleen had managed to secrete an extra present beneath the tree. Geraldine knew and was wriggling in delight.

The entire table looked on as the box was handed to Anna.

'This didn't come from Santa,' Kitty told her. 'Sure, Santa's only a man. It took a woman to do this.' Cathleen smiled at the words and hid her hand beneath the table.

The cream dress was a perfect fit.

'You look like the angel on top of the tree,' whispered Geraldine.

There was also a surprise for Cathleen. Tacit handed over his gift with an awkward shrug. It was a pair of leather gloves, as soft as cloth and the colour of wet slate. She thanked him with real warmth and colour seeped into his lean face.

'I remember the parcels from America when I was a child and the great fun we had out of them,' said Tacit. 'There's more of us Donovans in Long Island than there were ever in Dingle. Often the stuff would be useless. Gaudy ol' shirts that no man would wear but this one time my mother got a pair of gloves from her sister. I've always remembered the look on her face when she opened the package.'

It was the longest speech Cathleen had heard Tacit make.

'And they are *so* serviceable,' Aude chimed in, picking up a glove. 'I can see why you thought of your mother when you were choosing for Cathleen. Really a wonderfully sensible gift, Mr Donovan.' She hooked her arm through his. 'But do tell me about all your American relatives. Where is Long Island? It sounds charming.'

Later Kitty demanded 'Silent Night' from Dessie. His poignant tenor voice brought a tear to his mother's eye, and Reg was persuaded to have a go at 'Down at the Old Bull and Bush'. His voice was flat and nasal but the children sang the chorus with him and he finished with glowing cheeks. They were all laughing now and the girls were on their hands and knees pulling out the small collection of gramophone records from underneath the radiogram when Tacit began to sing. His voice wasn't as pure as Dessie's but it rang with a power that made everyone sit back and drink it in.

> I'll walk beside you through the world today
> While dreams and songs and flowers bless your way
> I'll look into your eyes and hold your hand
> I'll walk beside you through the golden land

Tacit focused on the Papal blessing hanging between the two windows as he sang. But once, at the start of the last verse, Cathleen thought she felt his eyes on her.

> I'll walk beside you through the passing years
> Through days of cloud and sunshine, joy and tears

She looked up and realized that she must have been mistaken. He was looking past her, out into the deserted street and across the rooftops and chimney stacks to a city sky fading from dull day to dark night.

'As I live and breath it's Josef Locke come among us.' Kitty was on her feet, pumping Tacit's hand. 'Who'd have guessed that such a sweet voice would come out of a stick of a face?'

'Mother!'

'What? A good word never broke anyone's teeth and I'll say as I find. Fair play to you, Tacit Donovan, if you can sing like that I don't care if it does take a month of Sunday's to get a sentence out of you.'

Later, much later, after everyone had left and the children were tucked up in bed, Cathleen stood where Tacit had stood. It was a cloudless night and she wondered if Father Jerry Brogan was looking at the same stars.

Forty-Eight

Father Jerry came back on a cold, still January morning, the second Sunday of the new year.

The empty flower beds in the park were rimed with frost when Cathleen and the girls walked down to the church. As they settled into their usual seats, the cold from outside penetrated the plastered walls. Anna and Geraldine huddled together for warmth, giggling because their breath clouded the air. As an altar boy emerged from the sacristy, swinging an incense holder, Cathleen dropped one of her new gloves. While she reached down to pick it up, she sensed Father Jerry on the altar. She raised her head at the same time as the priest raised his hand in blessing, and saw the face still touched by a Mediterranean sun.

The children didn't notice her sharp intake of breath, or that her head was suddenly bowed in silent prayer. She had to steady herself. Seeing him felt like being kicked from the inside. When she raised her head again she was in time to see Father Jerry turn away from the congregation and kneel before the altar. This is your way of managing, she thought, as he intoned the first prayers, making velvet of the Latin words. Mine would have been better.

There would be no communion today, no waiting around after church to see if he'd come out. She hurried the children up the road, promising them sweets from Reg if only they got a move on. But however much she avoided him in church, all that Sunday Cathleen waited for a knock on the door. She imagined him driving down Rosebery Avenue and hesitating, before parking badly in another street. She imagined him outside the door looking up, frowning as he worked out what to say. She dreaded him coming and wanted it all the same. Christmas could be survived because he was away – she already had the letter from Maeve describing the wonderful surprise visit – but this was a new agony. There was no knock and each time she looked out the window all she could see were grey pavements and a grey sky.

The Sunday passed into a Monday and the week into another. The nearest she was to Father Jerry was across the length of the table in The Sleeping Dog's committee room. Their eyes never met. Father Jerry had to leave early, although he was vague about where he was going.

Cathleen felt small, as though she were curling in on herself and if she curled any more she might snap. She told Pat that she was going to step down. I'm tired, she said. I'm asking Mary or Mum to babysit all the time. It's not fair on them; it's not fair on the girls. I thought I was ready for the world but I'm not. The shop and home are world enough for me.

Wait a month, instructed Pat. Things always seem worse in the winter. Cathleen told her that a month wouldn't change how she felt but yes, she would stay for a little while longer.

★   ★   ★

At the next committee meeting Cathleen arrived early to help Pat pin up the hem on a new dress. She had already decided that it would be her turn to make an excuse to leave before the end. She'd announce it right at the start and then he'd know he could stay. It was a ridiculous way of carrying on, but she didn't know what else to do.

The dress was still being pinned when Father Jerry arrived. He nodded at the two women through the glass in the kitchen door but Cathleen didn't lift her head.

Pat looked up at the ceiling quizzically. They could hear him move about in the room above. 'There's something not right with him. What do you think it is?'

'Me? I've no idea.' Cathleen kept her head down.

At the meeting everyone could smell sulphur, a rotten, cloying smell that seeped into the lungs. From the window they could see ugly swirls of fog licking around the dustbins by the back door.

'I better go home. I don't want to be caught in this.'

Already the back fence had disappeared and, as Cathleen struggled into her coat, the fog grew denser. It crept up the garden, swallowing the flower beds and washing line. When the telephone rang it had reached the dustbins. Christy gave Father Jerry the message.

'The parish priest says you mustn't think of driving back tonight. There's a bed made up for you in the presbytery and will you do first Mass in the morning?' Christy smiled. 'There's no help for it. It's yes to both, I'd say.' Father Jerry nodded, but didn't return the smile.

'You won't go out alone in this.' Christy was shocked to see Cathleen's hand on the door. 'Sure the good father would never let you go home on your own. Tell her, Father, tell her.'

'Of course, I'll walk with you.' Father Jerry found his coat and scarf. 'Of course,' he said again and neither of them looked at each other.

'Hurry on now, don't be letting the fog in.' The door slammed shut, banishing them from the light and warmth.

Cathleen took the lead, feeling her way along the wall. She stumbled when brickwork disappeared and turned into railings.

'Don't be silly. You have to hold on to me.' She felt his strong hand grasp hers. 'And I'm going first.'

He pulled her along, a silent, sullen force dragging her through the fog. London had vanished: no cars, no birds, no thundering trucks. The city's heartbeat was smothered. All that was left was taste and smell, all that could be trusted was touch. His hand was warm despite the damp cold.

He stopped. 'There's no more houses.'

'We must have reached the corner. The church and park should be in front of us.' They could see nothing. 'If we go left as far as we can, then right as far as we can, we have to hit St John's Street.'

They made quicker progress until Father Jerry stopped again. Cathleen assumed that they must have reached the point where they had to turn right. The fog was lifting a little. They could see black railings and there was a distant rumble. They were near St John's Street.

'I'm sorry.' Cathleen didn't ask what he was apologizing about: she knew. 'It was my fault. Entirely.'

There was an urgency in his voice and Cathleen guessed that he wanted to talk now, before they got back to the real world. Good. There were things she wanted to say too. 'Yes, it was and you made it worse running away from me.'

'I was running from myself.' She couldn't see the expression on his face but she felt a sudden spasm of anger.

'And the world only exists for you? You go without a word to me. You come back without a word. This didn't only happen to you. This happened to us.'

'That's what I'm trying to say. There isn't an us.'

Forty-Nine

Cathleen shook free of Father Jerry's hand. 'I didn't mean it like that. There can never be an *us*, I know that. And you don't even know that I'd want there to be an *us*. You're presuming an awful lot, Jerry Brogan.' This was not what she had planned to say. She wanted to make peace. She wanted it to be the way it was before and now she knew it would never be that way again.

'I heard your confession.'

Cathleen stood still. She couldn't move.

'I took the curate's place the night you ran out before getting absolution. The curate was ill.'

'You let me talk, without a sign it was you.' The cold had penetrated every part of her. 'You let me say all that. I was confessing to my God, Jerry Brogan, if He exists. You made me confess to you.'

'It wasn't like that. I didn't want to—'

'And then on the stairs . . .' She wasn't talking to him now and had stopped listening too. Her tears were icy on her cheeks. 'I hope it eats away at you until you have to make your own confession.' She threw the words at him and turned away. At the top of the road a bus was inching its way along and from the same direction came a muted honking. Cathleen ran. She ran towards the lights and noise and didn't care what was in the way. She was running blind. She heard Father Jerry call out but she didn't want to hear what he had to say.

From St John's Street, she was only three hundred yards from home and she needed to be home with her girls, but she had to get her breath back and was forced to pause at the corner. She looked back. There was only fog, wrapping everything up, hiding everything. She listened. There were no footsteps.

It was now just possible to make out the dark shapes of houses but from the right the road was washed with a gauzy light, like a candle seen through a veil. Reg had kept the shop open and an odd collection of standard lamps and bedside lights shone from every window. A row of paraffin lamps flickered on top of the sweet jars casting a golden glow into the sulphuric fog and Reg, wrapped up in a muffler, stood at the door with a torch in either hand.

Cars and buses hooted in appreciation as they passed. Reg was lighting the way home.

There would be no carrying on, no smoothing over. This was the end. But it wouldn't be a tidy end.

The postman had handed Cathleen a letter as she rushed the children to school and she was waiting to read it when the shop was quiet. Customers lingered, each one with their own story to tell: how they asked a lamp post for a light, or went to the wrong house. Reg stood behind the counter and bathed in their praise. How did he have so many lamps to hand? Cathleen smiled when she learnt that he had been waiting for such a night since 1952.

'Now that was fog.'

'And last night was a bit of mist off the mountain, I suppose.' Kitty arrived in a bad mood, jangling the doorbell. She had slept badly at Cathleen's 'You look washed out, girl.' She inspected her daughter critically. 'Fog carries all kinds of muck with it. I wonder if you're sickening. When I blew my nose last night the hanky was black and I hadn't even been out in it. You should knock all that committee work on the head, wearing yourself out.'

'You're right.'

'What?'

'I was thinking the same and it's not fair getting you and Mary to babysit all the time.

'Ah, now don't be so hasty, it's only getting interesting. Isn't there a dinner dance coming up? And when have I ever complained?' Kitty drummed her fingers on the counter. 'What's in that letter?' She pointed at the blue Basildon Bond envelope sticking out of Cathleen's skirt pocket.

Cathleen slit it open with a finger nail and scanned the contents.

'It's only from Maeve. The cows are out to grass again and Seamus went to town last Saturday night, you know stuff like that.' Cathleen's eyes flew down the page. 'And she's coming over.'

'You said she might.'

'No, she's really coming for Anna's First Holy Communion. She's bought the ticket.'

Cathleen could resign from the committee and go to another parish for Mass but he wasn't just a priest. He was *their* priest. Their lives were tied together and Maeve would want to see a lot of him when she was over.

A small wad of notes fell out of the envelope on to the counter.

'What's that for?'

'I'm not sure.' Cathleen read the letter more carefully and she found the answer in between complaints about Thady and news that Patsy Mulligan had put a bench outside the pub.

I love your two girls as if they were my own and doesn't
Seamus treat them like his own sisters and my mother lives
for news of them and prays for the sight of them.

The money was for their tickets. She was asking if the girls
could come back with her. Cathleen could follow along
afterwards.

Grandma Brogan must have been saving up. But no, it wasn't
the old woman, lonely for her grandchildren. Father Jerry had
left an envelope with Maeve at Christmas.

He'd surely not mind you knowing now. He said I was to
have a holiday out of it too, me who was only out of Kerry
twice in my whole life but he knew I had a hankering for
London and if the girls come back with me wouldn't that
give you a break Cathleen and make a gloriously long
summer.

Courtesy of Father Jerry, thought Cathleen. Her mother was busy
counting the notes. 'It must have been a thick envelope.'

Cathleen looked around. She didn't want Reg to hear. 'I'm
not taking his charity. I don't want it.'

'What else has he got to spend his money on?' Kitty was indig-
nant and she had no qualms about raising her voice. Reg's ears
went pink and he scuttled into the back room.

Cathleen shook her head but her mother persisted. 'Are you
going to take Anna and Geraldine to see their grandmother this
year? The hell you are. Scrimping and scraping, pennies put away
for every little thing. You're a powerful saver I'll give you that,
but money won't grow out of jam jars.' Kitty leaned over the
counter to make her point.

'It's a sin to turn it down. You'd be spitting in that old woman's
face if you do. She's going to be a long time dead, let her enjoy
her grandchildren while she has the chance.'

'You don't understand.'

'Don't I though! This isn't all about you. In fact, girl, it's not
even a bit about you. The priest's doing it for the Brogans. I don't
want to hear another word about it.' She slammed out the shop
door, knocking the open sign off its hook. Reg emerged from
his den in time to see Kitty sweep back in, the bell on the door
jangling furiously. 'You should take the help that's offered. And

now you've been sent that bundle I expect to see your wedding ring back on your finger.'

Fifty

Father Jerry stood outside the offices of *The Irish Champion* and looked up Fleet Street in the direction of St Paul's. Modern office blocks jostled for position with narrow brick terraces, greasy spoon cafes, pubs, bookshops, jewellers and the odd sixteenth-century timber-framed house.

He had no stomach for the meeting. It was a long time since he had a hangover, but he remembered what it felt like and it felt something like this. There was a heaviness to everything he did. Going away at Christmas had been a mistake. He wanted to suffer – it was the penance he had given himself – and needed physical distance from Cathleen, but she was still with him when he woke in the morning and last thing at night. He was ashamed to admit it, but she was with him on the altar too.

He sighed, thinking of the previous evening. It had left a taste in his mouth like too much beer and too many cigarettes. What a fool to seize the cover of fog, as if he could hide in it, and then to blurt out the wrong things in the wrong way. He had only found the courage to say what was in his heart once she turned away from him. Had she heard? He had waited for her to come back, to tell him that yes, it was a terrible mess, but now at least she understood.

He had got cold waiting and was glad to take himself off to the presbytery and it didn't matter that the blanket was too thin and the mattress too hard in the mean little room; sleep would have been impossible wherever he was.

It was hard to summon up energy for the meeting with the newspaper's editor but he was here and he might as well get on with it. The editorial office occupied the ground floor of a narrow building next door to The Cock Tavern and he found

Jack Daly in a back room behind a desk covered with paper. A stack of curling newsprint the colour of nicotine lay on top of a pile of discarded, dog-eared notebooks. Next to an ancient typewriter was a savage spike that had speared handwritten and typed letters, brown envelopes and crumpled balls of notepaper.

'You've guessed why you're here?' Jack Daly rubbed his hands. '*The Irish Champion* likes what you're doing. *The Irish Champion* is behind you!' The editor was on his feet now, chewing the end of a pencil. 'The Irish in Britain are a benighted community, neglected and sidestepped by their own and none more so than the lads on the buildings. If a mother in Roscommon was asked where her children were, what would she say? I've two in America, two still at home and two over. That's true, isn't it Father? Not even a name given to dignify the place where they are trying to scrape a living.' He sat down heavily. 'Just "over". As if they're at the bottom of the road and will be home for tea. But they aren't and they won't.

'Yes, sir,' he spat out. '*The Irish Champion* likes what you're doing.'

'Well, I suppose publicity is always welcome. What do you have in mind?'

'An interview. Very painless. Our readers are simple people, hard-working people. A dance on Saturday night, church on Sunday mornings and in between a week of grind. They don't need fancy writing. We'll do it now. I won't keep you more than ten minutes.'

He paused, tapped his mouth with his finger and then disappeared, coming back with a scruffy man in a leather jacket and a camera slung around his neck.

'What do you want? Quick head and shoulders?'

Father Jerry shifted uncomfortably as Daly looked him up and down.

'Action shot,' he said firmly. 'Priest among the navvies. Benediction over the bricks. Front page, if we have the right picture.'

Jack Daly rubbed his hands.

Tacit's men had grown accustomed to seeing a priest on site and Father Jerry was learning names and faces and getting used to the rhythm of the working day. He always stayed after Mass for a mug of tea, and even developed a liking for it's bitter, bark-like taste. He now knew enough to bring his own mug and a tanner for the youngster who still couldn't accept it without blushing.

He was also learning the vocabulary of the building trade. 'A decent skin' was a good worker and no one ever asked for a job, only a 'start'.

It was nearly a month since he'd seen Cathleen. She was coming to campaign committee meetings less frequently. It was better like this. The tension of seeing her regularly was too much. Even this was hard. Whenever he said Mass at her parish church he looked for her in the congregation. As soon as he stepped out on the altar, he scanned the pews, disappointed when she wasn't there, agitated when she was, and all the time scared that his face would betray him.

He had warned the men that they might have their photograph taken and with a heavy camera slung casually around his neck, the photographer looked satisfyingly like a professional when he arrived on site before a First Friday Mass. His approach was professional too.

'In front of the table, Father,' he directed. 'Have a go with the chalice. Above your head. Nice.' He loaded another reel of film while ordering a couple of the men to get in the picture and took a few photographs from the top of a ramp made out of scaffolding boards. Within minutes he was ready to go.

Father Jerry turned away. The men would break for lunch soon and Mass would begin. He imagined he would get some ribbing afterwards when he was having his mug of tea, but he knew too that they would get a vicarious kind of pride from seeing the photographs in the paper.

He noticed Tacit striding towards him. He doubted he was coming to Mass. Perhaps he should have told him about the photographer. He paused, considering. Yes, good manners alone meant that he should have. Father Jerry sighed. He'd confess his fault of course, apologize. He didn't want to fall out with the ganger but he was a hard man to know. There was no easy chat. Yet his men seemed to think well of him.

Something swung by.

Father Jerry frowned and looked up, unable to make sense of

the wire cable that was unfurling and dancing across the sky. The golden afternoon had been sliced apart. A cry slashed it to pieces.

Tacit was running towards a drizzle of concrete blocks. Every other man was running away. It seemed as though the sky was falling.

Silence. Then a shout went up: man down and it was Father Jerry's turn to run, his purple stole in his hand.

A body lay across a trench and a river of dark liquid was slowly sinking into the clay. The boy's blond head nestled on a mound of earth as if he'd decided to take a nap before serving tea. Beside him knelt Tacit Donovan, panting hard and bleeding from a savage cut across his hands.

'Oh God, Tacit, what the fuck was he doing there?'

'Get the priest,' growled Donovan struggling to his feet. The other men moved out of the way to make a path for Father Jerry. His lips were already moving in silent prayer.

'Back to work.' Donovan's voice was steady now. 'It's the priest he needs now, not us.'

No one noticed the photographer standing at the gate, zoom lens out, snapping away.

'It wasn't your fault. No one could say it was.' The wages clerk looked up at Tacit. They were in the office. The ambulance had just left with the body and there was paperwork to be done. Tacit had asked Father Jerry to join him. 'I saw it,' the clerk continued. 'An inch more and you'd have saved him. You damn near killed yourself.'

'I don't want to hear about that now and I don't want that to be the second thing the parents hear after they're told their son's dead.' Donovan's voice was harsh. He took a long slug from a bottle of whiskey, wiped the mouth and offered it to Father Jerry. He'd wrapped a towel around his cut hand. 'They don't want the word "nearly". What good is *nearly* to them? The second thing they should hear is that a priest gave him the last rites. You were in time, weren't you?'

Father Jerry nodded. He couldn't trust himself to speak.

'Maybe there's a point to having you on site, after all. Like in the trenches . . .' Tacit paused and took another swig of whiskey. 'When the men went over the top the Catholic priests went over with them.' He passed the bottle. 'You look pale, Father. Didn't you know this was the front line?'

Fifty-One

Cathleen was so sure it was the rent collector when the doorbell rang that she ran downstairs with money in her hand. Father Jerry was on the doorstep, gazing out at the traffic. There was cement dust in his hair and on the shoulders of his black jacket. He climbed the stairs to the kitchen without a word.

'I didn't know where to go.' He stopped and looked down at the cup of sweet tea Cathleen put in front if him. 'That's not true. There was no where else I wanted to go.'

Cathleen sat quietly, waiting until he was ready to speak. *Soon the girls would be home. Soon this moment will have gone.*

He drained his cup and told her what had happened on site. Slowly he reached out. She could feel his fingers burn into her hand.

'When you ran off in the fog did you hear what I said?'

Cathleen shook her head. He stood up and went to the window. 'It was my turn to confess and I made a mess of it.' She couldn't see his face.

'I love you, Cathleen Brogan.'

'What are we going to do?'

'Nothing.' He turned to look at her. 'But you should know how I feel. You have a right to know that.'

Fifty-Two

'Look at this. Will you ever look at this!' Kitty waved the *Daily Mirror* in front of Cathleen. 'It's your man himself! On the front page. Only on the bloody front page.'

'My man?' For a moment Cathleen assumed her mother was referring to Hugh Gaitskell. The week before they had been arguing about politics.

'Your priest! Who else? Father Jerry!'

'Oh God, has something happened to him?' Cathleen felt cold.

'Happened? Happened?' Kitty was dancing now. 'He's only a bloody hero, that's all.' She sat down suddenly. 'Oho, I'd like to see those craw thumpers back in Dublin now. I'd like to shove this –' she waved the newspaper in front of Cathleen – 'in the face of my mother-in-law, the Lord have mercy on the wretch. Never thought Kitty Cooney would amount to anything, did she? Never thought there'd be a priest in the family. And what a priest he is. That man is golden, haven't I always said it?'

'Mum! I still don't know what you're talking about.'

Kitty spread the paper out in front of Cathleen.

Although the quarter page photograph was grainy, Father Jerry was clearly recognizable. The photographer had been lucky; a shaft of sunlight had hit the priest's face at the very moment his hand was raised in a blessing. On the ground was the upper half of a young man's body. The head was turned away, an arm flung out as if to ward off a blow.

'Oh, the pity of it,' said Cathleen with feeling. 'He told me about this.'

'And you never said!' Kitty was scandalized.

'I didn't know about the photograph, or the newspaper, or any of that. I wonder if he knows himself, but I knew about the boy dying.' She looked again at the photograph; he said he was young. She hadn't realized how young.

'Read it out,' demanded Kitty. 'I haven't got my glasses.'

'"This weekend another young man full of hope and promise died on a British building site. He became just another number to be entered in the official record book. The grieving family of seventeen-year-old Joe O'Connor might find some . . ." Oh, Mum, just seventeen. The same age as Seamus.'

'Go on, will yer. Get to the bit about our priest.'

'"The grieving family might find some consolation knowing that in his last dying moments a priest was by his side. Father Jeremiah Brogan brings comfort to Irish labourers with a corrugated iron hut as a church and a rickety table as an altar. The *Daily Mirror* salutes you, Father B.""'

'Will you listen to that,' exclaimed Kitty. 'It salutes him! What a grand newspaper it is. Go on, is there any more about Father Jerry?'

'Not really. There's a bit about the true cost of building a better Britain. "See leader page twelve, also page eighteen Sheffield union leader calls for priests for the steel industry".' Cathleen scanned the other pages. 'No, he doesn't get another mention again, but I suppose that's enough. Front page of the *Daily Mirror*.'

'I can't stop.' In one swift movement Kitty gathered up all her bags.

'Not even for a cup of tea?' asked Cathleen, surprised by her mother's abrupt departure. 'Where are you rushing off to?'

'Over to Reg. I want to buy more papers before he sells out.'

Father Jerry discovered that other newspapers were interested in the story, each one taking their own angle. In one he was called a vicar and he wondered how the bishop would react to that, but he thought it probably wouldn't matter because the same article had turned him into Jeremy Brogue. Jack Daly's headline rivalled the nationals for type size: Champion Priest Hailed As Hero. But it was the description in the *News of the World* that made him groan. Here he was a priest with 'matinee idol good looks' rubbing shoulders with the 'roughest workers in Britain'. He imagined Tacit's face reading that.

The bishop sent a two-word telegram: well done. On the telephone he was more expansive. Father Jerry should prepare to move.

His instinct was to protest. After all, he'd only just started. He would only be handing over a fledgling organization, a fragile thing that needed nurturing.

'You're a fire starter and I want you to go start a fire some-where else.'

The bishop was wrong, thought Father Jerry, as he put the phone down, but a move was right for him. And Cathleen.

It was what they both needed but there would be no repetition of his cruelty at Christmas. She would be the first to know. He glanced at the clock. She would be in the shop now, near a telephone, if he could just find Reg's number, he could arrange to take her to dinner, a private goodbye in public.

He rang and suggested a time and place. When he wrote it in his appointment diary, he realized it was the evening after Maeve went back to Ireland, taking the girls with her. It was the first evening Cathleen would be on her own.

Fifty-Three

The wet week of Maeve's stay in London ended on the morning of Anna's First Holy Communion. Maeve took full responsibility for the clear blue sky.

'I said a novena.'

The church was crowded for the service. The doors at the back had to be kept open as the congregation spilled out on to the pavement.

'Of course, there's some here only because of him,' Kitty told the woman sitting next to her in the pew, as Father Jerry came out on the altar. 'On account of him being famous *and* he's only here on account of us.'

'Mum.' Cathleen glared.

'Isn't it the truth? And don't tell me he watches Irish dancing when our Anna isn't performing. Oh, there she is now.'

Anna, dressed in a simple white dress borrowed from the Italian family in the basement, looked angelic. The dark unruly curls were tame beneath the veil and the headdress of crushed velvet flowers. She took communion from Father Jerry's fingers with self-conscious piety and brought her hands together in prayer.

'The little mite.' Maeve had been in a state of quivering anticipation all morning. Tears streamed down her face

'The little cherub.' Kitty was crying too. 'The dote.'

Reg sat in between them, a broad smile across his face. He hadn't been sure about coming to a Catholic church, but he'd allowed Anna and Cathleen to persuade him.

Cathleen glowed at the older women's chant of praise for her daughter and discovered she had tears in her eyes too.

It was a long service but finally the three priests – the parish priest, the curate and Father Jerry – were ready to lead the children in a procession with the rest of the congregation following behind.

'I pity the mothers of boys,' Kitty observed to Maeve. 'What can you do with them on a day like this, except give their hair a bit of a brush?'

'I don't know.' Cathleen nudged her mother as an Italian boy in Anna's class walked past. He was wearing a cream suit and a white frilled dress shirt. At his neck was a cream bow tie, now nonchalantly undone.

'Oh, the Eye-ties don't count. They have the looks to carry off the style. Pour ginger hair and milk-coloured skin into that suit and it wouldn't look half the money.' Kitty sniffed. 'When are we going? I'm looking forward to marching around Clerkenwell belting out "Faith of Our Fathers".'

Anna handed Cathleen a new prayer book that had a one-pound note inside.

'Where did you get this?'

'The man.' Anna was impatient to be away. She wanted to march the streets of Clerkenwell too. 'You know, the man who builds things.'

Cathleen looked around and saw Tacit walking up Amwell Street. He was too far away to call his name, but it wasn't too far to run. She caught up with him just before The Sleeping Dog. He turned when he heard her footsteps and Cathleen was taken aback by the look on a face that was usually sealed shut. It reminded her of when the children were babies and their out-rageous, overwhelming delight when she picked them up. It was gone so quickly that she thought she must have imagined it. Tacit stood before her the same as always: serious, thoughtful and observant, nodding gravely at her mumbled word of thanks.

A strange man, Cathleen thought as she watched him walk

towards Pentonville Road. The only way he could have known it was Anna's Holy Communion was if he had seen the parish notice in *The Irish Champion* and worked out her age and put two and two together. That was a lot of adding up from a man they hadn't seen since Christmas.

Cathleen stayed behind and volunteered to help prepare the breakfast in the school hall. The children were noisy and ravenous when they trooped back. Once they settled in their seats the priests arrived. They could look forward to a much more substantial breakfast in the presbytery, but were first making a tour of the tables, talking to children and shaking hands with parents. They were making slow progress. Again and again, Father Jerry was asked for his autograph. Cathleen looked up and noticed that at the first table the parish priest was laughing and clapping him on the back, relishing the reflected glory, but by the time they had got to the third, his smile was worn down to an irritable mean line.

She looked up again and they were gone. She guessed that the parish priest had put his foot down. Finishing off a round of bread, she wondered if she ought to start on another loaf. She reached down for the butter knife and touched a hand.

Cathleen didn't move. Without looking she knew whose hand it was. He must have sent the other priests ahead. *This is ridiculous. We're in the middle of a crowded hall. There are children and parents all around. There's my child a few feet away dropping her fork on the floor. I should run over and pick it up.*

The voice in her head stopped talking. She wasn't listening any more to what she should do.

'Father!'

It was the headmistress. Jerry didn't move: his hand was hidden from view and still clasped Cathleen's.

'So good of you to come, Father. We saw you in the newspapers, of course. Class Six did a project on it. I was hoping we would have a chance to talk.' The headmistress paused; something seemed to be irritating her. 'Really, Mrs Brogan do get a move on. The children are quite starved.'

His hand was still pressing into Cathleen's. He would have to let go before she could butter any more bread.

'I'm afraid that's my fault. I was just catching up. How are my cousins doing in school?'

Cathleen glanced up and saw two small pinpoints of colour

appear on the headmistress's cheeks. It was clear that she had forgotten about the connection. 'Anna's a very capable child.' She nodded towards the trestle tables and seemed about to depart when Cathleen spoke up: there was unfinished business she could finish right now.

'Geraldine's not so settled. The toilet is a terrible worry. Not just for her, but all the reception class.'

The headmistress laughed again and made small flapping movements with her fingers.

'Such a vulgar subject . . . the Reverend Father doesn't want to hear—'

'Only the clever ones can use them,' continued Cathleen, ignoring the headmistress and growing in confidence. 'It doesn't matter if you put your hand up; if you're not sitting on the top table it won't get noticed. And they're so young . . .'

Father Jerry raised an eyebrow and looked directly at Cathleen. Only she knew that there was a smile just beneath the firm lips. Only she could feel the pressure of his hand on hers.

'Ah now, I think you must be mistaken. That sounds like the brutality the Christian Brothers dished out when I was a lad.' He turned the full heat of his warmth on to the headmistress. 'Not the kind of enlightened tutelage this school – this headmistress – is famous for.' Cathleen bit her lip.

'No, of course not. Really, Mrs Brogan, I'm sorry you got that impression.'

I bet you are, thought Cathleen. Father Jerry released her hand and led the headmistress away. He turned as he was about to go out the door.

'I'm looking forward to Saturday.'

Cathleen nodded and looked away. She became aware that someone was calling her name. Aude had arrived with her new camera and was lining up the family for a group photo at Anna's table, with Reg in the middle surrounded by all the women. Cathleen looked at the familiar faces without seeing them. I'm going mad, she thought. And I don't care.

Fifty-Four

'They're so excited,' said Mary encouragingly, putting her arm around Cathleen's waist as they waited at Euston to wave Maeve and the girls off. 'Remember when we were that little, wouldn't we have loved to do something like this?'

'I suppose,' said Cathleen. 'But don't they look small?'

The train slowly pulled out of the station and Cathleen began to walk beside it.

'I love you,' she shouted and she could see Geraldine's lip begin to quiver. 'And don't forget to wash behind your ears.' She mimed the action and was rewarded with a big grin from her youngest daughter.

'Come on,' Kitty ordered Mary and Cathleen. 'I'll treat us to a plate of something at the Golden Egg. There's one just around the corner.'

'Ah, not there, Mum,' Cathleen pleaded. 'Children get a free lollipop if they finish their meal there and the girls aren't with us.'

'Don't be silly,' snapped Kitty. 'We're going *because* the girls aren't with us. You've got fourteen nights of freedom ahead of you. Make the most of it.'

He was late. She inspected every lift load of passengers spilling out into the ticket hall of Holloway Road station. Anyone tall and dark captured her attention. Any man who walked with confidence.

At quarter to eight Cathleen wondered if he had rung Reg to say that he was held up. At eight there was footsteps from behind. She would tell him off and forgive him.

'Hello Cathleen.' She spun around to see the treasurer from the campaign committee. 'What are you doing here?'

She mumbled something about meeting a friend and was terrified that Father Jerry would turn up at that very moment. Why had she said friend? You don't call a priest a friend unless you're old and male and went to school with them.

Quarter past eight and she knew he wasn't coming. He had thought better of it. It was dangerous. People would talk. They would get the wrong idea. They would get the right idea.

She leant back on the red glazed tiles of the station wall and felt the grit of the city around her. The traffic never stopped. Holloway Road never stopped. He was going to take her to a little Italian place, he had said, near the station. He had always wanted a reason to go and now she was his reason. There was something he wanted to tell her.

Near *Caledonian* Road station.

She was in the wrong place. In a panic she bought a ticket and, too agitated to wait for the lift, ran down the stairs just in time to see her train growl into the dark. Five minutes until the next one, a dragging, lagging, lazy five minutes that stretched into the shadows of the tunnel. But it is just one station, she told herself, tracing the blue of the Piccadilly line with her finger. She rode in an almost empty train carriage and then in an empty lift. At last she was in the right station but it was at the wrong time. She didn't need to look at her watch to know that she was an hour late. He would never have waited. He must have given up long ago.

Cathleen ran past the ticket collector and into his arms.

Fifty-Five

They were too late for the restaurant and when he asked her where she wanted to go all she could think of was home. A taxi appeared and when they drove down St John's Street Cathleen could see that the shutters on Reg's shop were down.

'I'll come up, shall I?' Father Jerry paid the taxi driver and was looking at her as if she might send him away. Cathleen was able to climb the four flights to her set of rooms at the top of the house but when she reached her own door her legs began to quiver.

'You need a drink. We both do.' Father Jerry took the key from her hand and swung open the door to the sitting room. He moved towards the sideboard where he knew she kept spirits and ginger wine for special occasions. 'What do you want?' he asked.

Cathleen quietly closed the door.

'You.'

They had both known what she was going to say before she said it. Jerry held out his arms again and Cathleen curled into him, searching for his mouth with her lips. She kissed him hard as his arms locked around her, holding her tight, and then tighter still. Beneath her fingertips she felt his shirt and the starched crispness of his clerical collar. She kissed his throat and the sandpaper of his chin and then pulled away. Her mouth felt bruised and she remembered the first time they touched.

'We haven't had that drink yet. We need it.' I need it, she thought, looking about her. The room was different. The shadows seemed darker and the pool of light cast by the standard lamp sharper. Everything was more defined. She poured a large measure of whiskey and a smaller one for herself.

He took the glass from her hand. 'I don't know what I'm doing.' He moved away from her. 'When you didn't turn up, I thought it was a sign.'

'And when I did?'

'I thought that was a sign too.' He swallowed. 'You know I love you but . . .'

She took his hand and lead the way up the last flight of stairs to the two rooms squashed under the eaves and, although it was narrow and awkward, their hands remained tightly interlaced. They had been up here together so often. Jerry seemed to prefer the kitchen to the sitting room: he said that he liked the smell of cooking, the cluttered table that had to be cleared every time they sat down to eat and the children's drawings stuck on the wall. But it wasn't to the kitchen she was taking him now.

Cathleen opened the bedroom door.

Jerry stood on the threshold. Sometimes from the hall he had caught a glimpse of roses on wallpaper and a satin counterpane. Sometimes he had allowed his imagination to take him inside but he would have hesitated now if he couldn't feel Cathleen's hand in his. He was glad she hadn't turned on the light. He liked the wine-coloured shadows created by the street lamp glowing through the curtains and he felt in need of shadow.

'I'm a fool at this.'

Cathleen led him to the bed. 'I can hear you smile,' she said, but she was wrong. He wasn't smiling and his touch was hesitant. For the first time in his life he felt the sheerness of stockings between his fingers and that everything was spiralling away from him, out of control.

'It's going to be all right,' she whispered, shutting out the world beyond the bedroom with her words and the way she touched him. There was no church, no family, no duty and no sin. There was only skin on skin. There was only touching and being touched. There was only Cathleen.

'Teach me.'

She showed him the place on her neck that made her gasp in short rapid bursts and he wrapped his hands around her to feel the sharpness of her spine as he kissed her breasts. He was learning a new language of touch and sensation, and with it he was driving back the dark. Then, when he was above her, when he could see her mouth stretch open as though she was in pain, he kissed the small scar above her eyebrow. This moment, he thought, this moment now and forever.

Later he studied her sleeping face, half buried in the pillow, and very gently held up a section of her hair, allowing the light to shine through it. He let it fall through his fingers as he looked at her, and thought that he would lie like that all night, but at some point he must have drifted off to sleep because he woke with a start while it was still dark. For a moment he didn't recognize where he was, although he knew instantly all the places it couldn't be: not the gloom of the Diocesan House or his book-lined room in Verona, nor the whitewashed walls of the seminary dormitory or the lonely bedroom of his solitary childhood. No, he was drifting in a ruby night, silent except for the occasional late-night bus on the street below and the cadence of Cathleen's breathing. So, this is what it's like, he thought, sharing space and skin and air. I never knew.

He touched her arm and she moved, wrapping herself around him. I've come home, he thought. I'm home.

Fifty-Six

Cathleen opened her eyes. She knew from the light that it was early morning.

A chair creaked.

Jerry.

He was getting dressed. His black priest's shirt was open at the neck and his clerical collar was nowhere to be seen.

She rolled over on to her stomach and stretched. Jerry didn't look up. He was concentrating on a knot in his laces and frowning. She liked the way his uncombed hair fell forward and that his chin had grown dark in the night. She was just about to call over to him when it suddenly occurred to her that perhaps he had intended her to sleep on. Was he going to steal away, without a word?

I'm not ashamed, she thought, not of any of it. She sat up in bed, drawing her knees up to her chin. But if he is, oh dear God, if he is, I won't be able to bear it. I'll be able to tell just by a look. He can say anything he likes, but his eyes will give him away.

The shoelace snapped in his strong hands and he grumbled softly. He looked across the room and saw Cathleen watching.

'I'm sorry.'

Cathleen closed her eyes. Don't apologize, she thought.

He was beside her, kneeling by the bed, his arms around her.

'That wasn't how I meant to wake you up.'

Cathleen opened her eyes. 'Oh, so how were you going to do it?'

'Like this.' He held her face gently in both hands and kissed her forehead, her nose and then her mouth. Again and again.

Fifty-Seven

'So glad you agree, Mrs Brogan.'

Cathleen looked up at the committee's treasurer and blushed. Poor man, she thought, he must have thought my smile was for him. The sound of his soft lisp had been a pleasant background noise but she hadn't listened to what he was saying.

It was Monday, two whole days since she had seen Jerry and he should be here any minute. There were voices and feet on the stairs. Cathleen looked at the door. The heavy handle was beginning to turn and everyone else was looking too. Meetings only come alive when he's among us. It's as if we're holding our breath waiting for him.

The door swung open and Cathleen felt Jerry's eyes dart in her direction, making sure she was there. He only looked at her once. Then he was squeezing past chairs, laughing, touching elbows, greeting everyone. His eyes were everywhere but where she was sitting and then, before he sat down, one more fleeting glance. Cathleen looked away and focused on the tablecloth.

She looked up. He was saying something to Pat. His lips were smiling and words were coming from his mouth but his eyes were on her. How can the others sit here and not realize?

The meeting moved on, but now he was here she wanted it over. At last the chairman called for any other business. Cathleen's nails dug into her palm. *Don't let there be.* It seemed an age and her nails dug deeper, but finally the chairman announced the meeting over. Chairs were pushed back and everyone rose to their feet. Coils of sentences uncurled into light chatter and people seemed reluctant to leave. He was still sitting, sorting through the paperwork in front of him, as Cathleen slipped on her coat. It took an agonizingly long time for the others to file out the door.

'Cathleen.' Jerry was reading the minute book and frowning. 'Could you stay behind for a moment?' She waited until the door closed behind the last committee member.

He was on his feet and loose papers fell to the floor in his haste. Suddenly they were a hair's width away from a kiss and she felt his hands on her back, pulling her towards him.

'Tonight?'

Yes. Yes. She didn't know if she said it aloud. Their lips were touching.

A shuffling sound on the stairs wrenched them apart. Cathleen moved as if she had been scalded and her cheeks burned as if boiling water had been thrown in her face. Christy came through the door backwards, a brass tray in his hands.

'Now, it's nothing much, Father,' he said as he placed the tray carefully on the table, his eyes on the tea cup wobbling in its saucer. 'And I'm making a right hames of it. That woman of mine will roar blue murder if she could see the mess I'm making.' He looked up for the first time. 'But she can't and sure, my secret's safe with you.'

Cathleen couldn't meet his eyes. She knew her face was still red and she wondered what he would have seen if he hadn't been carrying the tray. 'Just a bit of old pie,' Christy murmured, sliding a plate over to Father Jerry. 'Will you have a bite yourself, Cathleen?' She knew he was smiling. She shook her head without looking up.

'Thanks, I'll just gulp this down and drive Cathleen home.' Father Jerry's voice was firm. 'I don't think she's feeling well.'

There must have been something in the way she looked, or in Father Jerry's manner that stopped Christy from saying more. Within minutes they were alone again.

'And now we're liars,' Cathleen whispered. She shivered as she felt his fingers draw a line down her back and trace the outline of her spine. He forced her to turn around and look at him.

'Yes.' He stroked her hair as if she were a child. 'Yes, if it means not hurting anyone.'

The rest of the week was impossible. He told her that as he was lying beside her, after he kissed her throat and grazed the soft flesh of her shoulder with his teeth. Absolutely impossible. But they had Saturday to look forward to. Saturday night would be theirs.

'What's going to happen to us?'

Cathleen didn't know she was going to say it until the words were out. She held her breath as she waited for his response.

'I love you. Whatever I do and wherever I'm doing it, I love you.'

It was no answer and they both knew it. She was scared he would say something else and she raised herself up on her elbows to close his mouth. As they kissed, she wondered about the words he'd used. *Whatever* was being a priest on the altar. *Whatever* was consecrating the communion wafer with a mortal sin on his soul. *Whatever* was the craziness they were living. But *wherever* sounded like some place far away from her.

When the doorbell rang late on Wednesday night she knew it was him even before she opened the door. Jerry stood in front of her, a shadow in the dark, but in the yellow glow of the street light she could see him smile.

'I had to see you.'

If the maids at the diocesan house noticed that his bed hadn't been slept in again, well, wasn't he always coming and going? And they weren't going to question a priest, thought Cathleen, sliding off his jacket.

She hung it up in the wardrobe where Mick's clothes had hung. They were all gone now, every last shirt, and Jerry's well-cut jacket looked lonely among the empty coat hangers.

But maids do gossip, thought Cathleen, as she closed the door. They are perfectly capable of that.

Fifty-Eight

When the doorbell rang on Saturday afternoon she knew he was back. They had planned to meet that evening. The Camden Irish Society were holding a dinner in Jerry's honour. She would be sitting next to him on the top table, but she knew their heads would be turned away from each another. I'll nod to whoever's on my right, she thought as she ran downstairs, and Jerry will have to chat to the person on his left, and all the time his hip will press against mine, and now and then his hand will drift from the tablecloth and, now and then, so will mine.

As she slid the bolt across, Cathleen wondered if she would have the courage to kiss him now in the shadows of the hallway, with her neighbours inches away in their own rooms. I will, she thought, swinging the heavy street door open. Every minute is precious.

Only it wasn't Jerry on the doorstep.

Reg held his trilby stiffly in front of him and what he said seemed like a terrible echo. There had been a telephone call and she was to come, but it was all right. Jerry had called for her to come across the road and wait for him to ring again.

She smiled and the colour came back to her face. It was bound to be something about tonight, she told Reg, and he shouldn't have worried on her account.

'There's been a telegram.'

That was enough to send Cathleen racing back upstairs to get her keys, two words drumming in her head: the girls, the girls.

Reg waited with her in the back room. His breathing was coming in short, sharp bursts as if he'd been sprinting. 'Father Brogan said he'd call back in ten minutes.'

Cathleen nodded. That had been half an hour ago. Whatever had happened, whatever terrible thing, would all be her fault.

The loud ringing shook them both as if they had forgotten what a telephone sounded like. Cathleen's hand hovered over the receiver. It had to be answered but she was scared to pick it up. Reg made no attempt to move away: he needed to know too.

'They're all right? You're sure?' Jerry answered her first, urgent questions impatiently. He said other things that she couldn't take in as she mouthed the same words to Reg. The small man nodded and returned to the shop counter, as she asked Jerry to stop and say it all over again.

'I didn't mean to scare you. I should have realized.'

Yes, thought Cathleen, you should have, but whatever had happened had passed over Anna and Geraldine and that was enough.

A telegram from Maeve had arrived that morning. Its message was stark.

EVICTION SAVE US FATHER.

It was such a simple message she couldn't understand why it didn't make sense.

'I thought maybe it was some kind of joke.' Jerry's voice was hesitant. 'I telephoned the local bank. I have an account there myself. I got the manager's number and he spoke to me. Not officially, of course, I don't suppose he should have said a word, but he said enough. There's no doubt, Thady's lost the farm. Mortgaged to the teeth. It's been going on years and I knew nothing.'

'But what's happening now?'

'The manager couldn't say. But it must be bad for Maeve to write like this.'

Cathleen twisted the telephone cord around her finger. *What have I sent my girls into?* She closed her eyes and thought of Thady lurching wildly with drink and despair and started to tremble.

'We'll get the girls out of there.' Jerry's voice seemed closer to the phone. 'And I'll see what I can do. Only I couldn't get train tickets. I've been phoning and begging and there's nothing. The whole of London is going to Dublin for the school holidays.'

Cathleen nodded, forgetting that he couldn't see her. She had her own ticket in a week's time but that now seemed far in the future. She pictured Geraldine in the confusion and unhappiness. Would she start hurting herself again? She should never have let them go.

'So I've booked two tickets on a flight to Shannon.'

'Flying?'

'Trust me, there's nothing to it. And this time tomorrow morning we'll drive up the boreen. I did the right thing, didn't I?'

Cathleen nodded again, as he told her what she had to do.

'Flying, eh.' Reg whistled when he heard the news. After sending Cathleen back home, he turned the sign on the door to closed and gave a young lad a shilling to take a scribbled message to Kitty. He pulled out the telephone directory and finally got the answer he needed. There was an airline coach going from Kensington and yes, there were seats available and yes, it would get her to the terminal in time. Reg put the telephone down. Fine and dandy, he thought, but she only had twenty-five minutes to get to west London. Even if she were standing in front of him with her suitcase packed, even if a taxi was revving its engine outside, she wouldn't make it. Cathleen Brogan might have a seat on a plane but she had no way of getting to the airport.

That priest should have thought of that. Like he should have left a decent message in the first place instead of scaring both of them half to death. The priest was hanging around a lot lately.

Reg wasn't entirely sure but he thought he'd caught sight of him early one morning, as he was hauling bundles of newspapers from the step. It was hard to tell because who ever it was hadn't been wearing a dog collar. But it looked awful like.

Still, Cathleen needed to get to Heathrow and there was one man who could get her there. Reg made another phone call. It was sheer luck he knew where to ring and it would take more luck to find him at home. Reg smiled as he heard a man's voice on the other end of the phone. Cathleen deserved a bit of luck, he thought.

Cathleen looked around her bedroom. Just throw a few things into a bag, Jerry had said. But how long will we be gone for and what will we face when we get there? Her best dress was still hanging outside the wardrobe, pressed and ready for the dinner. She touched the fabric lightly and then braced herself as she heard her mother's footsteps on the stairs.

'I'm ready to have apoplexy,' Kitty announced, flinging herself down on the bed. 'I could feel my heart racing when I saw a boy with a note and then when I read it! I don't know what I should be worrying about first: the Brogans and their money, my granddaughters in the middle of it, or you off flying!' She paused to catch her breath. 'Are they homeless? Are the girls out on the street? Here −' she waved a cardigan in front of Cathleen − 'my neighbour says you have to dress up warm when you're up in the clouds.' She jumped up from the bed. 'Are you not going to say a word?'

'Mum, I don't know any more. The telegram said eviction.'

'Ach, that's not allowed any more. We had enough of that in the old days.'

Cathleen gently manoeuvred her mother away from the bed and pulled out the suitcase stowed underneath. 'If I could only talk to the girls, tell them I was coming.' Cathleen crouched down, balancing on her heels, trying to reach for another case in the darkness under the springs.

'Is there no one in the village who would get a message to them?'

'Jerry − Father Jerry − has sent a telegram.' Cathleen's hand found the suitcase and tugged. It skidded across the lino bringing a few wispy dust balls with it and she recognized it as the one she had packed for Mick the morning he was ordered into hospital. She stood up and kicked it back underneath.

'Ah, well don't be fretting then. You're getting to them as quick as a human being can get.' Kitty jerked at her daughter's sleeve. 'The priest paid for the aeroplane, did he?'

Cathleen nodded.

'Did he say anything about wanting to be paid back?'

'No, no.' Cathleen coloured. 'I'm not sure, he didn't say. But I don't think he'd expect me to.'

'Thank the Lord for small mercies! That's one thing I don't have to worry about. How much is it costing, do you know?'

'Haven't an idea. Something huge.'

'Find out, will you?' Kitty grinned. 'You don't have to be asking, just take a peak at the tickets when he's not looking.'

The doorbell rang.

'That might be Mary. I called in at the shop but she'd hardly get away yet.' Kitty tugged at the sash window and put her head out. 'Well, would you Adam and Eve it! It's only yer man with his car. She's coming down. I've got her all ready.'

Thank God, thought Cathleen. He's come for me. He knew how nervous I was and he's come. Cathleen threw on her raincoat and fastened the suitcase. With Jerry beside me, I can do anything.

She ran down the stairs, her mother on her heels and flung open the front door. Outside was a maroon Humber and leaning on the bonnet was Tacit Donovan. He straightened up as soon as he saw her

'I don't understand,' Cathleen stammered. 'How did you know?'

'Reg.'

She felt herself blushing. 'He shouldn't have bothered you.'

'He should have.' Tacit took the suitcase and opened the passenger door wide. Cathleen followed meekly behind.

Kitty danced after her. 'You bring my granddaughters home safe, do you hear? And yourself.' She delivered a hard kiss on each cheek and cocked her head in Tacit's direction, speaking in a whisper that easily carried across the width of the car. 'I'm warming to him. He always turns up when he's needed, that one.'

Tacit honked the car horn as he turned the corner by the shop. Cathleen saw Reg's hand waving through the jars of coloured sweets.

★　　★　　★

They were in High Holborn before either of them said anything. She pointed out Gamages, the department store where she brought the girls every year to see Father Christmas, and realized that she was babbling.

'There's no need, Cathleen.'

'What?'

'You're as taut as wire and why wouldn't you be? There's trouble in front of you and you don't know how bad it's going to be. But you're doing the right thing by getting to your daughters just as soon as you can.'

'I don't know what I'm going to do when I get there.'

'You'll manage.' She looked up and realized that he was watching her in the car mirror. 'I'd say we're similar in that way. We're part of the same tribe, the people who get on and do things.'

Cathleen half smiled. She wasn't sure about managing right now. Everything seemed to be built on shifting sand. Still, it made her feel better to have Tacit's good opinion. They were silent as he expertly negotiated the tourists milling around Trafalgar Square and only spoke again when they passed Whitehall. He explained that Reg knew how to contact him because at Christmas they'd discovered he had once lived next door to Tacit's landlady.

'What's your name?'

'What?'

'I know so little about you and you've helped so much . . . I don't believe your mother ever called you Tacit.'

She couldn't be certain, but she thought her question brought a bit of colour to his cheeks.

'I was baptized John.'

She nodded. It was a strong, straightforward name: it suited him.

He delivered her to the entrance of the Europa terminal. I'll be fine, I'll be fine, she kept reassuring him when he insisted that he should stay until the priest arrived.

No, she shook her head. 'We're the same tribe, remember? I can do this.' She was adamant and she realized that she didn't want him to see the two of them together. *He'll sense there's something between Jerry and me. Please God no one else does, but I wouldn't risk Tacit.* With her suitcase on the pavement, she put her head through the passenger window again.

'Thank you, John. You've been a good friend to me.'

She was glad she had found out his proper name because there was a smile on his face that wasn't there before. He changed gear and seemed ready to drive off when he suddenly seemed to think better of it, and called her over. 'Will you call me when you get back? I mean it. I'd like to know you're safe and well.'

He turned away again and it was hard to catch his last remark. Cathleen watched his tail lights disappear. With the planes and the traffic and Tacit's head turned away, it was easy to mishear. But she felt she hadn't. She had sensed it before he said anything, when she saw his car outside the house that afternoon. Reg must have known it too because why else would he have called a man he had met only once.

Tacit Donovan. John Donovan. I'm not the woman you should be wanting as more than a friend.

Fifty-Nine

The sight of a plane soaring above in the darkening night sky made Cathleen feel nervous. But there's something magnificent about it too, she thought, just as there's something magnificent about Jerry. She turned back towards the terminal building to see him striding towards her. He was frowning.

'Come on, I've been waiting ages.'

'Mr and Mrs Brogan?'

Cathleen blushed at the Aer Lingus stewardess's scrutiny. Her hair was stiff with lacquer and her eyelids were the same shade as her uniform.

'Ah no.' Father Jerry undid his coat to reveal his clerical collar and smiled broadly. Cathleen knew that smile, and wasn't surprised when dimples appeared in the stewardess's flawless pancake

'Welcome aboard, Father. Is it your first flight?'

'No, I was on your inaugural. That was a great thing and I've flown a fair few times before.'

'Oh, Father, we'll be coming to you for advice,' she gushed.

'But my cousin here –' Father Jerry placed his hand over Cathleen's – 'is a novice.'

She looked down. His thumb, hidden from view, was making small circling motions on her palm. It was a sudden, intimate gesture: like the one he had used at the Communion breakfast. *The more nervous I am, the longer he can keep it there.*

It was dark by the time the plane slowly taxied forward. Cathleen felt a tremor of excitement and fear run through her.

'Are you all right?'

She swallowed and nodded, but jumped when part of the wing moved. That's supposed to happen, she told herself and looked to the cabin crew for reassurance. Wouldn't they know if something had fallen off?

There was a growl of machinery and then a flash of red and yellow as the engines fired into life. The plane surged forwards and upwards, pressing Cathleen back into her seat.

'Oh dear God, what's happening?' She clutched Father Jerry's arm.

'Think about something else.' He glanced at his wristwatch. 'Think about what we should have been doing tonight.'

She turned away so he couldn't see her face. Here we are flying in a bit of metal, she thought, going to God alone knows what, and all he wants is to be with me, and all I want is to be with him.

The lights of London were spread out below them now in a pattern so intricate that it seemed crafted.

'I never knew it could be so beautiful.' Cathleen strained to look out the window.

'Neither did I.' His hand was still on hers.

I'll settle for this moment, she thought. Forever.

'Ah Father, would you ever lead us in a decade of the rosary.' A voice from one of the seats behind cut through Cathleen's thoughts. 'Sure, it will make us all a little easier in our minds.'

'I will, of course.'

His hand left hers to scramble for the rosary beads in his pocket and he sat beside her intoning the familiar words.

Their plane was the last to arrive that night at Shannon and, although the walkways were still white-lit by fluorescent tubes, the airport felt as though it had already decided to go to bed. Cathleen left everything to Jerry and sat down to watch as he strode over to a car hire desk.

From a distance Cathleen watched as people gathered around him. She didn't need to see his face to know that he was cajoling, persuading, rewarding.

Suddenly she felt like crying. She thought of the agonies Maeve must be going through. A soft, simple woman; surely this would break her? And her mother-in-law losing her home and Seamus his job and all of them buried beneath the shame of it. She could imagine the gossip after Mass on Sunday morning. It would take a generation for it to fade away and looming over everything like a thunder cloud was Thady's bitter, brooding presence.

Cathleen shuddered and looked up to see Jerry walking towards her, swinging a key fob.

'Right. We'll be off.'

She fell in step beside him as the staff waved goodbye. In minutes he had gathered together a band of followers.

It's as if we're on holiday, she thought, hurrying to keep up, as if these are normal times and our being here is the most natural thing in the world.

'Do you know the way?'

'I've never driven the road before but sure, if we head south we'll find somewhere we know.'

'What time did you tell Maeve?'

'Soon. That's all I put in the telegram. She won't be expecting us until tomorrow at the earliest. We could even spend the night in a hotel and start off first thing.' He turned and looked at her. 'We could do that.'

'No.' Cathleen shook her head. She could picture slinking down corridors in bare feet, bed springs creaking through thin walls, and then back again before the chambermaids were awake. 'No. We have to get there as soon as we can. It won't matter if it's the middle of the night.'

'You're right.' Father Jerry took her suitcase from her. 'We have to get to whatever's facing us.'

They found their hire car easily enough, a Ford Popular with a thick tide of mud clinging to the wheel arches and they soon left the world of roads and street lights behind for the country-side where high black hedgerows, silhouetted against a black sky, rose up on either side of the car. Cathleen breathed in the smell of grass and the sweet smoke of a turf fire that was warming a home somewhere in the dark.

This is Ireland, she thought. Not her Ireland, not dirty,

garrulous Dublin that seemed to have been made up of broken pavements, rent books with pages missing and pub tables that needed a good wipe. This Ireland was another place, the place the songs were sung about. It was Mick's Ireland and Jerry's, and the Ireland she wanted her daughters to have. It was the Ireland that they were about to lose.

Sixty

The roads twisted in on themselves and she wondered how Jerry could be so certain that they were still heading in the right direction.

'What did you want to be growing up?'

She smiled. 'Where did that question come from?'

'Come on now, you're the passenger. Your job's to entertain me.'

'I'm not sure. Well, I really, really wanted to be Ingrid Bergman after I saw her in *Joan of Arc*.'

'Ah, but the black hair was against you.'

'There's always something to hold you back but I was great at the sword fighting with a bit of two by two lashed together. What about you?'

'Come to think of it Ingrid played a role in my career. My father loved her in *The Bells of St Mary*.'

'So?' She recognized the role he had slipped into: Father Jerry the raconteur. She had seen this side of him in the bar after committee meetings, when he could hold ten or fifteen together with a turn of phrase. Now he was performing just for her.

'So I was sent to see it twice in one week. Twice! Me who'd never been allowed so much as a glimpse of Hopalong Cassidy.'

'But why were you sent?'

'For the benign influence of Ingrid, the stern but beautiful Reverend Mother, and the saintly Bing Crosby, of course. I tell you it was a shock at the seminary to discover that there was very little singing involved. Even now if I'm stuck, I ask myself what would Bing do.'

'Did your father want you to be a priest very much?'

'Once a month he'd say a nine-day novena, once a year walk barefoot around Lough Derg and every night he'd go to church to light a candle and all in aid of my vocation.' Jerry's tone was still light. 'You could say it was his hobby. Mothers used to boil their potatoes by him. Three minutes past six he'd shut up shop, walk up the road to the church and twelve minutes past he'd walk back down again. Put the saucepan on when he was on his way up, and they'd be just right by the time he came down.'

'Is that true?'

'Yes and no. I've never boiled a potato in my life and I have no idea how long one takes to cook, but yes to everything else.'

They drove on in silence. 'It was all right you know, my Dad, the way he carried on.'

'No, it wasn't.'

'Don't pity me. He just got fixated. I could always escape to the Brogan farmhouse. I tell you playing for the Farran hurling team was better than watching films.'

'You still did what he wanted. You still became a priest.'

'He was pushing at an open door, that's all.'

On a distant hillside a few lights shone, while clouds drifted across the face of a yellow moon, large and low in the summer sky. Jerry pulled over when the road broadened out and a verge appeared on their left.

'What's wrong?'

The beam of their headlights illuminated a dry stone wall and a small animal scuttled away. Jerry switched off the engine. 'It's no good.'

His mouth was on hers, hard and urgent. She felt his fingers on the wool of her jacket, pulling her closer.

'I'm aching for you.' He was tugging at her clothes, impatient with buttons and zips, kissing her throat. Our world's being destroyed, she thought, and we're rushing it along.

Suddenly, a twin shaft of light from the west cut through the night. The headlights corkscrewed to the right and then to the left following the road down into shallow dips.

Jerry hesitated for a moment and then switched on the engine and his own lights as Cathleen turned her head away and pulled her jacket together. The other car slowed and Jerry gave the customary salute of acknowledgement. It was returned by a middle-aged couple who inspected them with curiosity.

'We better get on.' Jerry looked straight ahead as he pulled out and it wasn't until they reached the outskirts of a small village that he spoke again.

'I'm angry with myself for what I did back there, embarrassing us both. Dear God, sometimes I've no more sense than a schoolboy. It's how I feel when I'm with you.'

'My fault then.'

'No.' He looked at her sharply. 'Never that, hear me? Never that.'

Cathleen drifted in and out of sleep and woke with a start.

'Where are we?'

'Haven't an idea. But I've just seen a sign for Tralee. Would you light me a cigarette?'

'Can we share it?'

'I have plenty.'

'No, I'd like to share yours.' She sensed he was smiling as she inhaled deeply and passed it over to him.

'I can taste your lipstick.'

They drove on and for miles said nothing, Cathleen resting her head on his shoulder. Occasionally an overhanging branch rattled a drum roll on the roof of the car to tell them the outside world still existed. Will my girls know a difference in me? she wondered.

'What will we do when we get there?' She turned to Jerry, guessing it was nearly dawn.

'The best we can, Cathleen. Isn't that all we can do?'

All I have to do is be a mother and take my girls home. And be kind to Maeve and Grandma Brogan, I can do that much. I'm an outsider and a woman and no more will be expected of me, thank God. But everything will fall on Jerry.

'Not long now, five or ten minutes. No more.'

'I'm scared.' Cathleen bit her lip. 'For all of us.'

He took a hand off the steering wheel and she held on to it gratefully.

'I love you Jerry Brogan.'

He looked straight ahead. 'I haven't been called that since I don't know when. I'm Jerry to a few and Father to most. Jerry Brogan. I'd forgotten what it sounds like.'

'And what does it sound like?'

'Like winning at hurling and kissing you.'

'Jerry Brogan.'

'Cathleen *Acree.*'

Sixty-One

A dog barked as they drove up the boreen but turned and slunk away before they got out the car. There was a glow coming from the kitchen window.

The front door creaked open and they stepped inside, standing for a moment to listen to the house. Where are the girls? thought Cathleen. Without thinking their hands felt for one another, but as soon as their fingers touched they moved apart. Together they turned towards the dim light and swung open the door into the kitchen. Cathleen looked around remembering the room from the previous summer. In the grey light she saw the scrubbed pine table that they had eaten around, the sugan chairs with their rope seats, the flickering electric candle bulb underneath the picture of the Sacred Heart and an ancient turf bucket thrown in a corner. Little had changed except that someone had hauled two high-backed armchairs from the parlour and placed them in front of the range.

Maeve occupied one and Grandma Brogan the other. The old woman was asleep, her head low on her large square bosom, but Maeve had heard their arrival and was gripping the edge of the armrest, every muscle taut.

'The pair of youse!' Maeve's mouth opened in wonder. 'Here already? I knew you'd come, but here already.'

'How are you, Maeve?' Father Jerry strode over to her.

'Me? I don't know – but better for seeing you.'

'Anna? Geraldine?' Cathleen heard and hated the sharpness in her voice, but couldn't hold it back.

'Grand. Grand out.' Maeve moved towards Cathleen but she pulled away from her sister-in-law's flabby arms.

'Where are they?'

Maeve's wet eyes filled with tears. 'Believe me, they're grand. They hardly know a thing.' Her voice trailed off. 'They're sleeping, the dotes.'

Cathleen crept up the stairs to her daughters' bedroom. They looked untroubled in the tumble of bedclothes. Anna lay neat and straight with hair fanned out around her head, her little sister in a fetal roll beside her. Cathleen wanted to wake them, to pick them up and smell them, but no, she couldn't do that. She was tempted to slip her shoes off and get in beside them but she knew that wasn't possible either. Jerry would need her downstairs, and she needed to be there too. She had to know what was happening.

Maeve was still talking when she returned.

'Himself is out and Mam won't go to bed until he's back. He's been gone so long I suppose he could be in a ditch somewhere . . .' Her voice trailed off again as if she was scared to finish any thought. 'What am I thinking of? You'll be famished and parched.' She refused to listen to their protests.

'A cup of tea at least,' she continued. 'And we'll sit down in the parlour – we don't want to be waking Mam with our blather. It's destroying her, I swear to God.' Maeve lowered her voice to a whisper. 'I didn't say anything about the telegram because I was afraid another disappointment would surely kill her. But she'll get new heart from the sight of youse.'

Maeve scuttled into the back kitchen while Jerry led the way into the parlour. Last summer Cathleen had glimpsed the heavily patterned walls and dark, heavy furniture from the open doorway but she'd never been inside. It smelt like the water left at the bottom of a flower vase.

'The girls?' asked Jerry.

Cathleen nodded and stretched out a hand. He squeezed it as she looked around. The snap she had taken of Anna in her First Holy Communion dress was already on the chifforobe she noticed, among Jerry's sporting cups and a collection of photographs that stretched back forty years.

Maeve came in with a tray laden with thick slices of buttered soda bread.

'Eat now, you'll be starved with the hunger.'

Cathleen found she was hungry and they both ate with real relish. The ormolu clock over the mantelpiece chimed five times.

'We've ate, we've drank.' Father Jerry turned to Maeve and put an arm around her shoulder. 'Now, it's time to talk.' He directed her to a chaise longue pushed against a wall, the stuffing visible through the seams of worn velvet.

Maeve sat down reluctantly. Her eyes darted around the room and her hands seemed desperate for activity. 'The girls, Cathleen, how did you find them?' She didn't wait for an answer. 'Tired out, the little darlings. I've done my best.'

'I'm sure you have.'

'I hardly know what I'm saying but now you're here, ah sure nothing can be so bad ever again.' Maeve's eyes welled with tears. 'You'll sort it out, Father, won't you? It's a terrible mistake and no one will listen to me. How can we lose the farm? It doesn't make a bit of sense. Doesn't the world know what a great worker my Seamus is and that it will belong to him one day? It's his already, the hours he puts in. You tell the gombeens at the bank. You put them right.' Maeve had found a handkerchief in one of her pockets and was twisting it into a rope. 'They'll listen to you. Haven't we all listened to you? Always.' The tears fell in earnest now.

Cathleen looked across at Jerry. A muscle was working in his cheek but he was keeping his face under control as he knelt on the floor in front of Maeve and took her hands in his.

'You've been through so much,' he began.

It was a lullaby, Cathleen thought, and she could almost forgive her sister-in-law for her blind faith. It wasn't so much the words he used, as the soothing sound they made when he put them together.

'You've had to endure so much . . .'

The parlour door crashed open. The pictures on the wall jumped and Maeve let out a small scream. Thady was back.

Sixty-Two

'So it's the priest and the little widow woman.' Thady stood swaying in the doorway, a loose-lipped sneer pulling at his mouth. 'I saw the car and I wondered who was paying us a call. I should have guessed it was His Holiness himself. What's it feel like to be the only fecking saint that doesn't have to be dead before he's canonized?'

He attempted a mock bow that threatened to topple him over and he had to grasp on to the door frame for support. It was clear that he had passed out in his clothes, although his face suggested that he hadn't slept much. The darkness under his eyes looked like ink smudges.

'My mother and sister pray to you all the time. We even have a shrine.' A hand waved towards the hurling cups. 'So, what miracle is it today? Loaves and fishes? Water into wine? Sweat into money?' He paused and, without warning, aimed a strong, savage kick at the leg of the chaise longue, sending Maeve into a juddering fit of weeping.

'You sent for him, you old sow.'

Jerry leapt to his feet.

'Get back!' The angry howl reminded Cathleen of the way Thady had faced down the bull. 'As a child you were always where you weren't wanted, showing off, and you're no better as a man. This is my house for a few days more and I say feck off Jerry Brogan.'

'Enough.'

It was said quietly but it seemed to calm Thady. Grandma Brogan stood in the doorway, wrapped in a candlewick dressing grown, her thin grey hair dishevelled. She touched her son's arm. 'Lie down and rest.'

He stood for a moment swaying and Cathleen wondered if he would turn on his mother, but he allowed himself to be guided to the stairs. At the last moment he wrenched away.

'I'm going to ruin every last one of you.' His voice was strong and cold and he took time to look each of them in the eye. 'I'll bring youse all down with me.'

They stared at the door long after they could hear Thady moving above their heads.

'Four nights I've been begging him to lie down,' Grandma Brogan began and then turned away. She found her way to a dining-room chair and sank into it.

'You two here.' She looked up at Father Jerry and Cathleen. 'I heard voices and thought I was dreaming. Then I heard Thady and knew I wasn't.' She sat lost in thought for a moment. 'You're the two people I wanted to see most in the world and I wish to God you weren't here. We shouldn't have dragged you into this.' She closed her eyes and sighed.

Father Jerry looked down at the weathered face, cross-hatched with fine lines. When I was a child I never left her house without a little extra slipped into my school bag, he remembered. There was always a few home-made scones, or a jar of jam among the school books. And she was always there, in the background, making tea, milking cows, cooking, fetching, carrying.

He took her hands in his and was surprised by the strength in them.

'Aren't we family?'

'As long as you know there's no miracles to be worked here, son.' Her eyes were still shut. Jerry let her hands drop and straightened up.

Outside the countryside was waking up. Not far away a cow was lowing and, glancing at his watch, he realized that soon it would be time for milking. Thady had unnerved him and he suddenly thought of the shotgun that was kept in the back kitchen. Maeve brought it to him and he decided to lie it on the floor underneath the chaise longue. Tomorrow he would give it to Seamus to look after. He wanted it as far away from Thady as possible.

He urged the women to sleep if they could. An eiderdown had been brought for him and he promised that he would make a bed on the chaise longue but after the door closed he stood in front of it, lost in thought.

Was it envy that bound us together tighter than blood when we were growing up? With my pocket money and good shoes and the life I had living in town it must have seemed to Thady that I had everything. Oh, but I envied the Brogan brothers. They had each other and the smell of bread baking and the dogs at their heels. I even envied them their father, although he had a tongue sharp enough to clip a hedge. My own would hardly say a word between closing the pharmacy and winding the clock last thing at night. And I always envied them their mother.

But where did Thady's anger come from?

Father Jerry glanced towards the sideboard where two generations of Brogans were displayed. He hadn't noticed before but yes, there were more photographs of him than anyone else. He may not have been a frequent visitor over the years, but there was no doubt that he was a living presence in this house. I could almost feel sorry for Thady, he thought.

This won't do. He got to his feet to search for his breviary in his coat pocket and heard movements above his head. Thady again? He didn't relish another meeting but no, these were light footsteps and he imagined Cathleen in her opal petticoat getting undressed for bed. As he put his hand on the worn leather of his prayer book, he noticed a photograph taken the year he went to the seminary. Fresh-faced and bursting with confidence, he was surrounded by the hurling team and holding a trophy. He didn't notice any of the details; it was the innocence in his nineteen-year-old eyes that absorbed him.

He knelt on the hardwood floor and started to pray. 'O Lord Jesu wash me in the blood of your sacrifice, help me to repulse the attacks and deceits of the devil and . . .' He paused, seeing the next line in his mind. ' . . . being truly penitent forgive my sins and let me sin no more.'

He sighed and got to his feet. That was the problem. He couldn't confess a sin that he wasn't sorry for and which he had every intention of committing again. He kissed the small crucifix he always carried with him. *I love you. I love the priesthood and I love Cathleen Brogan.*

Sixty-Three

Cathleen woke him a few hours later with a cup of tea, the breviary still on his lap. It was about to fall and she rescued it, the small book's worn binding resting in her palm.

'How are you?' she whispered, crouching down beside the armchair where he had slept. She took one of his hands and pressed it against her lips.

'Mummy!' Geraldine stood in the parlour doorway, screwing tight little fists into her eyes. 'Mummy! I dreamt that you came in the middle of the night. And you did! You did!'

I'll never let them go away again, she thought, as she ran across to hug her and hold her in her arms. She was almost too big for it, but not quite. They can't go away again until they're old and have children of their own. She twirled Geraldine around and used the opportunity to inspect her arms and legs. There were no scratches that she could see, no finger-shaped bruises. Anna was still asleep. Cathleen stood undecided on the stairs. Should she wake her? It seemed mean to go off exploring without her, but Geraldine was insistent.

'Please! You've got to meet my special friend. Anna likes him too, but he likes me the best. He does.'

They met Seamus in the yard. He looked at her wild-eyed, as if he too had spent a sleepless night.

'You?' He shook his head as if to check that he wasn't seeing things. 'I saw the car and guessed Father Jerry but you're a week early.'

'Your mother sent a telegram. We came as quick as we could.'

'So that's what she was doing in town. She never said.' He lowered his voice so Geraldine couldn't hear but she didn't seem to be listening. She was tugging at her mother's hand, urging her to come on. An undercurrent of voices could be heard from the kitchen.

'The father needs to know there's nothing to be done.' Seamus spoke in an urgent, fierce whisper. 'Make him understand that, won't you? It's all gone. Long gone and good riddance.' He paused. 'I was going to write to you myself.' He stopped and pulled his thick dark hair away from his eyes. 'I was thinking maybe I could stop in your place just for a bit, if you'd have me. Just until I got a job and a room of my own.'

'Of course, you can.' It was an instinctive reaction and her reward was instant. There was hope in the way Seamus' chin jerked forward.

'I'll be free of Thady and the farm. It's the best thing that could have happened and Mam won't be on her own. Grandma can move in to our house.' He seemed to straighten up as he spoke and he grabbed Geraldine's hand. 'Quick now, let's find your friend before I go off to the creamery.' He turned back to Cathleen and nodded in the direction of the house. 'Thady won't go now. He hasn't been to Mass in a fortnight and he's a stranger to Patsy Mulligan's. For all his bluster the shame's eating into him.'

Cathleen nodded, trying to keep up with her daughter. The yard was still muddy from yesterday's rain and she had to pick her way between puddles and cowpats. Geraldine was wearing her Wellingtons and had no such reservations. My timid little girl, thought Cathleen, as she watched her run ahead impatiently, and balance on top of the gate as Seamus swung it open.

Cathleen recognized the field. The first few yards were an explosion of thistles and then it widened out to a green expanse of grass and ragwort. It was a place she still visited in her dreams and she knew without looking that in the distance was the gap in the hedge where the bull had appeared. Standing here a year later, she could still taste the fear in her mouth. She wondered what the next twelve months would bring. Another farmer's cows would graze in this wretched field and Seamus would follow in Mick's footsteps to London: that much seemed certain, but for herself and for Jerry? She tried to push the thought away. They had stolen a few days, and they couldn't steal it again. Something had ended when they got out of the car in front of the Brogan farmhouse. They were back in the real world and it was nastier than the one they were used to.

Her eyes felt sore and gritty. It was lack of sleep and seeing Thady again, that and being in this field. Cathleen shivered in the morning sunlight. Where had Geraldine gone? She could hear her daughter, shrieking and giggling as if Seamus was tickling her. A few steps further in, a few more ounces of mud on her shoes, and she saw them together on the other side of an over-grown gorse bush.

Geraldine had her arms around the neck of a large terracotta and cream bull calf and was squealing in delight as it licked her face. Seamus was scratching the top of its head.

'The girls have made a real pet out of him and he'd follow them anywhere. I've never seen anything like it. I swear we could put a lead on this one and take him for a walk.'

Geraldine's eyes widened. 'Yes!'

Cathleen studied the strong muscular legs and chest as the calf nuzzled Geraldine's neck. 'He's safe?'

Seamus nodded. 'Any calf this age is safe but they're usually silly, skittish creatures. This fella was born blind, he's a dote.'

'And he gets lonely because the other calves go off and play and he can't follow and he's in the field all by himself but now he has me. And Anna, she likes him as well, but not as much as me. So can I take him for a walk because he'll have to do that when we take him back to London, and it would be better if he could get used to it here?' Geraldine turned to her mother. 'I don't suppose they'll let me bring him to school but I can walk him to Myddlton Square in the morning and maybe the park after school.'

Cathleen and Seamus exchanged glances. 'But that's a lot of busy roads to cross.'

'Oh, he wouldn't mind that, not if he has me with him.'

'But you can't cross those roads on your own.'

'No.' Geraldine frowned. 'You'd have to come with me.'

Cathleen couldn't burst the bubble of her dream, not on their first morning together, not with Geraldine's smile lighting up her face. However, walking back to the farmhouse to see if Anna was awake, Cathleen did mention that London was a big, noisy city.

'I know.' Geraldine was matter of fact. 'But Uncle Thady has lost the farm and someone else has found it so he can't stay here anyway. So you see, he has to come to London and it won't be so bad because he has a best friend.'

'Has the calf got a name?'

'Well, it was Sammy for a day but we went off that and Anna wanted Simon after a boy in her class but that's a silly name for a calf.' Geraldine pulled a face. 'So, I think we've almost decided on Little Thady.'

Cathleen stopped in surprise. Last night's scene was still all too vivid. 'Why did you name him after your uncle?'

'It was Anna's idea. She thought Uncle Thady might like him better if they had the same name.'

'Well, he'll have to be down on the fifteenth.' Seamus snorted over supper. Thady had kept to his room for the rest of the day. By now all the adults had seen the letter from the bank. The fifteenth was the day the bank had set for repossession.

Only Maeve called it eviction. 'But that's what it is,' she argued tearfully. 'Just like in the days of the landlords. Why won't anyone believe me.'

If Cathleen thought she could keep anything from the children she realized her mistake that supper time. There was no other topic of conversation. Every word spoken referred back to the brooding presence hanging over their heads.

'Where are you going to live?' Anna asked her grandmother.

'Oh, I'll be fine, don't you worry about me.'

'But where are we going to visit next year?' Cathleen squirmed at her daughter's insistence.

'Father Jerry's going to sort out all that nonsense tomorrow, like the big, clever man he is.' Maeve beamed at the children while everyone else looked at their plates.

'Well, Seamus is going to live with us,' said Geraldine. 'So that's all right.'

Seamus' face flushed red to his ears and his embarrassment

grew as his mother tried to make light of it. Finally he pushed back his chair and stood up.

'There is no sorting for Father Jerry or anyone else to do. Some things can't be sorted. Grandma will live with you, Mam, and I'm off to England. There's plenty that's gone the same road as me.'

He looked up to see Thady grinning at him from the hall. His uncle put two fingers in his mouth and started to blow hard, until he produced a shrill, piping whistle. He carried on whistling as Maeve fled from the table in tears and Seamus stumbled after her.

'Aha, boy! That's the way to do.'

Thady selected a cap from the hall stand and went out the front door.

Sixty-Four

Later that evening Cathleen suggested to Jerry that they contrive to meet in the hay shed.

The shed had a corrugated iron roof. On three sides they were sheltered by tall walls of hay that still held a dusty warmth. The fourth was open and faced the back of the cowshed and pigsty.

Cathleen picked up a doll. Good, she thought as she slipped it into the pocket of her jacket. It was reason enough to be outside if anyone asked.

'What are you going to do tomorrow?' It was so quiet she felt she had to whisper.

Father Jerry sighed. 'Seamus is right, there's precious little I can do. I have no stake in this, but I can have a drink with the bank manager. They say that there's only one thing that counts in Ireland and that's what's written on a toilet door.' Cathleen frowned, not catching the reference. 'Pull.' Jerry made a face. 'Tomorrow we'll see how much pull I have in my home town. Not a lot is my guess.' He was standing a little apart from her, looking at the horizon, and the way his arms were crossed in front of him seemed like a barrier keeping her out.

'I've missed you.'

It was quietly said and when he didn't react Cathleen turned to make her way back to the farmhouse. Perhaps he was being reminded what it meant to be a priest now he was back among his own people. He was revered here, and untouchable. That was the life he had chosen and it was the life he was good at. So, where did that leave her: the little widow in Thady's hateful phrase. No. She put her chin up and walked away.

She felt a hand on her shoulder. Words were unnecessary as he pulled her back into the shadows.

'I've missed you too.' They kissed.

Cathleen moved away first. 'I better get back.' Jerry nodded and followed a few minutes later.

When he left the sanctuary of the hay shed, he didn't notice the half drunk bottle of whiskey propped up on a pile of hay bales. Or Thady's boots in the shadows. Or Thady smiling in the dark. He had two fingers in his mouth but he'd stopped himself from whistling.

Cathleen woke in the early hours shivering. She must have kicked the bedspread off during the night. Her nightdress was in a mess too: the bodice was open to her waist and the satin bows undone. No wonder she was cold.

She sat up. There was a sound. A stifled creak, like the weight of a foot on a floorboard. The curtains were askew and a shaft of moonlight fell across the bed but she couldn't see anything else.

Another creak. Louder. Closer.

There was someone in the room.

'Who is it?' Cathleen's voice didn't sound as though it belonged to her.

Silence. It was so quiet she could feel her heart beat.

'It's me, Mummy. It's only me.'

Anna. Cathleen scrambled out of bed and gathered her eldest daughter into her arms.

'Do you need something? The child shook her head as Cathleen led her back to the double bed where Geraldine was still asleep.

'I just wanted to see you were all right.' The child's voice was thick with sleep. Cathleen knelt on the cold lino and smoothed Anna's hair back from her face.

'You silly girl, why wouldn't I be all right?'

Anna yawned and turned into her pillow. 'Only he was a long time. He said he wouldn't be but he was.'

'Who?' Cathleen's voice shook.

'Uncle Thady, of course. He was by your bed. He said it was a game you were playing. A grown-up game that you liked playing.'

Sixty-Five

Cathleen watched Thady as they gathered around the kitchen table. He had thrown himself into an armchair by the fire and was studying the *Irish Independent* as if he was absorbed in farm stock prices and foreign news, not waiting like the rest of them for Jerry to get back from his interview with the bank manager. She wanted to shake the newspaper out of his sausage fingers and slap the ruddy jowls that fused into his shoulders. She hated him and she was scared of him too. She and the girls had to get away.

She had tried to tell Jerry that morning but, when it became obvious that they weren't going to get a moment alone, she wrote instead. Using a sheet of Grandma Brogan's blue Basildon Bond, she urged him to come back to London with them.

'Just a bit of a shopping list. Have a look at it when you're in town,' she said, when she slipped it into his coat pocket in front of everyone.

That had been two hours ago. They had been ghosts while he was gone, aimlessly waiting for the sound of his returning car. At the sound of tyres on the gravel Cathleen moved towards the door and they all surged forward. Only Thady stayed sitting, turning another page of the newspaper.

Jerry walked into the kitchen looking tired and defeated. There was a fragile mauve quality to his eyelids that Cathleen wanted to kiss better.

The girls were outside absorbed in a game and Cathleen could see them through the window. Good. She didn't want them listening to Jerry, they had heard enough already.

What had to be said was said quickly. The letter they had all seen was the last in a long line stretching back over years. The fat creamery cheque that came each month hadn't even covered the interest. The farm was gone. Maeve looked from face to face and when she couldn't find what she was looking for it seemed to Cathleen as though she broke, like a mirror cracking. It would have been better if she'd cried because they were used to her tears, but her silence was harder to bear.

Father Jerry had achieved one thing. A sale of effects had been cancelled. The women gasped when they learnt what that meant. After an advert in *The Kerryman* and posters in Mulligan's Bar, an auctioneer would have come to the house to sell off the chaise longue in the parlour and the foxed print of the Sacred Heart in the kitchen. The table they were sitting at would have gone under the hammer, together with the pots and pans they used to cook the dinner, and the willow pattern plates they had eaten it from. As a concession to Father Jerry they had been spared all that but it came at a price. The animals would be taken to market on Monday. Cathleen glanced up and saw Seamus' face. He looked as if he were in pain. He'll go too, she thought, he won't stay once the animals are gone.

Maeve spoke for the first time. 'But where is the money?'

'Only one man can give you that answer.' Father Jerry glanced over his shoulder. The armchair was empty. 'A lot of it must have passed over Patsy Mulligan's counter but the word is that most of it went on betting. I don't even know if you could call Thady a gambler because I don't think he lost the farm. I think he threw it away.'

'His father's farm,' said Grandma Brogan quietly. 'On the day I buried his father it was the best farm in seven parishes, everyone said so, and he built it up from very little. He was a hard man, I know that, he was hard on you as children, and maybe hardest on Thady.' She looked at Jerry and Maeve. 'But he worked hard too.'

'It was a good inheritance.' Father Jerry's voice was soft. 'No one could deny that.'

'The cows still need to be milked.' Seamus turned away now and put his cap on.

'They do.' Grandma Brogan nodded. 'I might even come a bit of the way with you. It's a long time since I walked the fields.' She put her hand out to her daughter. Maeve's tears were falling at last.

Seamus waited while Grandma Brogan found an old pair of boots to pull on. They walked out the back door together in silence. Today was one of the old woman's good days, when the pain in her knees was nothing more than a steady background ache. She shoved her hands into the pockets of her apron.

As they walked through the haggard at the back of the farm-house, she pointed out the spot Seamus had played the summer the builders had dumped a load of sand in the wrong place. That was back when his grandfather was still alive, when things were still being done, animals bought for their quality and not their price, and the farm had a working, beating heart.

Grandma Brogan had come to the farm as a bride of twenty with a dowry of seven hundred pounds and every step held a memory. This land had been her life.

They paused in front of the three-acre field.

'This way?' Seamus asked. 'Or would you rather go the long way around, up past the blackberry field and the pond.'

Grandma Brogan shook her head. She wouldn't trust her knees that far. No, she would pet Geraldine's calf and then turn back. It wasn't as far as she would have liked, but it would do. Grandma Brogan held her chin up. There was water in the air, not enough to be called a mist, but enough to put a shine on the grass and make skin feel as though it had been stroked with a soft sponge. It was the weather she loved the best and she felt better for it.

The gate to the three-acre field was already open. Seamus glanced back at his grandmother and frowned. 'The girls surely know better.'

They did. It was Thady who had left the gate open and Thady who now stood in the middle of the field. The blind calf was trotting towards him.

'Were you going to fetch the cows?' Seamus made an effort to keep his voice neutral. 'Only that's where we were going but if you'd rather . . .'

'I'm getting the cows all right. I'm getting the cows so that the fecking bank will never get them.' Thady waved the shotgun above his head. 'I'll even milk them too. I've a new way of doing it. I'll shoot the udders out from them. I'll burst the feckers open.'

'Dear God.' The old woman clutched at her grandson as if she was about to fall. 'Go back to the house,' she whispered. 'Go get help. I'll keep him talking.'

'Are you mad? I'll get the gun off him first.'

They moved towards him slowly, Grandma Brogan's mouth fluttering in silent prayer.

'Now, son,' she pleaded.

'Don't you son me.' Thady's eyes were wild. 'The only son you wanted is sitting at my table and making deals with the bank.

The son you wished you had wears his collar around the wrong way and his trousers around his ankles.'

Only the blind calf moved, nosing his way towards them.

'But did you know that the blessed Father Jerry has his hand up Cathleen's skirt?' Thady made an exaggerated sign of the cross. 'And does the little widow like it? Go on, give a guess.'

'Shut your trap.' Grandma Brogan was staring up into her son's face. 'Don't dirty other people with your thoughts.'

'But I seen them, mother of mine. I seen them kissing and groping in the hay barn.'

She hit him then, one resounding, stinging slap to the side of his face. The sound made the calf start but Thady smiled, an ugly, tongue-rolling smile.

With one hand still firmly griping the shotgun, he pulled from his trouser pocket a sheet of blue Basildon Bond paper. 'A present for you.' He let it flap in the damp breeze just out of reach. 'Seamus can come listen to me in Patsy Mulligan's tonight. Tomorrow I'll make a start on the bars in town but I won't rush it. I was thinking I'd go up one side of Main Street and then down the other, because there will be a different crowd in each bar, and every single one will be panting for what I have to tell them.'

He brought his face down to his mother's level and she felt herself tremble. She had been angry. Now she was scared.

'They'll drink in every word and be thirsty for more. And then they'll take it home with them. They won't believe me, of course. Just Thady Brogan blagging. But they'll look at Father Jerry sideways when he's on the altar. And then there's our little Cath-leen.' The old woman shivered as she felt her son's heavy, whiskey-clogged breath on her face. 'Every blackguard will know her for the tempting little tart that she is. What do you reckon, Seamus?' His head swivelled round to watch his nephew's reaction. 'Shall I tell them about her little titties? Do you think the good father twists them with his fingers until she cries? Is that her penance?'

'Stop it. Stop it.' Grandma Brogan was screaming at him now, lashing out with her fists. Thady seemed to relish each blow.

'Every time they hear the name Brogan they'll think of Cathleen and their mouths will water with the pictures I've put in their head. And you'll know, mother of mine.' He held up the sheet of paper again and then squashed it into her hand. 'Once you read that letter, you'll know every word is true.' He licked his lips. 'Such a lovely way of expressing herself. God! You'd think you were in bed between them.'

Grandma Brogan grabbed at him, clawing at his arm while Seamus made a lunge for the shotgun. Thady laughed as he batted them both off.

'Not so easy. I've a little bit of business here first.'

The calf had edged nearer, but some instinct made it veer away now, its back legs scuttling on the wet grass. Thady took aim and with one rolling, thunderous crack pressed the trigger.

The sound was still hanging in the air when Seamus charged. Thady was bigger, but Seamus was stronger, fitter and younger. The gun was his. The boy stood back, breathing hard as if he had been running. He lifted it up and looked at Thady through the sights.

Sixty-Six

Cathleen and Jerry were alone. The girls were still playing outside in the drizzle.

'Did you read my letter?' Cathleen turned her back on the window. Even if the girls peered in they wouldn't see her stroke the side of Jerry's face or see him close his eyes and kiss her hand. 'Please come back with us. I don't want to be here a moment longer. Thady scares me. I used to be mad with him but now I'm scared.'

'What letter?' He held her hand. 'I looked for the shopping list but it wasn't in my pocket.'

She stared at him. 'You can't have dropped it!'

'Why? What did you put in it?'

What had she written? Enough to damn them both.

'Did you put your name on it?'

He seemed relieved when she shook her head. If the oblong of blue was in town, drifting down Main Street, it wouldn't matter. The letter could be lying flat on the bank manager's desk and it still couldn't touch them. But here in this house, where her handwriting was well known and every detail would make sense, here it could destroy them. She had written the word want more often than the word love. She wanted him on the train back to London. She wanted him next to her at night.

Suddenly a hollow crash of thunder seemed to cut the air into pieces. Through the window Cathleen saw the girls look up and she motioned them to come in. When she turned back Jerry's face was white.

'That was a gun.'

He opened the door and was already running when they heard a second shot.

Father Jerry recognized Seamus' checked shirt in the distance and saw a shotgun in his hands. The strings of Grandma Brogan's apron were flying in the breeze and she seemed to be sitting or squatting, but he knew she was alive because he could hear the siren of her tangled words.

Thank God.

But he knew too that there were bodies in the long grass. He spurted forward and tasted iron. It was only later that he realized he had bitten a large chunk from the inside of his lip.

The first body was the young bull calf. The poor creature was still alive, quaking in terror as its life blood seeped from a bullet wound in the soft flesh of its neck.

Grandma Brogan was quiet by the time Father Jerry reached her and in her lap lay Thady. She was combing the dark whirls of his hair with her fingers as a gentle rain washed his face. Above his right eye was a small red hole, the size and shape of a sixpence.

'He was going to kill all the animals.' Seamus spoke in ugly gulps, as if he were swallowing air. 'And he said terrible things . . .'

'Shh, don't say any more. No one was ever able to help Thady while he was alive but now Father Jerry can.' Father Jerry very gently laid Thady on to the grass. He hesitated and then took off his jacket to make a pillow for his cousin's head. It seemed wrong somehow to let him lie flat on the ground. He looked up to see Grandma Brogan leaning on the shotgun that he had slept beside the first night they had arrived.

The old woman followed his gaze. 'Maeve wouldn't have it in her house. So we hid it in the turf shed.' She paused and looked down at her dead son.

Father Jerry nodded. He didn't trust himself to speak. There were words of comfort that should be said but he didn't know who he would be comforting. And there were other words he had to say and say quickly before the soul departed the body.

He ordered them back to the house, surprised that his voice could sound so commanding. Get Cathleen to call the guards, he instructed and then he turned back to the body. His hand was trembling as he closed Thady's eyes and recited the prayer that would pardon the sins he had committed through sight: *indúlgeat tibi Dóminus quidquid per visum.*

At first he thought Thady's face was splattered with mud but when he leant closer he realized that the dark marks that freckled his forehead had been left by gunshot powder. He blessed Thady's ears. What had he heard that he shouldn't have heard? To what had he refused to listen?

Had his nose led him to sin? *Odorátum.*

Had his lips? *Gustum et locutiónem.*

Had his hands? *Tactum.*

Had his feet? *Gressum deliquisti.*

Father Jerry brushed the sharp edge of a thistle away from Thady's hand as if it might hurt him and noticed for the first time a fragment of blue paper caught in the grass. He looked around and saw several more pieces. Some were tiny, no bigger than a stamp, while others were larger and torn roughly across. All were now a sodden mess of blue ink on blue paper. He walked back to the farmhouse. It was raining in earnest now and he was glad of it.

Sixty-Seven

Garda O'Sullivan sat in the parlour studying Seamus as other policemen prepared to take Thady's body to the morgue. 'A bad business.'

The boy nodded, sitting on the edge of the chaise longue. The guard allowed the silence between them to open up. Outside they heard the doors of the police van slam shut. Seamus wet his lips with his tongue and opened his mouth to speak.

'I have to go milk the cows.'

'All in good time.'

It was colder in the parlour than it was outside. There was a chill in the damp walls that couldn't be shifted, and Seamus started to shiver.

'It wasn't meant.' Grandma Brogan swung open the parlour door. The guard leapt to his feet, his hands stretched out to shoo the old woman back to where she had come from.

'Ah now, missus, I asked for a few minutes alone.'

'Well, I'm not giving them to you. I need him out here working.' She jerked her head in Seamus' direction. 'And you've no need of him when I can tell you what happened. It wasn't meant. It was an accident, that's all you need to know. The farm's lost and my son was mad with the grief of it. He went out to shoot the cows. There's a calf dead in the field. Did you find it?'

'We did.'

'I got the gun off him. He tried to get it back. It went off. That's the story.'

'That's *your* story.' Garda O'Sullivan took out his notebook.

'It is the only story you will hear because there is only one story to be told. There's animals to be cared for now and prayers to be said. I had two sons and I've lost them both. Give me the space to mourn them.' The old woman stood between Seamus and the guard. 'Now out of my house. Out!'

Seamus was taken away for questioning the next morning. Father Jerry followed the police car into town. He wanted Cathleen to come with him but she wouldn't leave the girls.

'I can't! They don't know what to do with themselves. Geraldine's been crying half the night and now Seamus being taken away, who they love like a brother.' She shook her head. They were alone in the hall and she kissed his cheek.

The pressure of her lips stayed with him as he drove through the country lanes, making him feel more alone. He couldn't imagine what he could do at the police station. As he walked through the double doors, Father Jerry recalled that he had once shared a classroom with the senior police officer. They had never been friends, but at least they hadn't fallen out. They had lived at different ends of town; himself in a middle-class home as the chemist's son and Callaghan in one of the grey council houses that were flooded by the river every couple of years.

He's losing his hair was Father Jerry's first thought as the inspector ushered him into his office. The balding head looked incongruous above a face that was still rosy-cheeked. The policeman bounced forward with an outstretched hand.

'Aren't we all very proud of you,' the inspector said with a smile. 'A ton of English papers were sold in the town the week you made the news. What is it that they call that prime minister over there? Super Mac, is it? Well, you were super priest around here. That's what the lads in the street were saying.'

Father Jerry shifted uneasily. He asked about the inspector's family. The boy from the riverbanks had done well and married the daughter of a big farmer. And there were three sons as well.

A sudden spasm of jealousy hit Father Jerry. Sons, he thought. I'd have liked to have had sons. I could go to matches with them and watch them play. And one – for a moment he could see the child's thin face, this son of his that he would never have – one would devour books, and be teased for it. And I'd have been the only one who understood.

'I'm glad you're here. To be honest, I don't like having that poor lad in the cells.' Callaghan shook his head. 'But my problem is that a man who should be walking and talking is waiting to be buried. You didn't see anything yourself? I see you were on the scene in pretty quick time.'

'I ran when I heard the shot.'

'Why?'

'I don't understand, wouldn't anyone run?'

The inspector leant back in his chair and a small smile spread across his face.

'Ah Jerry, you're not as long away as all that. If I was in a farmhouse, having a cup of tea and I heard a shot, I'd expect rabbit stew for supper.' The smile faded. 'Money doesn't bleed out of a farm without someone raising a voice. Tell me whose voice was the loudest? Seamus? Losing his livelihood and the hope of an inheritance. You'd have to be a saint not to be sore at that.'

I've walked into this like a fool, they have us both for questioning now. Father Jerry lit a cigarette to give himself time to think. 'You're right, I ran for a reason and the reason was Thady. You don't have to look further than him. It's well known what kind of man he was. Ask anyone in Farran. And since losing the farm, I'd say a kind of madness crept over him.'

'And what did you see? Take your time. You're in the field. You're running. Is Thady standing at this point? Is he?' Father Jerry shook his head.

'OK, so he was down already.' The policeman paused. 'Are you picturing it, Father?' Jerry nodded. 'Wet old day. Soft rain falling hard. You must have seen the shotgun. Who was holding it?'

Father Jerry closed his eyes. 'I don't think I can remember anything that will be useful to you.'

'I'll be the judge of that.' Callaghan grunted and turned to the file of papers on his desk. 'Mrs Brogan gave a very passable account of herself to my sergeant. An animal dead and a threat to the whole herd, God help us. Hot words. Thady likely with drink taken. Yes, you can see it unfold. She grabs for the gun to stop more harm and he doesn't give it up lightly. The man for all his youth – sure, he's only the same ages as ourselves – unsteady on his feet, the mother ranting at him. A struggle. A shot goes off and the old woman, God help us, watches her son die.' The inspector raised his head again to fix his genial blue eyes on Father Jerry. 'But I have a problem.'

'What's that?'

'I don't believe a word of it.'

The smile was gone. Father Jerry realized that a boy from the riverbanks had to be good to rise this far.

'Have you seen your aunt's hands recently? My sergeant doubts she could hold a gun, let alone fire one. And what's a strong lad like Seamus doing all the time while his grandmother is wrestling with her hulk of a son: standing by with his mouth open?' The inspector rose from his chair and perched on the edge of the desk. His voice dropped. 'You gave the man the last rites, Father. You saw his face. That shot didn't go off tight to his body in a fight'. His voice was almost a whisper now and he was bending over close to Jerry's ear. 'It was aimed.'

The policeman got up and walked back to his side of the desk.

'It's hard to kill a man with a small bore. Shot in the belly Thady would be in Tralee General. Even in the neck he'd live long enough to tell you his sins, that's for sure.' He tapped his forehead. 'Someone looked along the length of the barrel and shot him. It was no accident. Tell me, Father, who was holding the gun?'

Father Jerry stared at the floor. 'I've no more to say.' He spoke with more confidence than he felt. 'Can I take Seamus home?' He was surprised when he saw the brief nod. After everything that had been said, he almost imagined that the boy was about to taken away in handcuffs.

'As long as he doesn't think about going anywhere. Same goes for the grandmother, of course, but I'd be more upset if I saw Seamus catching the train for Dun Laoghaire. Or indeed yourself. Sorry, Father but I think we'll need to talk again.'

'Me?'

'You're an important man. Every blackguard in Kerry has heard of Father Jerry Brogan. And now you're an important witness. Someone did something in that field, Father, and that something has consequences. A price has to be to paid. We're in the same business really. Getting poor sinners to face the consequences.' The inspector walked Father Jerry to the door. 'You can tell Mrs Brogan she can bury her son. The dead can't tell us any more than we know already.'

Father Jerry thought he was free but the inspector had one final thing to say as he walked down the corridor towards the cells. 'Any jury would be understanding to a lad like Seamus. He should know that and you should tell him.'

Father Jerry and Seamus drove back to Farran in silence. The priest glanced at Seamus' expressionless face in the mirror and just before the Brogan farmhouse he pulled over on to the soft verge.

'Why are we stopping?'

'Because I thought there might be something you want to say to me.'

'Confession, do you mean?'

'A chat, confession, whatever you want.' Father Jerry felt for the purple stole he kept in his pocket and waited. Seamus lowered his head and a thick lock of hair fell in front of his eyes. He started to scuff the rubber mat on the car's floor. He's just a boy, thought Father Jerry, just a boy.

'I don't know,' Seamus began. There was a catch in his voice. 'I've never done it in the open. You know, with a priest seeing me and all.' His chin was now almost digging into his chest.

'Don't worry about it. See that bit of hedge there, in front of us? You stare at that and I'll stare at it too. We won't see each other at all.'

Seamus nodded.

'Forgive me, Father, for I have sinned.'

Father Jerry took out the stole, kissed the gold keys of Papal authority embroidered on one end, and placed it around his neck. He waited and slowly, very slowly, Seamus began to speak.

Sixty-Eight

From the kitchen door Cathleen could see Jerry walking among the moss-covered apple trees in the thin strip of orchard that stretched from hen house to hay barn.

'Meet me,' he had whispered, as she cleared the supper plates and scraped the remains of thick cut slices of ham into the dog's bowl. 'Please,' he'd added, as if she needed persuading.

Maeve was in a red-eyed trance. It hurt Cathleen to watch her sister-in-law like this. It hurt her too that no one was talking. Grandmother and grandson moved around each other like circling cats.

They were all waiting. Would the police or the bank move against them first? It would happen sometime and that sometime had to be soon. They all knew it and still no one was talking.

Cathleen balanced a bowl of washing on her hip and walked out through grass that had been allowed to grow too long. My alibi, she thought, and looked down at the children's clothes. No one could see from the house that they were already dry as a bone.

She passed an old car tyre swinging from a tall elm at the edge of the orchard. It moved as she touched its warm surface and she heard a twig break. Jerry was behind her. She swung around, hitting him in the stomach with the bowl and spilling half its contents. Their heads almost collided as they both made a grab for the washing and she noticed he needed a shave. It was a relief to be near him but she longed to reach out and feel the roughness of his chin, to have his arms around her.

'I've missed you,' he said quietly. 'We're in the same room and I miss you. I'm sitting down to dinner right next to you. Our plates touch, for God's sake. You stretch out for the salt and I can breath you in and I'm still missing you.'

'Good.' She straightened up. 'That's what you're supposed to do.'

He smiled wearily and pressed a hand to his forehead. 'This place is grinding me down. I'm losing all sense of who I am. Of what I am.' Cathleen bit her lip and waited. 'I used to be so certain.' He shrugged. 'I don't know what to do any more.'

'This is about us?'

'No!' His head shot up in alarm. 'No, no, don't ever think that. You're the only person I can talk to. Whatever I'm doing. Wherever I am. Remember?' She nodded and waited again. He had moved around and his back was now to the sun so she couldn't see the expression on his face.

'I could send Seamus to jail.'

'How?'

'Well, there's the gun for one thing. I'm almost certain it was in Seamus' hand when I ran into the field. I know my aunt had it afterwards but . . .'

'What did you tell the Garda?'

'Come on, I'm Irish.' His tone was mocking. 'If the eleventh commandment is don't get caught, then the twelfth must be don't tell. It's an instinct we're all born with: I said I didn't remember.'

'And do you?'

'I think I do, but you're right. I couldn't send anyone to jail on what I *thought* I saw. Not that alone.'

'You've answered yourself. There's nothing you know for certain unless . . . Oh God, Jerry.' Cathleen stood in front of him, suddenly aware of where their conversation was leading. Her hand flew to his mouth. 'Please, no more. Don't say another word.'

'It's a sin to let the old woman take the blame. She was like a mother to me when I needed mothering. The guards are going to make someone pay . . .'

'Stop it, Jerry. I don't want to hear any more.'

'I thought I could tell you anything.'

'Not this.' Cathleen turned away 'You'll never forgive me if I let you tell me this.'

Jerry frowned as he followed her with his eyes. She was dropping clothes out of the basket and not stopping to pick them up. He felt cheated and angry. What did that last remark mean?

The knowledge hit him like one of Thady's vicious kicks. She knew there's only one way he could be certain about Seamus' guilt and he'd come close to blurting it out.

Priests die rather than break the seal of the confessional. Nothing justified it, not even saving a life. Sin was too small a word for it and the penalty was too big even to contemplate: excommunication. Automatic. Final. *Latae sententiae.* Only the Pope could break it and only then after the priest had served years of penance in a monastery. Had his passion for Cathleen brought him to the brink of that? She thought so. She ran away rather than let him inch closer to it.

He looked around at the hedges of hawthorn and wild blackberries. Somewhere far away, two fields at least, maybe three, a dog was barking and he could just make out the low throaty complaint of the herd returning home. These were the last days. Nothing would ever be the same again. He knew now that he loved the right woman, but what right did he have to love anyone?

Sixty-Nine

There was heat in the air on the day of the funeral. The sky was a grey tarpaulin pulled tight over the valley and the sun a sullen, hazy ball.

'Very un-Irish weather,' complained Father Jerry, fingering his collar as he stood up to look out the kitchen window.

Cathleen could see he was nervous. His hands had made small choppy movements at breakfast as he moved the black pudding and rashers of bacon around his plate.

Thady's body had left the police mortuary that morning and was now resting in front of the altar at the village church. Father Jerry had been down once already to check that everything was in order. It was a break with tradition but nothing about Thady's funeral would be traditional.

Cathleen wondered how many would come. In the normal course of things the countryside around would have emptied itself into the church to pay their respects. Would they stay away now because of what had happened? Or come in their hundreds because of what had happened? She couldn't decide which was worse.

Cathleen looked around as she entered the church. The pews were filling up. It seemed every family in the vicinity had sent at least one representative. Farran was doing its duty.

Maeve was holding on tightly to her mother's arm as they walked up the aisle to the front pew. Seamus walked a little behind, head bowed.

Father Jerry was distracted on the altar, as if his mind was elsewhere. His sermon, usually so expansive, was short and subdued. Cathleen had seen the notes he had made, full of crossings out and amendments, and knew that he had abandoned most of what he had intended to say.

'We all knew Thady Brogan,' he began. 'And whatever our personal relationship with him was like, we regret his death and the manner of his dying.' Father's Jerry's eyes were fixed on the back wall of the church.

'I have known him all my life and I cannot tell you I understood him or the things that troubled him. But he is going where he will be understood, where God's love can wash over him and there is no more pain or suffering.'

'Unless he's gone to the other place.'

The coarse whisper carried clearly to the front pew and Cathleen could see Grandma Brogan's arthritic fingers clutch her rosary beads tighter.

And then it was over. Father Jerry had no more to say and the rest of the Mass was conducted with spare economy. Within minutes of the final blessing Cathleen and her daughters were in the graveyard.

Seamus was standing a little apart from the rest of the family and Cathleen felt he looked even younger wearing the suit she had sent over that first Christmas when her mother was nagging her to get rid of all Mick's clothes. That morning he had sought her out to ask again if he could stay with her in London.

'I'll be over just as soon as the guards let me.' He paused. 'If they ever do.'

'Have you talked to your mother?'

He grimaced. 'No, she hasn't mentioned it because she's scared what I'll say and I haven't because . . .' He shrugged. 'I want to be gone.'

As she stood in the graveyard, Cathleen found her anger towards Thady mounting. She had found a scratch on Geraldine's arm that morning and she wanted to rail at her brother-in-law for spreading his misery so wide. Their suitcases were in the hired car. They were going to the station straight from the graveyard.

Cathleen was holding Anna's hand when the first trowel of soil clattered on to the coffin and she felt her daughter flinch. They both remembered that sound and Cathleen glanced over at her mother-in-law. How can she bear burying two sons? Because there was still Seamus. That was the only way she could bear it, knowing he was still free to go on.

She turned her head to look for him and saw that he was behind her, a little distant from the main body of mourners but not alone. In ones and twos, man after man was detaching himself from his own family, or knot of friends, to stand by Seamus and then move away again. She recognized many from church on Sunday, from outside the Jehovah's house and the dance at Maeve's house last summer.

The Yank was the first, and he stood in front of Seamus and offered the boy a cigarette. It was the first of many he was offered that day, although they all knew that he didn't smoke. It was the offer that was important.

Then each man moved to Maeve and Grandma Brogan.

'Sorry for your trouble.'

They came to her next. She was included in the circle of bereavement and the familiar phrase never sounded more appropriate.

The first drops of rain fell as the coffin was lowered into the grave. There was no thunder or lightning, just heavy raindrops that fell from a sky bruised with dark clouds.

'Fat rain!' the Yank announced.

Some laughed but they soon stopped laughing and charged back to their cars for shelter as the rain made mud out of paths and forced the sides of the newly dug grave to cave in on top of the coffin.

'He's burying himself,' commented one man, nodding in the direction of the grave, as he hurried past Cathleen, pulling his cap down over his eyes. 'He wouldn't trust us to do the job.'

'Aye,' mumbled his companion. 'It's Thady Brogan weather right enough.'

★   ★   ★

The Killarney lakes lay cold and beautiful beneath the mountains. I should have brought Cathleen here, thought Father Jerry as he drove past on his way to meet the bishop. It was three days since she and the children had left and he felt her absence as something physical, like a weight he was carrying. She would have loved it here.

And she would have given him courage. He wasn't sure why he had been summoned.

The bishop's handshake was perfunctory and the cup of tea that arrived at Father Jerry's elbow tepid and metallic tasting, brewed too long in the pot.

'You're a rising star.' The bishop's opening statement sounded more like an accusation. 'And rising stars can't afford the whiff of a scandal.'

'Not a sniff of the brown stuff,' agreed the stocky, mohair-suited man sitting beside him.

Father Jerry swallowed and said nothing. The two men were looking at him, but he couldn't think of anything to say. He disliked their man-of-the-world vulgarity.

Outside, past the heavy velvet curtains and leaded windows, the sun had broken out from its covering of clouds. I am a good priest, he told himself. Whatever they say, I'm a better priest because of Cathleen. Sitting here, in front of these two men, he needed that idea to sustain him, but his mind flashed back to the orchard. He had come close to telling her things that no one should hear. Even this bishop shouldn't have been able to prise those words from his lips.

A better priest?

He looked at his shoes. Yes, he thought. Yes. It was a test of the pair of them and they had passed.

'You know Tomo Murphy?' The bishop's gritty voice interrupted his thoughts as he gestured at the man beside him. Father Jerry shook his head.

'You've been away too long. The Taoiseach's right-hand man.'

'Ah, now I wouldn't be laying claim to that,' the politician wheezed, his heavy jowls covered in a mesh of broken thread veins.

The bishop frowned. 'I've been misinformed then, and so have all the Dublin papers.' The words were a rattle of irritation. 'In any case you're well aware of the Brogan family's troubles? Yes? Right then, we all know where we are.'

'It's a sad business.' The politician leaned forward; his eyes squeezed half shut. 'You and your family —' he tapped his chest for greater emphasis — 'I feel for you here.'

Father Jerry relaxed. This was going to be all right: it was about Thady. It was about the farm. It wasn't about the woman he loved.

'I realize that after the newspaper report people will be aware . . .' began Father Jerry.

'Aware! It's the talk of the county and it'll be the talk of the country if we don't put a lid on it.' The bishop looked over the top of his glasses. 'A dead body and a farm broken up! There's many that will think one is as bad as the other.' He sniffed.

'The Gardai . . .' Father Jerry began and trailed off. He didn't know what he was going to say.

Tomo Murphy leant forward. 'The bank had no business lending to a man like your cousin, none at all.'

'Arah.' The bishop waved his hand impatiently. 'Why wouldn't they? You can't ask a bank not to act like a bank.'

'All the same, it's the work of gombeens and I speak for the common people when I say it. What say you, Father?'

'It's terrible,' Father Jerry agreed. 'My aunt will lose her home.'

The bishop looked across at the politician and then back at Father Jerry. 'And how is your aunt bearing up under all this?'

'As well as could be expected, I suppose,' Father Jerry added. Something was happening here, he thought; something that he couldn't quite grasp.

'But not well.' Tomo Murphy jumped in. 'Let me say there's great sympathy for her here.' He touched his own chest again. 'She reminds me of my own dear mother. Dying was the only bad thing that woman ever did.' He sighed heavily. 'You won't think me a terrible man, Father Brogan, if I say my mother was a saint.'

'No, of course not.'

'And I've heard many fine things about your aunt, the poor creature.'

'Tell me, Brogan —' there was a different tone in the bishop's voice — 'did you not come into a substantial inheritance when your father died?'

'Well, I suppose . . .'

'We priests don't have a vow of poverty so let's have no supposes here.'

Father Jerry hesitated. 'I don't know about substantial though.'

'Let me ask you frankly what you did with it?'

'Well, not much. There was the Maynooth Missions to China . . .'

The bishop looked up sharply. 'You're not telling me that you've given it away. You're not telling me that?'

'No, some, of course. But really no, not as much as I should have.'

'And it's in the bank, I suppose,' Tomo Murphy cut in. 'The very same bank that made such a disgrace out of lending to Thady Brogan. Now then, now then . . .' He turned to the bishop. 'Wouldn't you see a certain rightness in all this?'

Father Jerry suddenly realized what the two men had in mind.

'Land!' Tomo Murphy's fist thumped the table. 'Irish land. What finer investment could there be?'

'Buy the farm, you mean, or pay off the debt? I don't have that kind of money. My father had a pharmacy, not a palace.'

'All things are possible.' The bishop put his fingertips together. 'You've made a name for yourself in England.'

'You have, Father, you have,' the politician agreed. 'And the common people respect you for it. I expect vocations to soar.'

'It would be a pity for anything to spoil your advancement,' the bishop murmured.

'I don't understand how it can be done.' Father Jerry's voice was quiet.

'It can be done.' Tomo Murphy beamed at him. 'It's a poor farm, farmed poorly.' He lowered his voice as if they were in danger of being overheard. 'God have mercy on Thady Brogan's soul but these things have to be said. It won't fetch market value.'

'Why wouldn't it?' Father Jerry shifted in his chair. 'It's a good farm for all Thady didn't work it well enough. It was a good farm in his father's day. There's plenty that would bid for it.'

'I don't think so.' Murphy shook his head.

'No?'

'I think we could guarantee the bank that, in fact, there would be no bidders if it came on the open market.' The bishop's tone was dry.

'When the Church and the state come together –' the politician rubbed his hands together – 'who is to resist us?'

'But first loose ends have be tidied.' The bishop looked up. 'The old mother, God help her, claims responsibility and that's a tidy explanation, especially as it avoids you having anything more to do with the Gardai. From now on, the only time you go near a police station is when you're asked to bless a new cell. Do you understand?'

'And Inspector Callaghan?' Father Jerry swallowed. 'Does he want tidiness?'

'He wants promotion and I think he'll find that the two are the same thing.'

'What will happen to my aunt?'

'Why the poor woman, her mind must be addled with grief. Gethsemane will do her the world of good.'

Of course, thought Father Jerry, Gethsemane House, the county mental home.

'The Gardai might proceed against her,' the bishop continued. 'They must make their own decision. I'm no lawyer, negligence perhaps, or a manslaughter charge but I think we can rest easy that Callaghan won't rush proceedings when his elderly defendant is secure in Gethsemane. We can let the Almighty be her judge and jury.'

'Now, if we've resolved the present, we must look to your future.' The bishop smiled. 'And you have a very big future.'

He sat back and listened. As the bishop mapped out his plans, Father Jerry was making his own decisions. Once this is over my future is with Cathleen. I don't want us ever to be apart again.

'That's it?' Seamus looked up at the priest. 'I'm to stay here, while she goes into that awful place. All decided is it?'

'Yes, all decided.' Grandma Brogan's voice was firm. 'We have much to thank you for, Father. I know it and Seamus will know it by and by.'

'How can you talk like that.' Seamus turned away. 'And you? He threw the words bitterly at the priest. 'How could you let it happen?'

'Because not letting it happen seemed worse.' Father Jerry looked across at the old woman, sitting tall and straight at the other end of the kitchen table 'Can you forgive me?'

'Of course. The farm's safe and Seamus' safe. I had stopped praying for both but you came and saved us.'

The boy stood up between them. The anger had faded from his face. 'We're both trapped then.'

Grandma Brogan seized her grandson by the shoulders and forced him to look at her. 'You'll have a ton of work to do every

day of the year, but the farm! Seamus you've got the farm and
no uncle fighting with you over every blade of grass.'

He hung his head. 'But you . . .'

'I'll be grand. This is the best that could be done.'

She turned to Father Jerry. 'And you can wipe that hangdog,
guilty look from your face, Jerry. Yes, it was Seamus' bullet that
killed Thady, but I'm the one who told him to shoot.'

Seventy

C athleen and the girls were back in London a week before
the first letter from Father Jerry arrived

She picked up the envelope from the hall mat as they were
leaving for school and imagined him smoothing out Grandma
Brogan's blue notepaper, the fountain pen inking his fingers.

'Mummy! What are you doing?' Anna tugged at her. 'We're
going to be late.'

'Sorry, I was miles away.'

'You mustn't do that.' Geraldine frowned. 'You have to be here
with us.'

Cathleen forced herself to wait until she had taken the girls to
school. Whatever it says, she thought, I mustn't be disappointed.
He won't have said all the things I want him to say. How can he,
when I don't know what they are myself. What's the best thing
he could say? Perhaps that he's found a desert island somewhere,
and she smiled at the thought of a golden beach littered with
gramophone records from the Home Service radio programme.

She slit open the envelope and four pages spilled out. Dear
Cathleen. Only 'dear', she thought. If I wrote to the parish priest
I'd call him 'dear'. She scanned the rest of the letter quickly.

Only the last lines were hers.

> I am lonely for you. Whatever I'm doing. Wherever I am.
> When my mind should be on the business in hand I think
> of you, and what you would say if you were here. If I've

done wrong I hope you will forgive me but we have so
much to talk about.

She hurried back through the letter, trying to make sense of it.
When she read every last word she studied the calendar above
the sink. This would be the second morning that kind, brave, old
Grandma Brogan had woken up in Gethsemane. She thought of
her home-cut hair and the set of rosary beads gripped in her
sandpaper hands.

Something else hadn't made sense on the first reading. Jerry
had been to see the bank manager three times and he hoped that
he would never have to go inside a bank again. She read this
page of the letter twice before understanding. That he had a
fortune was hard enough to take in – it had to be a fortune to
clear the mortgage – but that he had spent it on the farm was
harder still.

Cathleen remembered the Yank's words on her first day in
Farran. Other places were called after the church on the hill or
the river that ran through it, but Farran just meant land. Getting
land was like winning a war, losing land was murder. Was holding
on to it a holy duty?

Cathleen held the letter to the side of her face. What could we
have done with that fortune, Jerry? What kind of desert island could
we have got for ourselves? When she got up she noticed the two
new pillows she had bought the day before in Chapel Market. They
were for Seamus' bed. He wouldn't be needing them now.

If Mary hadn't decided to sleep over it wouldn't have occurred
to Cathleen to meet the train. They had been playing cards on
the Saturday night. Aude was there in another new outfit and
she had brought a set of fashion magazines with her. She tapped
the cover of one.

'I'm getting very bored at Alibone's. It's just not stretching me
any more. I was thinking I might get a job here. *Vogue's* much
more my style.'

Mary laid down her cards. 'Are you going to leave? Because
if you are, will you have a word? Will you? I can't bear it at
Crawford's any more. And the teacher says that my Pitman's the
best in the class so I'll have a good reference.'

Cathleen happened to look up at that moment and saw the
expression on Aude's face. It would have been better for Mary

if she hadn't mentioned the teacher's high opinion. Aude had given up night school months ago, declaring she was far too busy.

The moment passed and Aude was all smiles again. 'Dear heart, I was only thinking.' She shivered theatrically. 'I wonder if you'd jump into my grave so quick. Anyway, Uncle says he doesn't know what he would do without me so I'm not sure I could leave the poor poppet in the lurch.' She flicked through the magazine. 'After all, you can't get my experience in classes.'

After Aude left, Mary grabbed a blanket and made a bed for herself on the sofa without asking.

'You don't mind, do you?'

Cathleen nodded and turned away. There was no privacy. If it wasn't her family, it was the neighbours listening to the feet on the stairs and Reg thinking that the sweet jars hid his lookout post on St John's Street. There was no space for Jerry and her. They had been lucky to snatch a few golden days together but if they wanted a future it had to be away from everything they knew. But Mary staying overnight meant she could leave the children for an hour or so in the morning. Jerry was coming back on the early train. She pictured him on the platform, cold and lonely in the grey light of a London dawn.

'If it's all right with you, I'll go to first Mass. It's Thady's Month's Mind and I thought I might if you're here. I'll just slip out.'

'Is it really a month since that old so-and-so died? I'd be dancing in the street if he was my brother-in-law, not praying for him. Do what you like, just don't wake me.'

It was another lie to add to the rest. She would be there as the train pulled in and he'd have to wipe the sleep from his eyes before he could trust what he was seeing. The few minutes they'd have together would be enough to warm them for the rest of the week.

'Must be someone special to be out this early,' said a porter at Euston Station, grinning at her.

She didn't reply, although she suspected the look on her face said enough, because he went away laughing. Hugging her coat around her, she pulled back her hair. She must remember to wash her face before going home. Mary was bound to raise an eyebrow: early morning Mass and make-up didn't go together.

A pigeon landed near her foot and she wondered if the bird was trapped inside the station forever and if the glass roof was now its sky. She heard the rhythmic rattle first and then smelt the smoke as soft flakes of soot fell on her coat. The Holyhead train was steaming in. A flock of startled pigeons flew up into the air as the porter tipped Cathleen off his cart with a grin.

There were so many people, slamming doors and rushing, far more than she had expected, and she cursed herself for not staying near the barrier. In this crush she might easily miss him. She saw a man in a dark coat near the front of the train and started to run in his direction when she heard a laugh from behind. She would have known it anywhere but she still couldn't see him. A woman with three tearful children moved out of the way and suddenly there he was, striding down the platform with his head flung back. He was flanked on either side by a bevy of priests that he must have met on the boat, laughing and making them laugh. It was a posse of smiles and genial black slappings. One short-legged, round-bellied cleric at the back was almost skipping in his effort to keep up.

Cathleen slid into the shadows, moving from pillar to pillar on the other side of the platform in the hope that they would go their separate ways at the barrier, but no, they seemed to be travelling as a clump. One did peel away though: an exuberant clapper of backs with iron-coloured hair and an American accent.

'Chancing into you sure was a piece of luck, Brogan. You took miles off that journey.' There was more laughter and place names were flung about – Paddington, Austin, Drogheda – and promises to meet up. It was at that moment, while he was shaking hands, that Father Jerry glanced across the platform and his eyes met Cathleen's.

He froze, then looked away. When he looked back he had lost some of his colour. With a small, almost imperceptible movement he shook his head.

Cathleen moved back into the shadows and counted to ten before walking with painful slowness back to the barrier. It was long enough. When she looked around the knot of dark-suited men had vanished. The porter who had given her a seat earlier saluted as she walked past.

'Lover boy not turn up?'

'No, he didn't.' She tried to smile but it was hard and the effort pulled her mouth to one side. It was hard to shake off the look in Jerry's eyes. She expected him to be startled, shocked even, but she wasn't prepared to see his fear.

*   *   *

The telephone was ringing when she opened the door to the shop. Reg was at the counter but he didn't move to get it. 'That's your priest, I expect. He's been on twice already this morning.'

Cathleen was blushing as she picked up the receiver. Yes, she understood it was difficult. It didn't matter. She understood completely. He was repeating himself and talking so fast and so loudly she was scared Reg would hear both sides of the conversation. Yes, he would be around just as soon as he could, but not before Sunday. Sunday dinner, then? Yes, Sunday.

'We have a lot to talk about.'

She put the receiver back before turning around.

'You never used to take personal calls.' Reg sniffed when Cathleen put the phone down.

'I know,' Cathleen said, flustered. 'It won't happen again . . .'

'Oh, it's all right. Only it is there for business. Suppliers might want to get through.'

Cathleen nodded. They both knew that wasn't true.

'And then there's my customers,' Reg continued. 'They rely on the phone being here in an emergency. On me taking messages.'

Cathleen turned away. 'That's not something I'm likely to forget.'

'No, of course not.' It was Reg's turn to be embarrassed. 'I shouldn't have said anything. Was it important? What Father Brogan wanted?'

'No,' said Cathleen. 'Not important to anyone else.'

Seventy-One

K itty and Mary invited themselves over when they heard that Father Jerry was back.

'You wouldn't deny us,' Mary said with a grin. 'Come on, Cathleen, you have him to yourself all the time!'

Cathleen looked from her mother to her sister. Although she longed to make an excuse, there was no way she could say no. Jerry had his cluster of priests and she had a family that stuck like glue. If they didn't work hard to stop it, their lives would pull them apart.

Ireland had helped her to make the only decision she could. Seeing him vulnerable, wracked by doubts like any ordinary man, made her even more certain. He loved her, she knew that now, but it was only in Ireland that she realized he needed her too. Together they could be strong and they were going to need every ounce of strength if they were to face the future together.

'All right if Aude pops around after?' Mary didn't usually bother to ask. 'Only I might have a bit of news and I won't have seen her all week.'

'You've got it?' Kitty spun around, like a cat.

'I don't know, don't make a fuss,' said Mary crossly. 'They've asked to see me again, that's all. So, maybe I've found a way out of Crawford's.' She shrugged and tried to looked casual. 'I'll let you know on Sunday.'

Cathleen guessed from the look on her mother's face that the new job had nothing to do with Alibone corsets.

The doorbell rang and the girls ran downstairs to answer it.

'It's the father,' Anna called out and Cathleen sighed with relief. She hoped he would be early and here he was a good two hours before the dinner would be ready. He must have realized that this would be their only chance to be alone. The sitting-room door on the floor below opened and closed and she assumed that the girls had gone back to playing records, leaving him to make his own way up. Sure enough, she could hear Chubby Checker and guessed that her daughters were already twisting away in their pleated Sunday best.

Her back was to the kitchen door as it swung open.

'Jerry, I've missed you so much.' She didn't want to spoil it by turning around too soon. First, he would kiss her neck and then he would hold her and tell her the things she hadn't heard in a month. There was flour on her hands and she would have to be careful not to touch him.

'Jerry?' No response.

She could hear the floorboard creaking under his weight, but he hadn't moved. What could be so bad that he had to hold back like this: more news from Ireland?

Cathleen swung round and looked straight into the ageing face of the parish priest.

'What's that?' He was feigning a deafness Cathleen was sure he didn't have. 'You were expecting someone else, I suppose, so I won't keep you. Only if you were seeing Father Jerry, ah Father Brogan that is, if you were seeing him today – and you're probably not, although I heard he was back – but if you were, you could ask him to call in at the presbytery on his way home. There's a favour I'm after needing.'

The priest looked around the kitchen and blinked at the sunlight streaming through the window. 'But you're probably not. Seeing him. Or he's busy, I expect, so it doesn't matter, but if you do.'

'Yes, Father.'

'Yes, yes,' said the old man absently. 'I'll be on my way so.'

Cathleen wiped her hands and showed him out. As she passed the sitting-room door on her way back to the kitchen, she noticed that Adam Faith had replaced Chubby Checker on the record player. 'What do you want if you don't want money? What do you want if you don't want gold?' Both girls shouted the last word of the last line. 'Bye-bee.' Listening to them through the door, Cathleen wished she could join in their laughter. I've cried too much, I can't cry over this, she told herself, but the rabbit twitching of the parish priest's mouth stayed with her. It will always be like this.

Father Jerry was so late that Cathleen wondered if he was coming at all.

'You're going to have to serve up soon,' Kitty announced. 'Otherwise it won't be fit to eat.'

Cathleen gave in and had just carried down the last tureen of vegetables to the sitting room when the bell rang. The girls scooted down to open the front door and their chatter and squeals could be heard all over the house.

'Look, he's bought us more sweets,' said Anna.

'And you've started eating them already,' said Cathleen, slamming down the peas on the table.

'My fault,' murmured Father Jerry. 'I didn't think.'

'I know that.' Cathleen glared, as she waved him towards the seat at the head of the table.

'Shhh, ordered Kitty. 'You can't be talking to a priest like that!' She turned towards Father Jerry. 'Don't mind our Cathleen. She always was contrary.'

'Mother!'

Father Jerry's smile broke into a laugh, but his eyes told Cathleen to be careful. There are traps for me here, in my own home. I can't be too familiar with a priest. He's trying to get through this the same as I am, she thought catching his eye again, but there's danger in everything we do.

She was shocked when he put his coat on while the plates were still on the table. Eating and running, he called it, and apologized, but he was expecting a telephone call back at the Diocesan House. As she got up to show him out, she thought of the way he looked at Euston station and decided not to mention the parish priest's visit.

'Forgive me,' he whispered outside the sitting-room door. ' I have to go.' She held her face up to be kissed and felt his lips high on her forehead, near her hairline. 'We'll talk soon.' She felt herself dismissed.

Suddenly he was beside her again. His mouth on hers: hard and hungry. His coat fell open and she was enclosed by it. He broke away and twisted her around so that he could see her face under the bare bulb in the hall.

'I told myself I wasn't going to do this. I really thought I could leave without this.' He kissed her again, softly this time.

'When? When can I see you?'

'Soon. Tomorrow night, maybe. Or the next night. Soon.' He turned to leave. 'I have news.' He nodded towards the sitting-room door. 'I was dying to say something in there but . . .' He shook his head at the impossibility of it. 'I have so much to tell.'

He was running down the stairs now and Cathleen had to lean over the banister. 'Good news? At least tell me if it's good news?'

'For us? It's the best news.' The front door slammed.

Seventy-Two

W hen Cathleen stepped back into the sitting room to clear the rest of the table, she realized that a pile of plates had already been taken up to the kitchen. She looked from her mother to her sister. Had one of them heard? Had one of them seen? Kitty was at the window, drawing the curtains.

'Aude's just got off the bus.'

'Good.' Cathleen said it with real relish. She couldn't think of a better way of taking her mind off what Jerry wanted to say.

As soon as Aude was through the door, Kitty started.

'Sit down, girl, you look tired out. Hard week at work?'

Aude was taken aback. This was not Kitty's usual greeting. Cathleen felt a sudden cramping guilt as she admired Aude's new candy-striped tunic and noted the carefully applied frosted lipstick. She gets dressed up to come here. Mary at least had the Palais de Danse on Friday nights and the young lads whistling after her in Chapel Market on weekdays. And then there was Mass on Sunday mornings. More than once her young sister had got a date on her way back from communion.

Aude joined in none of these activities. The church, of course, was out of bounds, but the dance halls too were avoided. 'Such a silly crowd,' she'd explained more than once and, after the Campaign dance in the school hall, she had refused all invitations to attend Irish functions. 'Very amusing but a bit too yokel for me.' Cathleen remembered Aude sitting by herself while everyone else was on their feet. She wondered if there was a well of loneliness hiding behind her air of bored sophistication.

'Very busy at work, are you?' Kitty was enjoying herself. 'Need another pair of hands? Any openings for our Mary?'

'Mum!' Mary had suddenly woken up to her mother's baiting tone. 'Never mind her. It's just that I've a bit of news.'

'Oh yes?' Aude's smile was polished.

'I'm out of Crawford's at last. I've a new job starting tomorrow.'

Aude stiffened slightly but the tight smile remained in place. 'Oh darling, I am *so* pleased for you. Where?'

'It's for a magazine company.'

'Tell her which one. Go on,' said Kitty.

'*Women and Girl*, you know the one?'

'Lovely. Gone a bit downhill lately, hasn't it?' Aude yawned. 'I'm told nowadays old ladies buy it for the knitting patterns. Do you get it, Mrs C?'

'It's still better than typing in a knicker factory.'

Kitty delivered the line she'd been saving up with the finesse of a three card brag player who had just turned over the third three.

Aude didn't saying anything but started to root in her handbag.

'I don't know why, but that reminds me, I've had the photos

of Anna's big day developed.' The children looked up and they all gathered around.

Truce, thought Cathleen as she was handed a snap of Geraldine squinting in the sun.

She was wrong.

'Now, here's a little oddity. I was just snapping away you know, snap, snap, snap. Really I don't have a clue and not a thought in my head but I've captured something quiet interesting here.'

She handed the photograph to Cathleen first. There she was in profile standing by a table, bread knife in one hand. There was Father Jerry also in profile. They were smiling, looking at each other and they were holding hands.

Kitty was looking over her shoulder. Cathleen heard a sharp intake of breath, but her mother's voice sounded matter-of-fact. 'I've seen one like this before. A double what's-it. Two photographs in one. That's what it is.'

'I expect you're right, Mrs C.' Aude's smile grew wider. She had made a complete recovery from the news about Mary's job. 'There's always an explanation for these things. Only it's a new camera and it doesn't let you take a snap unless you wind it on. Isn't it clever?'

Mary was demanding to see now, had her hand out to take the photograph. She was passing them on to Anna and Geraldine who were sitting on the sofa studying each one carefully.

Mary will know, thought Cathleen. And my mother already knows. My life is about to crash and there's nothing I can do about it. She turned away, unable to face them.

Kitty was moaning softly, her dentures moving backward and forward in her mouth. Mary's hand was still outstretched but she dropped it as her mother struggled to reach an armchair.

'Whatever's wrong with you?'

Kitty was breathing rapidly now, her eyes darting around the room.

'A hot flush,' she croaked. 'This is a bad one, I've put on a brave face but I suffer terrible with them. Jaysus.' She raised herself up. 'A sup of something for pity's sake, that cup of cold tea will do fine. Give it here.'

She spilled it. Her hand was shaking so much it was inevitable. More went on Kitty's skirt than in her mouth but most splashed on to the photograph that she held in her hand.

'Holy Mother of God, see what I've done!' Kitty wiped the

back of her mouth with her hand. 'Let's see if I can dry it off.' A handkerchief came out before anyone could stop her. 'Nah, I'm making it worse. Aude, your picture's ruined.'

Cathleen glanced at her mother's face and looked away again, ashamed. *I'm reduced to this, a kind of farce.* Her mother and Aude were still sparring.

'Go on, give me the negatives and I'll have it reprinted for you.'

'Couldn't hear of it, Mrs C. I could always make a copy for you though.'

'Give it to me.' It was a test of wills, Kitty's hand outstretched in a claw.

Mary sighed. 'Oh give in, Aude. No one ever wins when she's in that mood.'

Cathleen turned away, as her mother clutched the strip of negatives that Aude had thrown over to her. If it wasn't for the children she'd tell her where she could put the negative.

Cathleen was even more certain that the decision she'd reached was the right one.

Kitty was quiet for the rest of the evening. Later when she and Mary were about to leave, had their coats on and were standing at the door, she opened her handbag.

'You see what I have here?'

The sisters looked at each other and nodded. They knew that their mother always kept her post office book near at hand.

'I just wanted to say,' Kitty continued, 'that I haven't got much, but there's enough, if one of you took it into your head to go away for whatever reason, whatever the cause.'

'Who's going away?' Mary wanted to know. 'The new job's only at Waterloo.'

'Please God, no one is going anywhere,' said Kitty crossly. 'I'm just saying *if*, that's all. I'm letting you know, that I have the train fare to visit.' Her handbag snapped shut. 'Whatever happens and wherever you go, I have my savings book.'

'And you won't let go?' Cathleen was looking directly at her mother.

'That's it.' Kitty's gaze never wavered. 'I might not like what you do. I might hate it. But I'll never let go.'

'That sounds like a threat,' said Mary.

Seventy-Three

It wasn't until Wednesday that Father Jerry drove into Robert's Row. He glanced at his watch and hoped that the girls would be asleep. Tonight he didn't want to share Cathleen with anyone.

The sitting-room light was on but was she alone? A neighbour let him in and he climbed the stairs quietly. Outside the door he hesitated. He had gone to confession the day before and hadn't realized how much he had given away until the other priest had spoken.

'There's a woman involved, isn't there? You haven't told me everything.' That had been enough to make him stop, but the Jesuit had persisted and he remembered what the old priest had said. 'Living without sex is easier the older you get. It's living without women that gets harder, living without a comfort of the mind.'

The sitting-room door opened to his knock and Cathleen was in front of him, holding him, and it was almost like the first night they were together. He felt again the conviction that had overwhelmed him when they first made love. *This isn't wrong. This can't be wrong.*

She said very little. Instead she drew him into the room. He could feel the pressure of her hands reaching up to his shoulder blades, and he rested his own on the small of her back. Their breathing was slow and in time with each other. They kissed. Tonight they would build their future together.

'Do you want to hear the news?' he whispered, touching her neck with his lips. She nodded, but first they kissed again. He tried to pull away, but she wouldn't let him. He kissed her forehead. She closed her eyes and he kissed her eyelids. 'My Cathleen. My love.' He was supposed to go through his whole life and never say those words.

'This feels so right.'

'Is that your news?' Cathleen held his hand and pulled him over to the sofa, laughing softly. 'I could have told you that.'

He began slowly, choosing every word with care. Cathleen had to understand what he was saying. Everything depended on her seeing the future he could see.

'There's a new life waiting for us. We just have to reach out and grab it. It's in Birmingham. I know it means leaving London, I know it means taking you away from everything you know.'

'That doesn't matter.' Cathleen sounded certain. 'Much better a fresh start for both of us. Birmingham, Alabama if you like. Birmingham anywhere, as long as it means we're together.'

Jerry closed his eyes. This was what he wanted to hear. 'I've been promised a fine house in Sutton Coldfield.' He knelt down beside her. 'Oh Cathleen, there's an acre of garden. Think of the girls playing in that. Can you picture them?'

'But I don't understand. Who's giving us a mansion?'

'I'm to start the campaign up there, make it a national thing, stretch it out, make it more than it is now. I'll be on the move a lot.'

He got to his feet. It was hard to judge Cathleen's expression. 'But I've been thinking that you might not want . . .' He turned around. 'I'll go either way with you on this, but I was thinking you might not want to move up there once you hear the other news.'

'Which is?'

'Hold on now, I want you first to have a good picture of Birmingham in your head. It's a grand place and good schools nearby. The girls would fit in very well, I'm thinking, but we wouldn't be there long. A year tops, and I would be away a good part of that year too. So, you might think it better not to disrupt them, when we would be going back home so soon.'

'Where's home?'

'This is our future. This is where we'll make our home. The bishop needs a new administrator. The present one retires in about a year and the post is mine. I'll be in South Kerry with my own establishment. It's God's own country down there, wild and beautiful. The salmon jumping out of the rivers into the frying pan.' He grinned. 'I love Farran but God did his best work in South Kerry. And there's more.'

'More? You have my head reeling with all the futures lined up in front of you.'

'Lined up in front of *us*.' Jerry's voice dropped. 'The bishop's a young man, a few summers over sixty. He was young when he was appointed but he has cancer. Diagnosed last spring and he's doing fine and it should stay that way for a good while yet.'

'He wants you to succeed him?'

'It's more a case of better me than the other eejits. And there's no guarantee of course, nothing written in stone.'

'But if it was known you had his blessing . . .'

'Exactly.'

'You'd make a great bishop, Jerry. You would. You would.'

'I don't know about that, but there's our future, Cathleen. There's our life. And it's not a bad one. The worst that can happen, the very worst, is that the bishop thing is a Will o' the Wisp that comes to nothing and we live it out in one of the best places on earth.'

'But Jerry, you've asked me to picture this future and I don't see myself in any of it. There's no place for me.'

He pulled Cathleen to her feet. 'Oh, but there is. This way we can always be together. Nothing will separate us again.' He held her face in his hands and kissed the scar above her eyebrow gently. 'Cathleen, you'll be my housekeeper.'

Seventy-Four

'You haven't said anything.' Jerry frowned. 'I know it's a lot to take in, but are there no questions you want answering? Nothing you want to say? I love you, Cathleen. You complete me.'

'I believe you.' Cathleen reached out to touch him. 'And I know how rare it is to feel like this. I loved one man, I never expected to love two.'

'Well then?'

'These weeks, these few precious weeks, I didn't want to think about anything but us. I didn't want a future. I just wanted what we had. And if I could have chosen I would have those moments for ever.' She shrugged. 'But you've laid a whole carpet of futures out in front of me.'

'And you hate it?'

'Oh, wouldn't it be easy if I hated it.' Cathleen swung away from him. 'I wish I hated it. I wish I hated the sound of the house in Birmingham and hated the thought of us two walking in the gardens. Don't you know how well I can imagine the times we'd have together? And the great work you would do!'

She turned to face him again.

'And I could play my part. Dear God, I'd be good at it.' She was angry now. 'And I know better than you what it means to be a priest's housekeeper. The butcher would save the best joints for me. Men in suits would tip their hats as I passed by and their wives would call me by my first name and invite me to tea.' She paused to catch her breath, to calm herself.

Father Jerry sat down again. 'You're not finished?'

'No.' She took another deep breath.

'Don't destroy us.' Father Jerry held her hand tight. 'Cathleen, whatever you do, don't destroy us.'

'I won't.' She shook free of him. 'But your future will.'

'It's a way of being together.'

'It's a lie. You could almost persuade me with the way you roll words together, but nothing could change that. I would make your bed and when no one was looking I would creep into it. But I'd have to make sure I was first up in the morning. I'd have to make sure that my girls didn't get sick in the night and come looking for me. Or a curate didn't catch a glimpse of me sliding out of your room.'

'It won't be easy, I know that. Every moment we've had together has been snatched from our other lives, but that doesn't dirty what we feel for each other. Our love isn't sordid. Remember that and fight for it, Cathleen. What I'm offering is a chance to grow old together.'

She moved away so he couldn't see her face and to make sure she couldn't see his. There was something twisting inside, some kind of fist that was yanking at her. 'Maybe I'd do it if it was just me. Maybe I'd kid myself that it was a price worth paying but it would be a trap for both of us. It wouldn't be long before I resented you. God Almighty, Jerry, I can feel it rising up inside me already. And it would only get worse.

'You don't even realize what you're asking. No friends – how could I get close to someone and have this great hole in my life that I couldn't talk about. I'm young. What if I got pregnant? What if I wanted your child?' She turned to face him. 'You might have an answer for all that. You might persuade me that somehow it would work, but there are two obstacles even you couldn't get over.'

'You're wrong. There's nothing we can't do if we love each other. What are these obstacles; I'll show you the way.'

'Can't you guess? Anna and Geraldine. I'd never let my daughters be part of that kind of life. You shouldn't even ask.' Cathleen lowered her head. 'Shame on you for asking. Shame on me.'

'Don't say that.' He was on his feet now, holding her by the shoulders. She was afraid that he might wake the girls, asleep in the next room. 'Don't tell me there's no hope.'

'There's hope.' Her breathing slowed. 'But we've broken the rules, Jerry.'

'So? You think the men behind closed doors don't break the rules when it suits? This Thady business has opened my eyes to that. The important thing is that we aren't breaking God's rules. I can't believe that what we're doing is a sin in heaven.'

'But we live here on earth. I say let's carry on breaking the rules. Let's turn our backs on the men behind closed doors. Leave the priesthood, Jerry. Live with me. Marry me. Be a father to my daughters, not a priest.'

'What would we live on? How would we live?' His voice sounded hollow.

'Like anyone else. You're an educated man. You could teach. You could do anything.'

'We'd be outcasts.'

'Together we could do anything, you said it yourself. And I don't think my mother would be so easy to escape from. I think she was trying to tell me that the other day.' Cathleen's heart was beating fast. 'We'll move away. You made Birmingham sound nice. We won't get the big house, of course, or the acre of garden, but maybe a couple of rooms. And, in time, a place of our own.' She reached out to him. 'It's an ordinary life. A good life. You could hold me in public and I could say your name and not be scared someone might hear me.'

'Cathleen.'

She could barely hear what he was saying, his head was down and it seemed as if his voice was about to break.

'Will you leave the priesthood, Jerry?'

He looked up. He was crying.

'I would, Cathleen. I would, but it won't leave me.'

Seventy-Five

It was the last Feis before Christmas and, although Kitty knew they would be coming home with medals, she wasn't taking any chances. Sitting next to Reg in the front row, she had wound one set of rosary beads around her hand while another dangled like a necklace underneath her cardigan.

Cathleen stood at the edge of the hall. She had just made a running repair on a seam that was in danger of coming apart. It would be the very last outing for the cream dancing dress, outgrown at last. She wasn't sorry: it was bought with too many tears for her to like it.

She heard the hall door open, heard the rattle of the security bar as it clanged closed, but didn't turn around. There would be plenty of others in the audience to give the late arrival a disapproving look.

'Hello Cathleen.'

She hadn't heard that voice in over a year. Suddenly she was in the car again, next to him, and she remembered the things that were said and the things that weren't. A lot had happened since he'd driven her to the airport.

'Hello, John.'

She turned to look into Tacit Donovan's face.

'I saw it advertised and I came on the chance.'

A mother of one of the dancers brushed by. 'I don't know what's going on. The judges are giving all the prizes to the Luton girls. I heard one has a niece who's a nun in Bedford . . .' She turned, noticing Tacit for the first time. 'Oh, it's yourself. Wasn't such a great show at Stroud Green last week, was it?'

Cathleen frowned and glanced up at Tacit.

'I've taken a few chances lately. This is the first one that's paid off.' Cathleen saw something shift in his face. 'You've changed parishes.'

It was a statement not a question. She nodded. They went to Mass at St John's now.

'We still live in the same place.' She meant it to be a light remark but it sounded more like an accusation.

'I know.'

He looked away and Cathleen knew that he'd waited outside Robert's Row, and gone away again without ringing the bell. Whatever he wanted to say, it was costing him a lot to say it.

'I was back home recently, to bury my mother, God bless her, and it set me thinking. I suppose what I'm saying is the things I was thinking have lead me here.'

She waited for him to say more, scared that if she were to interrupt now he may find it impossible to begin again. But what he did say startled her. 'There was a lot of talk about Father Brogan back in Dingle. He has a regular column in *The Kerryman* and he's on the radio too. I suppose your paths rarely cross now.'

'Never.'

Cathleen turned towards the stage, her eyes focusing on the flying steps of a dark-haired girl. At the back of a kitchen drawer, under the rubber bands and next to a wedding photograph that wasn't good enough for the album, were two plain white cards. The first had arrived during the grey days of the previous autumn in an envelope with a Birmingham postmark. There was no name or date: just two sentences. 'Wherever I am. Whatever I'm doing.'

The second card arrived two months ago. It was the same message, written by the same hand, but this time the envelope was smudged with the postmark of the Irish postal service.

All we had was one week, Cathleen thought, as the jig came to an end. There was no way we could ever have more. I was looking for a new life: Jerry wanted his old one with me in a corner of it. And how could he ever be happy being plain *Mister* Brogan when he'd known the glory of being Father Jerry?

The clapping stopped and chairs were scraped back. It was the interval. But I'm glad we had that week, Cathleen thought. It had taken her a long time to be glad. She was angry at first, even though she didn't know who to be angry with, and then a great aching loneliness swept over her as if she was back in the hospital ward, telling Mick to go play in the fields again. But that too had gone. Almost.

And what was left? She glanced around the hall. Her daughters were here somewhere, although she couldn't see them for the moment, but she could see her mother talking to Reg, her hands waving and ropes of rosary beads flaying the air. What was left was enough.

'There's a Christmas fair in my parish church next week. Tombola. Santa Claus. I thought the girls might like it.' Tea was being served in the corridor and they joined the queue. He waited until everyone had filed back into the hall before speaking again. 'Only there's something I have to say before you even think about coming with me. I have to be straight with you.'

Seventy-Six

'The dogs in the street must know how I feel, but I don't know if you do.' Tacit turned away. Cathleen was aware that each word was a struggle.

'What do you want?'

'Everything.' The smile was self-mocking. 'I want every contract in London. I want to be ganger on the new tube line. I want the motorways and the ring roads and the bypasses. I want every tower block in Westminster to have Tacit Donovan's mark on it. I want you holding my arm and your girls holding my hand. Like the song says, I want to walk beside you. I was going to tell you that I'd settle for less.' He shook his head. 'But now I see you again, I know it wouldn't work. I had a picture of you and me at the church fair and I thought that would be enough, for a while at least. But I don't want you as a friend Cathleen that much I know. And if you won't take my arm I'd rather walk alone.' He paused and turned so that he could see Cathleen's expression. 'Don't be kind.' His voice was harsh. 'You're a nice woman, Cathleen, but I'm asking you not to be nice. Don't tell me something because you think it's what I want to hear.'

She looked up and saw the muscles in his neck tighten as he waited for her to speak. His mouth was set in a tense line. Cathleen didn't trust herself to find the right words. Instead she touched the side of his face and felt a tremor arc across the cool cheek. He was holding his breath, she thought. Holding himself back.

'But I promise you this: there'll be no Mrs Donovan if there's no Cathleen Donovan. I'll grow old with you or I'll grow old alone.'

He paused and for a moment his stern exterior seemed about to crumble. 'Have you no answer for me?'

He was the one with the words today, thought Cathleen.

'Are youse two ever coming?' Kitty yanked open the hall door and gestured furiously. 'For the love of God, they're on next.' There was no time to say any more. Kitty was holding the door open and hissing at them to hurry, hurry. Cathleen couldn't see Tacit's face, but she could sense that he was retreating inside himself. Soon he would make an excuse and go. He wouldn't embarrass either of them by staying. What she said now would shape everything else they did and their lives to come.

Reg, sitting in the front row, had turned around to wave them forward. Kitty was standing in the gangway with her back to them and her eyes fixed on the stage.

Reg saw Cathleen spin on her heel and face a startled Tacit. He saw her stand on tiptoe and reach up. He saw too the look on the ganger's face as she kissed him.

'Will that do as an answer?'

Tacit nodded. Together they stood at the back of the hall and watched as Anna and Geraldine appeared on stage together. Anna in green and Geraldine in the cream dress.

Tacit reached for Cathleen's hands as the Brogan sisters danced their way to a medal.